Great Moments in Fiction

Great Moments in Fiction

THE WALT DISNEY PARADE
OF FUN, FACT, FANTASY AND FICTION

WITH ILLUSTRATIONS BY THE WALT DISNEY STUDIO

Purnell

Contents

Verses from the song "Westward Ho The Wagons" copyright © 1955 by Wonderland Music Company. Verse from "John Colter" copyright © 1956 by Wonderland Music Company.

"The Happiest Millionaire" adapted from the screenplay by A J Carothers, based on the play by Kyle Crichton and the book "My Philadelphia Father" by Cordelia Drexel Biddle and Kyle Crichton, published by Doubleday & Company, Inc. Lyrics from the screenplay by Richard M. and Robert B. Sherman.

Library of Congress Catalog Card Number: 77-116696. Copyright © 1970 by Walt Disney Productions. All rights reserved. Stories and pictures in this book previously copyrighted © 1969, 1959, 1958, 1954, 1953, 1944, 1941 by Walt Disney Productions Inc. Published and printed in England by Purnell & Sons Ltd.

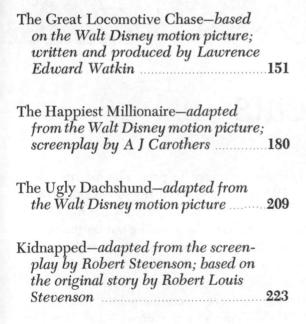

Aristocats

MADAME ADELAIDE BONFAMILLE stood before her mirror and tilted her head to one side, the better to admire her new hat.

"Outrageous!" she said.

Madame smiled and turned to Duchess the cat, who was curled up on the faded rose velvet sofa in Madame's little sitting room. "Don't you think it's an outrageous hat, Duchess?" she asked.

Duchess purred her approval. Like Madame, Duchess loved outrageous, elegant things.

"You're quite right, my dear," said Madame. "I'll keep it." She took the hat off, put it into the box and began to cover it carefully with layers and layers of tissue paper.

Duchess continued to purr. The cat truly admired Madame. She loved the soft hands which could stroke a cat's fur in precisely the right way. There were blue veins standing out on the backs of those hands, but the fingers were still nimble. The skin of Madame's face was like fine silk which has been pleated into a thousand tiny wrinkles, but there were roses blooming in her cheeks. Madame was as vain as a girl, and she moved almost like a girl. She was straight and graceful and quick.

But Madame was old. Duchess knew it. Sometimes she listened, half-dozing, as Madame told her of the golden yesterdays. Once the great and glittering people of Paris had come to visit Madame. They had come to chatter and gossip of large and small events. They had come to be amused and to be amusing. They had waltzed and flirted to the msuic of violins which played in the salon.

Now that was all gone. The glittering gossips had vanished as the years had overtaken them. The scuttling of dry leaves was heard in the courtyard more often than the sound of footsteps. And it had been many seasons since the strains of violin music had echoed in the house.

Yet there were pleasures. There was the phonograph in Madame's sitting room, spinning out its thin tunes. There were the trips to the bookshop to buy the newest and most exciting romances. There were the visits to the milliner to try on the most astounding hats. And there was a drive every fine afternoon in the Bois de Boulogne.

Madame always looked forward to the drives. Many Parisians had taken to the motorcar. They rattled about with much noise and confusion, and often with loud cries of alarm and anger. Madame did not care for motorcars. She preferred her carriage. Frou-Frou, the horse with the ridiculous name and the curly mane, still stepped along proudly for her mistress. And Edgar, Madame's manservant, gladly put off his butler's livery and became a coachman during these afternoon outings.

Madame and Duchess never discussed it, but they were both very happy. Madame might be vain, but she was also wise. She had spent her time well, tasting whatever joy came her way. If there were bitter moments in her life, she did not dwell on them. And she was grateful for all of the small delights which remained to her.

As for Duchess, she had everything a cat could dream of possessing. She had her youth. And she had breeding. Duchess was an aristocat and she knew it. It showed in her beautiful blue eyes and her fine white coat. It showed in the way she used her lovely tail and the way she held her head and the way she walked. She was graceful, but she never swaggered.

Duchess also had Madame, and that was no small thing. Madame did not treat the cat as a pet. Madame and Duchess were friends. Madame confided in Duchess.

Then there was Edgar. The butler could do wonderful things in the kitchen. He knew all of Duchess' favorite dishes, from cold salmon to thick cream.

Dearest of all to Duchess were her kittens. Duchess loved them fiercely. She loved them even more than she loved Madame. Since this was quite natural, Madame did not object. She understood perfectly.

Now Duchess watched Madame fold the last bit of tissue paper around the new hat and put the lid on the box. "I think Monsieur Hautcourt will not approve of this hat, eh, Duchess?" said Madame. "We will put the box out of sight, and then it will not trouble him."

Duchess blinked. So Monsieur Hautcourt, the lawyer, was coming to the house? That might be amusing. Monsieur and Madame had been friends for many years. He advised Madame on all of her business affairs, and on many things which were not business at all. Monsieur often disapproved of the way Madame spent her money. However, Monsieur himself had just invested a small fortune in a motorcar. He liked to speed around Paris like a mere youth, and frequently he sang at the top of his lungs.

Madame returned to the mirror and touched her hair. "We must look our best for dear Georges," she told Duchess.

Duchess wondered why. Monsieur did not see well. He would hardly be able to tell whether they looked their best or not.

Way off, down in Edgar's kitchen, the doorbell sounded. Duchess heard Edgar's steps cross the hall. The front door opened and there was some muffled conversation. Then came the unmistakable sound of Edgar helping Monsieur up the stairs.

Monsieur always required help, but he had his own vanity. He would not use the little elevator Madame had had installed.

Mounting the stairs took quite a time, but at last Edgar knocked, opened the door and announced Monsieur. Monsieur tottered into the room to greet Madame—and to pet Duchess dutifully.

Edgar went out and closed the door behind him. Duchess sat and watched her mistress and the lawyer. At first they simply chatted, as they usually did. They spoke of champagne which had been poured many years ago and of waltzes which were long over. Then Madame became more serious.

"Georges, there is a legal matter to discuss," said she.

Monsieur was delighted. Legal matters were what he liked best. "Whom shall we sue?" he asked brightly.

"No, no!" The idea of Madame suing anyone was ridiculous. "I simply want to make my will," she told the lawyer.

Monsieur did not think a will would be nearly as exciting as a lawsuit. However, he sat down at Madame's little desk, drew some paper toward him and prepared to behave like a hard-headed legal advisor.

Madame had given careful thought to the matter of her will. "Georges, I have no living relatives," she said.

He knew it.

"If anything should happen to me, I want Duchess and her kittens to be well cared for. Certainly no one can do this better than Edgar."

Monsieur was aghast. "Adelaide!" he cried. "Surely you don't wish to leave your fortune to your servant? Why I've never heard of such a—"

"No, no!" interrupted Madame. "Not to Edgar. I wish to leave my fortune to my cats."

How like Madame, thought Duchess. She was a true friend.

"It can be very simply arranged," Madame went on. "The cats will inherit first, and Edgar will be appointed their guardian. Then, when they have lived out their lives in comfort and ease, the money that remains will go to Edgar."

Monsieur Hautcourt did not like it. Duchess could see that. However, it was Madame's fortune, and she could do with it what she wanted.

Monsieur Hautcourt settled his spectacles firmly on his nose, picked up a pen and began to write.

9

The kittens had enjoyed their afternoon romp in the courtyard. They had had a fine game of hide and seek around the chestnut tree. But the shadows were long now and the air was chill. It was time to go in.

Toulouse, the oldest by a few minutes, was first in the rush for their little cat door.

"Wait for me!" cried Berlioz.

Marie wouldn't hear of it. "Me first! I'm a lady!" she said, and she pushed through the door ahead of her brothers in a most unladylike way.

"You're not a lady." Berlioz laughed and pulled her tail. "You're nothing but a sister."

Marie flounced away into the salon. Toulouse and Berlioz scooted after her and caught her before she could scramble up into Madame's very best chair.

"You're tickling!" shrieked Marie. She tugged at Berlioz' ribbon with all her might.

"That's not fair!" gasped Berlioz.

"Females never fight fair," was Toulouse's comment. He charged in to give Marie the swat she so richly deserved.

Outmaneuvered, Marie cried for her mother.

Duchess came quickly, but without undue bustle. "Marie, darling! You must stop that. It is really not ladylike. And Toulouse! And Berlioz! Such behavior is most unbecoming to lovely gentlemen."

"Aw, we were just practicing biting and clawing," said Berlioz.

Duchess shuddered. "Aristocats do not bite and claw. That's horrible!"

Toulouse did not think it was horrible. "Some day we might meet a tough alley cat." he told his mother.

Duchess thought this was possible, but not likely. "That will do," she said. "It's time to forget

10

these silly ideas and think of improving your-selves. You want to grow up to be lovely, charm-ing ladies and gentlemen. Now Toulouse, you go and start on your painting."

With her own hands, Madame had put up an easel in the corner of the salon. There were paints there, always ready for Toulouse. Madame and Duchess were in agreement; Toulouse had real talent. He must be encouraged.

Edgar thought it was dreadfully foolish to per-mit a kitten to dabble his paws in expensive oil paints. Edgar saw nothing but senseless daubs in the designs which Toulouse created on the canvases Madame provided. But Edgar had been with Madame for a long time. He knew better than to disagree openly with the old lady.

Now Toulouse took his place in front of the easel. He thought for a moment, then began to mix his colors. There was zinc white, of course, and a little alizarin crimson. There was cobalt blue and bright orange and black.

Toulouse began to paint. He worked quickly, sometimes drawing a clean line with his right front paw, sometimes backing away from the can-vas and hurling a blob of color.

Marie giggled. "Oh, look! It's Edgar!"

It was indeed Edgar. The butler would never have recognized himself. He had not learned to see things as cats saw them. But Duchess and Marie and Berlioz knew a portrait of Edgar when it appeared on the canvas. It was plain as day.

"Old pickle puss," laughed Berlioz.

Duchess did not like that remark. It was not kind. Edgar took very good care of her and of her kittens. She quickly sent Berlioz to the piano to practice his scales, and Marie had to take her place on top of the piano to sing as Berlioz played.

Edgar objected to the kitten's music almost as much as he objected to Toulouse's art. But again, no one asked his opinion. So he stuffed his ears with cotton whenever one of the practice sessions began.

The cotton was in place when Edgar carried in the supper tray. Edgar was humming a little tune. It had nothing to do with the kitten's tune. It was Edgar's own music—tired and a little dull, like Edgar himself.

"Good evening, my little ones!" Edgar inter-rupted the practice and put the tray down on the floor. "Here's your favorite dish," said Edgar. "I prepared it in a very special way."

There were three small blue bowls and one larger bowl for Duchess. The kittens ran to sniff and investigate.

"Creme de la creme a la Edgar," the butler an-nounced.

Duchess was delighted. There was nothing nicer on a cool spring evening than a bowl of warm cream. And if Edgar had taken the trouble to fix it in a special way, it would be delicious indeed.

Toulouse and Berlioz put their noses to the cream and began to lap it up.

"Sleep well," said Edgar warmly. Then he flushed and looked awkward as if he had said

something rude. "I mean, eat!" said Edgar quickly. "Eat well!"

How odd, thought the Duchess. Why should Edgar mention sleeping? Bedtime was still a long way off.

Edgar went away, leaving Duchess and her family to their supper. And Monsieur Roquefort, the clever and friendly mouse who lived behind the baseboard, put his nose out to see what was going on.

The kittens were most happy to see Roquefort. Next to their mother and Madame, he was their favorite friend. If anyone had told them that most cats chased mice, they would have been horrified.

Roquefort cleared his throat and greeted Duchess with his usual gentle courtesy. Then he remarked, ever so softly, that something smelled good.

"It's creme de la creme a la Edgar," Marie told him.

Duchess was always hospitable. "Won't you join us, Monsieur Roquefort?" she asked the mouse.

Roquefort had been expecting this. From behind his back he produced a cracker, and he tried to look like a mouse who always carried a cracker about with him. Roquefort liked to dunk.

Toulouse nudged his bowl with his nose. "Have some. It's good."

Roquefort thanked the kitten and dipped his cracker into the cream.

13

It *was* good. It was very good. Roquefort dipped his cracker again and again. And soon the cracker was gone.

"My compliments to the chef!" said Roquefort. "Delicious! This calls for another cracker." Roquefort started for the hole in the baseboard. "I'll be right back," he promised.

But Roquefort did not return. In fact, Roquefort did not quite make it all the way into his hole. Before Duchess' astonished gaze, the little mouse stumbled and reeled. He went down on all fours and stretched out. His tail twitched twice. Then Roquefort was asleep.

"My word!" murmured Duchess.

Roquefort snored a tiny snore.

"Mama, he's sleeping!" exclaimed Berlioz.

"How rude!" said Marie. "Mama, isn't that rude, to go to sleep in the middle of a dinner party?"

"Now, now, Marie. Monsieur Roquefort must be very tired. And it is also rude to criticize a guest, you know."

Subdued, Marie returned to her supper bowl, and now Duchess began to eat.

Roquefort had been right. The cream was delicious. And very soothing. Supper was hardly over before Duchess felt her eyelids grow heavy. Toulouse yawned. Marie sat quietly, leaning against the leg of the piano.

Duchess hid her own yawns behind her paw. "I think, my darlings, that we must go to bed early tonight," she said. "We seem to be quite sleepy. I am sure Madame will not mind if we leave her alone for one evening."

For once the kittens did not argue about their bedtime. They followed Duchess up the stairs. Berlioz stumbled as he went. And before Ma-

dame even came down to her own dinner, which she ate in solitary elegance in the big dining room, Duchess and her kittens were curled up in their basket, sound asleep.

* * * * * * * *

Edgar looked at himself in the mirror. He did not appear to be a criminal. He appeared to be what he was—a middle-aged butler who was beginning to get thick around the middle.

Edgar adjusted his hat. Why should he look any different? He was the same as he had always been. He was Edgar. He served the meals and drove the carriage and polished the brass knocker on Madame's front door. He was Edgar, who supervised the cleaning woman when she came twice a week, and who counted the teaspoons after she left. He was Edgar, who often listened at doors, and who learned some very interesting things that way.

"So the cats will inherit first?" said Edgar to the mirror. "Ridiculous! So I'm to spend the rest of their lives waiting on them, eh? We'll see about that. They will have to be here to inherit, and they won't be here. They will never be here again."

Edgar, satisfied that his derby sat perfectly straight on his head, turned away from the mirror. He picked up his umbrella, clicked out his light and opened the door. The house was midnight-dark, and Edgar moved through it without making a sound. He knew every inch of the way. He did not even need to touch the wall as he came down the stairs from the third floor.

Duchess and the kittens were sleeping deeply

in their basket on the second floor landing. The effect of the pills which Edgar had dissolved in their cream would last a long time. Edgar knew the cats could not wake before morning.

Marie made a small noise when Edgar lifted the basket. Toulouse half-opened his eyes. Then he closed them and went back to sleep.

Edgar stole down the back stairs and out through the kitchen to the garden. Across the garden was the carriage house. Frou-Frou the

16

horse was there, and so was Madame's carriage. And so was the motorcycle which was Edgar's delight on his days off.

Edgar deposited the cats' basket gently in the sidecar of the motorcycle. Frou-Frou watched sleepily as the butler wheeled the motorcycle out without starting it. It occurred to Frou-Frou that Edgar was behaving strangely. Why was he taking out the motorcycle in the middle of the night? And what was in the basket? But Frou-

Frou knew that in time all things usually explained themselves.

Frou-Frou dozed off again, and Edgar rode away through the empty, cobbled streets of Paris.

Edgar rode and rode. He went quickly, but not so quickly that some late-roaming gendarme might stop him and—horror of horrors—ask why he was speeding through the night with a basket of cats in his sidecar. He drove until the rooftops of Paris had dropped out of sight behind the horizon, and even the Eiffel Tower had faded into the mists.

Perhaps it was not strictly necessary to go so far to dispose of a family of cats, but Edgar was nervous. He wanted to make sure there would never again be a sign of Duchess and the kittens in the old house near the Bois.

In the end, Edgar went too far. He went out to the farm country, where every plot of land was guarded by at least one faithful and alert dog, and he ran afoul of Napoleon and Lafayette.

Napoleon the hound was the first one to hear the roar of the motorcycle on the country road. The dog had been asleep under a cart near a haystack. But he slept lightly, as befits a watchdog.

He raised his head and listened. The motorcycle was coming on fast. The motor made popping little backfires as the machine soared up a small hill.

"Lafayette!" called Napoleon. "I say, Lafayette! Wake up! Cycle's coming!"

Part of the haystack stirred and a beagle put his nose out into the night air. "It's a motorcycle with two cylinders," reported Napoleon. He was the expert on vehicles of all types.

Lafayette the beagle looked even wearier than usual. "We bit six tires today," he told Napoleon. "And we chased four motorcars, a bicycle and a scooter." Lafayette felt that the game of chasing passing vehicles could be overdone.

Napoleon wasn't listening to Lafayette. He was listening to the approaching cycle. "It's got a chain drive," was his verdict. "Sounds like a squeaky wheel on the front."

Lafayette tried to crawl back into the haystack, but Napoleon would have none of that. "You go for the tires, and I'll get right to the seat of the problem."

Lafayette grumbled and blew hay out of his nose. "How come you always grab the tender part for yourself?" he asked.

"Because I outrank you, that's why," growled Napoleon.

The motorcycle was just approaching the bridge that spanned the small stream at the edge of the farm.

"Sound the attack!" ordered Napoleon.

Lafayette threw back his head and let out a deep, baying cry.

"Charge!" yelped Napoleon.

Poor Edgar hardly knew what happened next. One moment he was riding along, calm as could be, with his derby squarely on his head and his umbrella strapped on behind the seat and the cats asleep in the sidecar. The next moment the shadows beside the country lane became two monsters with fierce, howling, bellowing voices and teeth that looked many inches long.

Edgar stepped on the gas and the motorcycle leaped forward. But it did not leap any more nimbly than Napoleon and Lafayette.

After the first frightful moment, Edgar knew that he was beset by dogs, not monsters. But this was no help. One of the brutes went for the rear wheel of his motorcycle. The other attached itself to the tail of his coat.

Edgar tried to get another spurt of speed out of his cycle. The machine responded by running off the road, down into the bed of a small stream and up the other bank. Now Edgar bumped through a plowed field instead of skimming along a road.

A windmill suddenly appeared to block Edgar's way. The butler swerved his motorcycle, and the dog who was attached to his coat flew through the air and landed in the sidecar.

This was much closer to the dog than Edgar wanted to be. He swerved again and turned, and this time he ran down into the riverbed and under

the little bridge. The basket with Duchess and the kittens bounced out of the sidecar and disappeared into the darkness. The motorcycle zoomed up onto the road, and the sidecar separated itself from the motorcycle. Edgar wheeled around and headed back toward Paris. He was without his sidecar. By this time he was also without his derby hat and his umbrella. Part of his coat was missing, too. He was wet and shaken and badly frightened.

But he had gotten rid of those infernal cats.

* * * * * * * * *

Duchess awoke just before dawn. She was cold —colder than she had ever been in her life. Her fur was damp, and when she moved her paws there was no velvet cushion under them. Instead, mud oozed up between her toes. Reeds rustled overhead.

"I am not at home!" said Duchess.

Such a thing had never, never happened before. Duchess always awoke to find herself safe and snug in her basket.

19

She looked around wildly. "Children?" she called.

No one answered.

"Children? Where are you?"

Something splashed off to the left, and Duchess felt a terrible fear.

"Berlioz! Toulouse! Marie! Where are you?"

It was Marie who answered first. She was huddled under a bush, still more than half asleep. "I guess I had a bad dream," she mumbled. "Did I fall out of bed? Mama, I'm cold!"

Duchess hurried to nuzzle her and hold her close. "Now don't be frightened, my little one," she said.

Duchess herself was frightened, but she kept her voice calm.

"Mama! Mama!"

Berlioz straggled out of the reeds that edged the river.

"Over here, darling!" called Duchess.

"I'm wet," Berlioz complained. It was not a necessary remark. Anyone could see Berlioz was wet—thoroughly wet.

"Don't worry," soothed Duchess. "Everything is going to be all right."

But where was Toulouse? As Duchess tried to smooth Berlioz' fur with her tongue, her eyes darted this way and that.

There was a little light now. Duchess saw the basket, atilt on the ground under the bridge.

In the river, a frog croaked a welcome to the new day.

"Mama!" squeaked Berlioz.

Duchess managed a shaky laugh. "That's only a little frog, my love," she told her son. "He cannot hurt you. Now you two darlings stay here. Do not move. I am going to look for Toulouse."

The kittens obeyed. They were too cold and miserable to think of doing anything else. Duchess picked her way across the marshy ground to the basket.

Toulouse was a lucky one. There were no two ways about it. Of them all, he was the only one who had remained snug and warm inside the basket.

"Toulouse!" cried Duchess.

The kitten looked up at her in bewilderment.

"Why didn't you answer me?" asked Duchess.

"I was having a funny dream," said Toulouse. "Edgar was in it. He was carrying our basket."

"Edgar?" At first Duchess was surprised. But then, when she thought of it, it was quite natural. Why shouldn't Toulouse dream about Edgar?

Toulouse yawned himself awake. "In my dream, we were all riding in Edgar's motorcycle," he told his mother.

The little frog in the river croaked again. Downstream another larger frog answered.

Toulouse looked around him. How strange everything was. Duchess was there, as she always was when he awoke. Marie and Berlioz came scampering up. But where were they? Certainly not in their usual place on the second floor landing of the old house near the Bois.

"Was it a dream?" asked Toulouse, wondering. "Where are we? Did Edgar bring us here?"

"Edgar?" repeated Duchess again. "Oh, darling, that can't be. You know Edgar always takes good care of us."

"Maybe you fell on your head, Toulouse," suggested Berlioz.

It was an unkind remark, but for once Duchess did not scold about it. She knew Edgar had not brought them to this terrible place where it was cold, and where frogs made rude noises. But it was a mysterious business. They had gone to sleep in their basket in Madame's house, and they had awakened in a wilderness.

But they were together. That was the important thing. And together they would get back to their own place. Duchess would manage it, although at the moment she had no idea how to begin.

"What's going to happen to us?" Berlioz asked suddenly.

"I want to go home to Madame!" Marie's voice was a forlorn wail.

Duchess felt a pang at that. Poor Madame! She would be so upset when she found that her dear friends were gone.

The sun began to come up. As sunrises go, this

one was rather run-of-the-mill. Still, Duchess had led a sheltered life. In Madame's house the blinds were not opened until Edgar came up from the kitchen with Madame's coffee. And Madame did not awake with the dawn.

Duchess stepped into the basket and Marie and Berlioz crept in after her. The aristocats settled down to enjoy the moment as much as was possible under the circumstances.

The clouds on the horizon glowed very red, and Duchess thought that was rather marvelous. Then the red faded to pink. And where it was not pink, the sky was a nice shade of blue—much like the blue of the kitten's bowls. Finally the sun appeared above the tops of the trees and little

fingers of morning gleamed along the reeds beside the river. There was a splash and the frog was gone, to be heard no more.

Duchess stepped out of the basket and decided that things were not so bad after all. The place might be chilly and wild, but it was not dangerous. It was just an ordinary little stream with ordinary reeds and a couple of very ordinary frogs. And, Duchess knew, they could not be so far from Paris. Whatever had happened to them, it had happened in a single night.

Several pale pink flowers floated down and settled on Duchess' head.

The aristocat looked up and found herself staring at another cat.

Duchess looked down again quickly. The other cat was plucking blossoms from an apple tree that grew beside the bridge and throwing the flowers down on Duchess. In the eyes of that other cat— bright, playful green eyes—Duchess recognized a glint of admiration.

"Yeah!" said the other cat.

The remark did not seem to call for an answer. Duchess kept still.

"You're some cute cat!" said the one on the bridge.

Duchess thought that this was very forward of the other one. They had not even been introduced!

The other cat took care of this right away. "I'm

Abraham DeLacey Giuseppe Casey Thomas O'Malley," said he. "I'm O'Malley the alley cat."

Duchess thought that last remark was quite unnecessary. She could see that this orange and black creature with the impudent grin was an alley cat. Of course, Duchess had never really known an alley cat. But one sees all kinds in Paris when one drives out with Madame in the afternoon.

"Your name seems to cover all of Europe," said Duchess coolly.

The alley cat picked a flower and tossed it down. Duchess made no attempt to catch it.

"I'm the only cat of my kind," said the newcomer. "I'm king of the highway. I'm prince of the boulevard. The world is my backyard."

"You have a large estate, Monsieur," murmured Duchess.

"It is. It is." O'Malley came down off the bridge and stalked toward Duchess. "I've only got myself and this great big world," he told her. "So I don't worry about what road to take, whether it's to Calcutta or to Rome. It's the road of life. Sometimes it even leads to home sweet home. That's Paris."

At the mention of Paris Duchess was all attention. Above all, Paris was where she wanted to be. So, when the alley cat asked what her name might be, she answered him with charm and courtesy.

"Duchess?" said O'Malley. "Beautiful! Beautiful name. Love it!" He came very close to Duchess and peered into her face. "And your eyes! Why, your eyes are like sapphires. So sparkling! So bright!"

Duchess had known this for a long time. She was not carried away by the flattery. "Very pretty," she said softly. "But really, Monsieur O'Malley, I am in a great deal of trouble."

O'Malley tried to look very gallant. "Trouble?" he cried. He seemed delighted. "Helping beautiful dames—er—damsels in distress is my specialty. What's the hang-up?"

Duchess had not heard about hang-ups but she could guess O'Malley's meaning. "It is most important that I get back to Paris," she said, "so if you would be so kind and show me the way . . . ?"

"Perish the thought!" cried O'Malley. "I won't show you the way, your ladyship. "I'll *take* you to Paris. We'll fly there on a magic carpet!"

The kittens had been crouched in the basket watching the scene with enormous interest. Now, at the thought of a journey on a magic carpet, Marie could keep still no longer.

"Wonderful!" she mewed, and tumbled out to join her mother.

Berlioz came out, too. "Do you really have a magic carpet?" he wanted to know.

"Are we really going to ride on it?" Toulouse asked.

The magnificent Mr. O'Malley seemed to shrink three sizes. "Kittens!" he gasped. "You have kittens!"

"But yes, Monsieur," answered Duchess.

"Mama, do I have sparkling sapphire eyes like you?" Marie wanted to know.

"Of course, my darling."

"Where's the magic carpet?" Berlioz demanded.

O'Malley was crushed. He had met this divine creature. She was sheer beauty from the tips of her shapely ears to the end of her marvelous tail. And what did she turn out to be? A mother cat with three lively, curious kittens!

And O'Malley knew that one could rely on kittens not to understand the poetry of certain situations.

"Well, now," said O'Malley.

"You said we could ride to Paris," insisted Toulouse.

"Did I say that?" asked O'Malley. "Well, what I meant, you see, was that . . ."

Duchess understood. Poor Monsieur O'Malley! What an awkward position to be in.

"What I had in mind," said O'Malley, "was kind of a sports model."

tens followed. All except Toulouse, who paused to hiss at O'Malley in a very rude way.

"I'm a tough alley cat, too," boasted Toulouse.

"I'll bet," said O'Malley. "You must be a real tiger in your neighborhood."

Toulouse wanted to tell O'Malley what a real tiger he was, and how he practiced all the time, but Duchess called him and he had to be off.

"See you around, tiger," said O'Malley.

"A magic carpet built for two, perhaps?" prompted Duchess.

"I wouldn't take up much room," Marie protested.

"Be quiet, Marie," warned her mother. Duchess turned to O'Malley. "I understand perfectly, Monsieur," she said.

The kittens huddled close. They knew without being told that, for some reason, there would be no magic ride to Paris.

"Come along, darlings," ordered Duchess. She started up the bank toward the bridge. The kit-

The aristocats vanished beyond the bridge. O'Malley stretched out on the bank of the river. For some reason he felt an emptiness inside of him. Oddly enough, it wasn't in his stomach—which was where O'Malley's empty feelings usually were.

"That's quite a family," said O'Malley.

There was no one to hear, so no one gave O'Malley any argument on that.

"You're not really much of a cat, O'Malley," said he to himself.

No one agreed. But no one disagreed, either.

"Come to think of it, you're a rat," said the alley cat. "Right?"

"Right!" answered O'Malley.

No cat wants to be a rat. O'Malley streaked up to the road and called after Duchess and her kittens. "Hey!" he cried. "Hold up there!"

The aristocats stopped and waited for O'Malley to catch up to them.

"I said I'd get you to Paris, and I'll do it," said O'Malley. "Don't you worry about a thing, Duchess. Leave it to me and my magic carpet!"

* * * * * * * *

Monsieur Roquefort awoke half in and half out of his hole. It was a dangerous and undignified position for a mouse to be in. Roquefort hastened to change it.

But even after he had gotten completely inside the hole and was stretched out on the bed which he had made for himself out of a discarded candy box, Roquefort had trouble sorting things out.

Some things he remembered clearly. Edgar had come in with the tray. He had been waiting at the entrance to his home for Edgar's appearance. Then Duchess and the kittens had begun their supper, and they had invited Roquefort to join them. And the creme de la creme a la Edgar had been delicious. It had turned his dry little cracker into a dinner fit for a king.

The cracker! That was it! He had finished his cracker and had started back to his hole to get a second one. And then. . . And then. . . And then what?

No matter how he tried, Roquefort could remember no more than that. He had wanted a second cracker.

Roquefort sat up and felt his head. It seemed

larger than usual this morning, and it ached. What on earth was wrong with him? Could he be coming down with something? A touch of the flu, perhaps?

Roquefort decided that he would risk a journey to the upper regions of the house. Perhaps there was something in Madame's medicine cabinet which would be good for a small mouse with a touch of the flu.

Roquefort peeked out of his hole. It was still early. The sun had not yet come over the wall to touch the east windows. The tray with the cats' supper dishes was gone and the door to the hall stood open. Yes, it should be safe enough. Roquefort ventured forth.

Roquefort had gotten only as far as the music cabinet when Madame screamed.

The mouse froze. Had he been seen? But no. The scream came from upstairs.

Roquefort heard Edgar run up from the kitchen. He couldn't hear everything that followed but he heard enough to alarm him. Madame was in tears. Duchess was gone. The kittens were gone. Even the cats' basket was gone from its place on the landing.

"Call the police, Edgar!" cried Madame. "There has been foul play!"

Edgar tried to reassure Madame. He went through the house, upstairs and down, calling to the cats. Madame called, too. But there were no answering mews from Duchess or the kittens.

And, as Madame pointed out, Duchess would hardly be able to leave and take her basket with her!

Roquefort retreated to his hole to ponder. He decided that he did not have the flu after all. He did not have time to have the flu. Duchess and the kittens were missing, and Madame was quite right. The cat would not go away and take her basket. Her kittens, perhaps. But never the basket. It wasn't possible.

Despite his rather insignificant position in the Bonfamille household, Roquefort was a mouse of some intellect. He had nosed his way through many of the books in Madame's library. Now he

28

wondered what the great detective Sherlock Holmes would do in a case like this. No doubt he would think deep thoughts. He would consider motives. He would deduce. Also, he would question suspects.

That, Roquefort decided, was what *he* would do. He would question suspects. He would find out what had happened to Duchess and the kittens.

And who was a suspect? Well, there was Edgar. Edgar had prepared supper for the cats. No doubt it was Edgar who had carried out the tray with the dishes. Edgar might very well be a suspect.

But then, how would one go about questioning the butler. Come to think of it, if he saw Roquefort, Edgar might put out a trap for the mouse.

Better to leave Edgar alone. Instead, Roquefort would discuss the entire affair with Mlle. Frou-Frou. Of course the horse had not actually been in the house. But she was a mare of uncommon good sense, and she kept her ears open. She might know something.

Roquefort took himself out to the carriage house.

It turned out to be a wise move. Mlle. Frou-Frou listened with keen attention when Roquefort told his story. The mouse left out no detail. He told of the supper tray and the delicious cream. He told of his own collapse, and how he

had awakened in the morning with a headache, and how Madame had screamed. He told of the search through the house for the kittens.

"And not a trace," finished Roquefort. "Even their basket is gone."

"So that's what Edgar put in his motorcycle!" exclaimed Frou-Frou. It was the first word she had said since Roquefort started his recital.

"What?" said Roquefort.

"The basket," Frou-Frou said. "It was very late last night. I had been asleep and then awake and then asleep again when Edgar came in. He was wearing his derby and carrying his umbrella, the way he does on his day off. You know?"

Roquefort nodded.

"I was surprised because I knew it had to be the middle of the night," Frou-Frou went on. "He never makes a lot of noise, but I think he was walking even more quietly than usual. He had a basket with him and he put it into the sidecar of the motorcycle. Then he took the motorcycle out without starting it."

Roquefort looked at the place where the motorcycle stood. There was no sidecar.

"He didn't come back until early this morning," Frou-Frou told the mouse. "I can't imagine what happened to the sidecar. He lost his hat and the umbrella, too. And his coat was torn."

"He did it!" exclaimed Roquefort. "He stole Duchess and the kittens."

Frou-Frou agreed that it looked bad for Edgar. It also looked bad for the cats.

"I suppose he put something in their cream," suggested the horse.

Roquefort recalled his own collapse and agreed. No doubt there had been something in the cream—something to make Duchess and the kittens sleep.

"But what's the motive?" demanded the mouse.

Frou-Frou had never heard of motives and she was an honest enough horse to say so.

"I mean, why would he do such a thing?" explained Roquefort. "What would he gain?"

Frou-Frou couldn't answer. She was only a horse, and many of the ways of men were strange to her. But no doubt Edgar had had a reason to steal Madame's cats and take them away.

Where had he taken them?

* * * * * * * *

The magic carpet which O'Malley produced for Duchess and the kittens did not really fly, but it was admirably suited to the needs of two cats and a trio of kittens. It was an aged, chain-driven milk truck which came clanking down the road.

"Now this is going to stop for passengers," O'Malley told the aristocats when the truck rattled into sight. "You kids get over in the bushes at the side of the road and leave the rest to O'Malley."

Duchess and her kittens had nothing to lose. They hid themselves beside the road and O'Malley launched himself through the air with such skill that he landed right on the hood, just in front of the windshield.

"*Sacre bleu!*" shouted the truck driver.

O'Malley hissed and spit and howled and arched his back so that he looked at least twice as big as he really was.

Brakes screeched and the truck motor coughed and died.

O'Malley fled from the hood of the truck and streaked into the bushes to join Duchess and the kittens.

The truck driver climbed out of his cab. He was muttering to himself. He had never before been attacked by a cat on the Paris road.

O'Malley chuckled. It had gone perfectly. Now the driver went to the front of the truck to crank the balky old thing back to life.

"Come on, Duchess!" whispered O'Malley. "Kittens! Hurry up!"

And while the driver was bent over the crank at the front end of the truck, the cats were getting in at the rear end.

They were all safely aboard before the driver managed to coax the old motor to go again. Unaware of his passengers, he climbed into his cab and they jounced on toward Paris.

Duchess turned her enchanting blue eyes toward O'Malley. "Monsieur O'Malley, you are amazing!" she exclaimed.

"True!" admitted the alley cat.

"How can we ever thank you?" asked Duchess.

O'Malley shrugged it off. "My pleasure entirely," he told the Duchess. "But helping fair damsels has whipped up my appetite. Is anyone ready for breakfast?"

Were they ready for breakfast? They certainly were!

"What breakfast?" cried Toulouse.

"Where is it?" Marie wanted to know.

O'Malley nodded in the direction of a canvas sheet covering something in the truck. "It's right under the magic carpet," he told the kittens.

"Another magic carpet?" Marie was quite excited. Monsieur O'Malley had such a way of talking about magic carpets, and his magic carpets had such a way of turning out to be something different entirely. She wondered what he would do now.

"We have to cook up a little spell," O'Malley told her. "You really have to use magic for this one. You ready?"

All three kittens nodded.

"All right," said O'Malley. "Now to make the magic begin, you wiggle your nose and tickle your chin."

Three little noses wiggled. Three small chins were tickled.

"Now close your eyes and cross your heart, and presto! Breakfast a la carte!"

O'Malley swept aside the canvas cover, reveal-

ing huge cans of milk. The lid was loose on one can, and a nudge from O'Malley was all that was needed to send it tumbling to the floor of the truck.

"Hurray!" cried Berlioz.

"Look, Mama!" exclaimed Toulouse. "Milk! Isn't Monsieur O'Malley just great?"

Duchess didn't answer. There was no need for an answer. Of course Monsieur O'Malley was great—and of course Monsieur O'Malley knew it at least as well as anyone.

* * * * * * * *

Edgar had had a busy day. All morning the house had swarmed with police. They had done all the things which police do when confronted with a puzzling mystery. They had questioned Madame, who wept a good deal. They had questioned Edgar, who did not weep at all. He had been most helpful. He had told how the cats had their supper in the salon at the usual time. He had told how they had retired early to their basket. He had told of Madame's dinner in the dining room, and how he had gone to his room soon after washing the dinner dishes.

"I read for a little while," Edgar told the inspector in charge of the case. "It was after eleven when I put out my light."

All this was true. Edgar had put out his light after eleven.

No, Edgar had not noticed any strangers lurking near the house.

No, there had been no unusual visitors of late. "Monsieur Hautcourt came to see Madame yesterday," said Edgar. "But Monsieur Hautcourt often comes to visit."

The police were baffled. How had the catnapper made his way into the house? No locks were broken. All the windows were intact. Besides, Edgar had closed the shutters and barred them at sunset.

At last the police went away. Edgar chuckled. He had been clever. He had said enough, but not too much. He had made the right impression. He was a faithful servant, and fond of kittens—almost as fond of kittens as Madame herself.

The afternoon papers came out and Edgar's

glee increased. The story of the catnapping was on the front page. The very first paragraph of the story reported that the criminal who had stolen Duchess and the kittens had not left a single clue.

Humming to himself, Edgar tucked the newspaper into his pocket and went out to the carriage house to feed Frou-Frou.

And in the middle of that task, a dreadful thought struck Edgar!

Good heavens! He *had* left clues! He had left clues scattered all over the countryside.

First there was the sidecar. Suppose someone noticed that it was missing? Suppose someone began to ask questions about it? How would Edgar explain it? One did not simply mislay a sidecar.

Then there was the derby. Everyone knew that Edgar wore a derby. Of course he could go out and buy a new one, but the police might be watching. They might have a man trailing Edgar. What would he say if someone asked him why he was buying a new hat?

And the umbrella. No doubt the dogs had gotten the umbrella. What if someone found them with it and began to wonder?

Last of all, there was the coat that the dogs had torn. Luckily Edgar had a number of coats. He put the torn one into the trash bin at the end of the alley.

So much for the coat. But the sidecar, the hat and the umbrella had to be retrieved. The hat and the umbrella might be damaged beyond repair. No matter. Edgar could not take any chances. If they were found way out in the countryside there might be some very nasty consequences.

Edgar got through the rest of the day as best he could. He was jittery, but Madame was too upset to notice. She did not take her dinner downstairs. She had a tray brought up to her sitting room. Then she went to bed to lie awake and think of Duchess and the kittens.

Edgar waited until it was very late. He sat in the darkness of his room until the clock struck one. Not a footstep sounded on the street outside. Edgar could see from his window that the gar-

35

den behind the house and the narrow lane beyond that were completely empty. If the police were watching the house, their man had to be posted in front.

Edgar took his fishing rod from the closet. With his shoes in his hand, he went down the back stairs. He got the kitchen door open without once rattling the bolt. Carrying shoes and fishing rod, he crossed the garden.

Frou-Frou and Roquefort were waiting in the carriage house. Little Roquefort, who could get about without being noticed, had been watching Edgar all day. Madame might not have noticed that the butler was having a fit of nerves, but Roquefort noticed. Madame could not know that the butler sat alone in his darkened room, waiting for the hours to pass, but Roquefort knew.

Roquefort had come to the carriage house at eleven to take counsel with Frou-Frou.

"That sneaky, crooked, no-good butler!" spluttered the mouse. "He's sitting in his room with his clothes on and his light out. He's going somewhere tonight. Frou-Frou, I've got to do something."

Frou-Frou agreed. Something needed to be done. "But Roquefort," she protested, "you're only a mouse. What can you do?"

"I can go *with* Edgar," said Roquefort. "When he took Duchess away, he went on the motorcycle. He'll take the motorcycle tonight. He'll have to. I'll hide and go with him, and if I'm lucky he'll lead me to Duchess and the kittens."

Frou-Frou thought it was a wonderful plan. For a moment she envied Roquefort. Being tiny had its points. Roquefort could hide almost anywhere. A fair-sized mare like Frou-Frou could not play such clever games.

The mouse and the horse heard the clock strike midnight, then one. Then Edgar started across the garden.

"Here he comes!" squeaked Roquefort, who had been watching through the window.

"Hurry!" Frou-Frou stood still while the mouse scampered across her back, then slid down her mane and made for the motorcycle.

"For goodness sake, be careful!" warned Frou-Frou.

Roquefort intended to be careful. He had already chosen a hiding place. He concealed himself inside the taillight of the motorcycle. The glass on the light had been broken for some time, and Edgar had not gotten around to fixing it.

Again Edgar wheeled the motorcycle out of the carriage house without starting it. He went down the lane to the corner before he even put on his shoes. And he trudged on for almost a mile before he decided it was safe to start the motorcycle and get out into the country.

When the motor of the cycle roared, the journey quickly became rough for Monsieur Roquefort. There is nothing on the inside of a taillight which even the cleverest mouse can hold on to.

Roquefort braced himself with his legs as the motorcycle took a corner at top speed.

Roquefort dug his little nails into the hole left by a missing screw when Edgar accelerated to roar up a hill.

Then the motorcycle came to a street where the cobblestones were old and worn. The motorcycle shook and rattled. And poor little Roquefort bounced like a rubber mouse and was thrown clear of the light.

Roquefort rolled across the cobblestones and splashed into a puddle. The breath was knocked out of him. He barely had the strength to sit up.

Edgar and the motorcycle disappeared down the dark, empty boulevard.

* * * * * * * *

Monsieur O'Malley had proved himself a cat of parts when he stopped the milk truck for Duchess and her kittens. Certainly it was not his fault that the cats had scarcely finished their breakfast when the truck driver looked into his rear view mirror and saw his uninvited guests.

The truck came to a jarring halt. The driver shouted terrible things. He screamed that the cats were tramps. He called them *cochons*, which means pigs. He even threw a great heavy wrench at them. They ran to safety in a culvert.

The terrible man drove away at last, and the cats continued their journey on foot. O'Malley

offered to stop another truck so that they could ride further, but Duchess wouldn't hear of it. She was an aristocat, and she was not accustomed to finding herself in places where she was not wanted.

Night came upon them before they reached the city. O'Malley could make himself comfortable anywhere. It was he who found the big drainpipe set into the side of a hill. Obviously it had been put in to carry off water from someplace above them. It was dry now, and the sand which had collected on the bottom was soft and clean. O'Malley, Duchess and the kittens moved in to take shelter for the night.

The kittens were very weary, and they were hungry. But they were angry, too, at the thought of the horrid truck driver.

"That man called us tramps!" complained Berlioz.

Toulouse chuckled. "He's not so great. He couldn't throw worth beans."

Duchess remembered the ugly, heavy wrench flying through the air. What if it had hit one of them? She shivered. "What a horrible, rude human!" she exclaimed.

O'Malley wasn't upset. "Some humans are like that, baby," he told her. "They don't dig us cats. You've got to learn to live with it."

Live with it? Duchess didn't plan to do any such thing. "I'll be glad when we get back home," she told O'Malley.

This started a whole new train of thought running through O'Malley's brain. If the humans Duchess knew were so great, how had the cat and her kittens wound up miles from home, dumped under a bridge?

"You know, Duchess," said the alley cat, "It may be you're not wanted back home."

"Not wanted?" Duchess couldn't believe that even an alley cat could suggest such a thing. "Of course we are wanted," she told O'Malley. "I am Madame's dearest friend."

"Then who gave you the old heave-ho?" asked O'Malley. He wasn't trying to be unkind. But it seemed to him that a word of warning might be in order. "Someone tossed you under that bridge. It happens in the best of families. One day you're the pet of the household and the next day nobody wants you. So you're out!"

"Madame would never throw us out!" declared Duchess.

Toulouse had the answer. "It was old pickle-puss Edgar," he announced.

Duchess put a stop to that right away. "Toulouse, that's enough. Edgar would never do such a thing!"

"Someone did," O'Malley pointed out.

Duchess did not answer, and the cats settled themselves to sleep.

They were sleeping so soundly, hours later, that they did not even stir at the sound of a motorcycle put-putting down the road from Paris.

* * * * * * * *

Edgar returned to the scene of his crime with great stealth. He left his motorcycle by the side of the road and walked the last half mile, carrying his fishing rod. He even took off his shoes

again. He found the dogs, Napoleon and Lafayette, asleep beside a haystack not far from the little bridge.

When he saw the dogs, Edgar could have murdered them with glee. Napoleon was stretched out in his sidecar and Lafayette had retrieved the cats' basket and was snoring away in that. Napoleon had taken possession of the derby and the umbrella.

Edgar reflected that it would be marvelously simple to shoot the dogs and make off with his possessions. However, Edgar did not own a gun. Even if he had, he did not want to rouse the countryside. He would have to rely on cunning —and his fishing rod.

Edgar hid himself in the haystack and set to work. He let out some line and maneuvered the rod until he snagged his derby. He reeled the hat in without making a sound.

That wasn't too hard. Now Edgar went after his umbrella. He got that, too, without disturbing the dogs. Napoleon twitched slightly, but he didn't wake.

For the sidecar, Edgar used a different strategy. He put the umbrella and the derby on top of the haystack and wriggled his way down inside so that he was completely covered by the hay. Then he reached out, groping ever so gently, until he felt the edge of the sidecar.

Carefully, carefully, Edgar tilted the sidecar. Napoleon growled in his sleep.

Edgar waited a minute, then tilted the thing still further.

Napoleon slid out onto the ground and Edgar pulled the sidecar in under the haystack.

Napoleon sat up with a puzzled "Woof!" Something was very wrong here. Where was his marvelous one-wheeled bed? Where was his hat and his umbrella?

There was a squeak behind Napoleon. The dog looked around and saw the haystack, which had always stood in one place as sensible haystacks do. It was going away. A pair of running legs showed beneath it. And it had not only legs. It had a single wheel that squeaked as it turned.

In the cats' basket, Lafayette floundered awake. The squeak had reached his drowsy brain. For a few seconds he, too, watched the retreating haystack.

"Hey, Napoleon!" he growled. "Let's get it."

Napoleon didn't think so. He chased almost everything on wheels. He chased carriages and bicycles and motorcycles and automobiles and trucks. But Napoleon had never heard of a one-wheeled haystack, and he was not about to chase it!

"We can't win them all," he reminded Lafayette.

Then he shoved the beagle rudely out of the cats' basket and settled down to spend the rest of the night in solid comfort.

Duchess, O'Malley and the kittens were on the move before dawn. By eight o'clock they

had come to a small market town. O'Malley advised Duchess and her family not to show themselves in the place. They were valuable cats. Someone might take a fancy to them, and that would certainly complicate their journey.

So Duchess, Marie, Berlioz and Toulouse skirted the edge of the community. As for O'Malley, there was little worry that someone would try to adopt *him* by force. He sauntered into town and made a quick tour of the open-air market. When he joined Duchess and the kittens on the far side of the place there was a fine plump fish clenched in his jaws.

Duchess knew that O'Malley must have stolen the fish, but she felt it would be rude to mention this. Besides, her family was hungry.

The fish disappeared, head, tail and all that happened in between, and the travelers went on.

They walked and walked. Whenever the kittens grew tired, they would stop in the shade of a tree and rest for a while. Then they would walk again.

By late afternoon Duchess was beginning to fear that they would never reach Paris. Was it possible that they had gone in the wrong direction? Monsieur O'Malley seemed very sure of himself. He claimed to know every road from Avignon to Madrid. Still, even the most experienced cat can make a mistake.

Duchess wanted to stop at one of the farms to ask directions. O'Malley was against this. He said he knew the road. Besides, the farm cats who kept down the mice in the barns never went anywhere. They were an ignorant lot. They wouldn't know Paris if someone put them down right on the steps of Notre Dame.

Duchess was terribly weary and on the point of crying. Then two geese came toward them, waddling along in a no-nonsense way.

"Let's ask them," suggested Duchess.

O'Malley was shocked at the idea of asking a goose anything, but he had no chance to argue. Marie bounced forward and greeted the geese with her sweetest meow.

The geese seemed pleased at the sight of the kittens. They stopped gladly and introduced themselves in very bad French. They were, they said, the Gabble sisters, Abigail and Amelia. Back home in England they employed themselves by instructing the younger geese in their barnyard on the finer points of behavior, such as waddling and, when the occasion called for it, hissing. They also gave swimming lessons. But this was vacation time, and they had de-

cided to improve themselves by taking a walking tour of France.

"Of course we don't always walk," explained Amelia. "Sometimes we swim."

"Whenever we come to a river," added Abigail.

The two went off into gales of giggles, and O'Malley decided that it was time to get the train back on the track. He stepped up and told the sisters who he was, taking care to mention every one of his wonderful names. And he called the Gabbles chicks!

The Gabbles giggled again.

"We're not chicks," said Abigail. "We're geese!"

O'Malley pretended to be amazed. "I wouldn't have guessed it," he told them. "I thought you were swans."

The Gabbles went off in another delighted giggling spree, and Amelia bent close to Duchess and whispered, "Your husband is charming—and very handsome!"

Whereupon O'Malley quickly informed them that he wasn't Duchess' husband. He wasn't anyone's husband.

Most single ladies do not care for confirmed bachelors. The Gabbles quickly changed their minds about O'Malley. He wasn't handsome after all. His eyes were too close together. And they were shifty. His smile was crooked and his chin was weak.

Marie peered up at O'Malley, wondering if these things could be true.

Duchess came to the rescue. "Monsieur O'Malley is our very dear friend," she explained gently. "We have been lost in the country, and he came to our rescue. He has agreed to see us safely home—to Paris."

Well, that was different. Any cat who would go out of his way for a stranded lady and three helpless kittens could not be all bad. And of course the Gabbles knew the way to Paris. They had just come from there.

With this settled, the Gabbles took charge. They lined the cats up, putting O'Malley at the end of the line, since even the best of males have been known to cause trouble. Then off they went like a class of children, singing a little song.

And when they came to the top of the nearest hill, there was the Eiffel Tower. The cats were almost home.

The Gabbles left them then, but not before promising to come and visit Duchess on their next trip to the Continent. O'Malley again became the leader of the party and the cats walked on.

There were no more stops to rest. They were too eager. But it was very late when they reached a shabby district which was completely strange to Duchess, but which O'Malley seemed to know quite well. Marie appeared to be walking in her sleep, and Toulouse no longer scampered. He trudged.

"Monsieur O'Malley, is it much further?" asked Duchess. "My children are very, very tired."

O'Malley looked at the poor little ones and agreed. "We'll never make it tonight, Duchess," he told her. "I've got a real keen pad near here. Why don't we stop over and rest, and then get a fresh start in the morning."

"A pad?" questioned Duchess.

"An apartment," explained O'Malley. "A home—of sorts. A place to lay the weary head. What do you say, Duchess?"

Duchess said yes. It was the only thing to say.

O'Malley led the way down some very dark and narrow alleys. Then he nosed a door open and went up some very dark and narrow stairs. Then they were out on the rooftops of Paris. They picked their way along ledges and around chimneys and came at last to an open skylight.

"Here we are, baby," said O'Malley proudly. "It's not exactly the Ritz, but it's peaceful and quiet."

Hardly were the words spoken when there was a sudden blare of music from the skylight.

Duchess jumped and Marie scooted to hide behind her mother.

O'Malley wasn't disturbed. "Sounds like Scat Cat and his group have dropped by," said he.

"Friends of yours?" asked Duchess.

"Old buddies. And real swingers—cool cats. But not exactly your type, Duchess. Maybe we'd better find some other place for tonight."

Duchess wouldn't hear of it. If this Scat Cat was a friend of O'Malley, she wanted to meet him. And she wanted to see O'Malley's pad.

So the aristocats joined the party which was noisily going on in O'Malley's garret room. She met Scat Cat and his group—a truly fierce-looking band of alley cats who did the most amazing things with music. Tired as she was, Duchess was at her charming best when she greeted them. And alley cats though they were, the group made her welcome. Scat Cat outdid himself; he planted a respectful kiss on Duchess' paw.

Then the party went on, and even the exhausted little kittens were fascinated by the singing and the playing. Scat Cat had, somewhere and somehow, acquired a brass horn. He tootled it loudly. One of his friends had an old bass fiddle, and another did violent things to some drums. It was unlike anything the aristocats had ever heard, and it was exciting.

But the alley cats knew when enough of a good thing was enough. Besides, O'Malley had quietly slipped them the word that Duchess and the little ones had hiked a long way that day. One by one the alley cats picked up their instruments and stole away. When they were gone, there remained only Duchess, O'Malley and three sleepy kittens.

Duchess tucked her children into the big sagging bed that stood in one corner of the garret. O'Malley perched on the edge of the skylight and watched.

Suddenly it came to O'Malley that being a single cat might not be all that it was cracked up to be.

"Happy dreams, my loves," whispered Duchess. She left the kittens and came to sit beside O'Malley just outside the skylight. Together they watched the moon come up over Paris.

"Thomas, your friends are really delightful," murmured Duchess.

O'Malley turned his head so that the aristocat would not see his grin. For the first time she had called him Thomas, and not Monsieur O'Malley.

"They're kind of rough around the edges,"

and the neglect and the clutter of years. He saw
that the bed in which the kittens slept had a
broken leg.

O'Malley saw all of these things, and he
thought of the house in which Duchess and her
kittens usually spent their days.

"Hey, Duchess," he protested, "this is the low
rent district, remember?"

"Oh, it is really very nice," said the enchanting
Duchess. "All it needs is a little tidying up,
and perhaps a bit of the feminine touch."

O'Malley gulped. "Gee!" he said.

That remark didn't require an answer. Duchess
smiled and was quiet.

"Your eyes really *are* like sapphires!" declared
O'Malley after a bit.

Duchess didn't answer.

"That was pretty corny, wasn't it?" said
O'Malley.

Duchess didn't think it was corny. Any woman
loved being told that she had sapphire eyes—
even little Marie.

Which brought the subject of the kittens into
the conversation—and how fond the kittens were
of O'Malley.

O'Malley was pleased to hear it. He liked the
kittens, too. And he thought it would be wonderful if they had a—well—sort of a father around.

admitted O'Malley, "but when you're in a jam,
they're right there."

"You were right there when we needed you,"
said Duchess gently.

"That was a lucky break for me," O'Malley
answered.

"And you let us use your home—er—your
pad," Duchess pointed out. "It's really very
nice."

O'Malley turned to look at the streaked walls
and the putty crumbling away from the window
panes. He saw the place where a board was missing in one corner of the floor. He saw the dust

46

There was no mistaking his meaning. O'Malley was offering to take the job. He wanted to join the family, to help raise Duchess' kittens, to be with Duchess forever.

Duchess sighed. How wonderful that would be. In the last two days, Duchess had learned a great deal. She had learned that there was more to life than being an aristocat. Life required courage. That was at least as important as a fine pedigree. And if one was to live worthily, one had to be kind. And Abraham DeLacey Giuseppe Casey Thomas O'Malley, the alley cat, might steal fish from a market or waylay trucks on the Paris road, but he was kind.

What's more, he was fun. With O'Malley about, there was no way of telling what would happen next.

"Oh, Thomas!" purred Duchess.

O'Malley grinned his most mischievous grin. "What about it, Duchess?"

"If only I could," breathed Duchess.

O'Malley's grin disappeared. Was this the beginning of a very polite turn-down?

"Why can't you?" demanded O'Malley.

"Well you see, Thomas, there is Madame," said the Duchess.

Thomas did not see. What had Madame to do with it?

"I could never leave her," said Duchess.

What blather! What complete and utter nonsense. "Madame's just another human," O'Malley pointed out. "To her, you and the kittens are nothing but a bunch of house pets."

"Oh no, Thomas." Duchess paused to choose her words with care. She had to make Thomas understand how it was with herself and Madame. "We are friends," she said at last. "Madame tells me everything. She would not know what to do without us."

O'Malley could see that Duchess really believed this. He did not understand it. He had never felt this way about any human. Certainly no human had ever felt this way about him.

O'Malley was too downcast to speak. How could he argue with a thing like friendship? Especially a friendship which he did not understand.

Duchess said goodnight then and slipped away to curl up beside her kittens. O'Malley watched the moon travel across the sky and considered the difference between alley cats and aristocats —and humans.

The inspector of police had promised that he would do his best. His men would not rest until they had found Duchess and the kittens. But promises are only promises. The inspector could do no more than his best, and that was not good enough.

Madame Adelaide Bonfamille felt weak and useless, and for the first time she felt old. The phonograph in Madame's sitting room was silent. The new novels from the bookshop were untouched. Madame took to her bed.

The doctor came and felt Madame's pulse and looked at her tongue and listened to her heart. He looked very wise and very sad, and he went away again without even writing a prescription. He knew of no pills or poultices which could cure loneliness.

Edgar stayed downstairs as much as possible, and he was not sad at all. By ten in the morning he had already paid a visit to Madame's wine cellar. He had selected a bottle of Madame's best sparkling burgundy. He had taken one of the fine crystal goblets from the pantry and had come to rest in the salon, sitting on Madame's finest chair and propping his feet high on the keyboard of the piano.

Edgar drank a toast to himself. Then he drank a toast to his own future. A brilliant future it would be. Once Madame's forture was his, the sky would be the limit. Edgar would have all the finest things of life. He would have wine at ten o'clock every morning, if he happened to feel like it.

And O'Malley remembered Duchess and her kittens abandoned beneath a bridge far from home. If Madame was so fond of Duchess that she could not operate without her, why had Duchess been taken out in the dark of the night and stranded in the countryside?

Either Madame was a phony, O'Malley decided, or something very wicked was going on at Duchess' house. Tomorrow, when Duchess and the kittens returned home, O'Malley would go along. He would see what happened when the aristocats presented themselves at their own front door.

48

Edgar drank greedily and the bottle was soon empty. No matter. There was more wine. There was plenty of wine. Edgar made a second trip to the cellar and was soon back in the salon opening the second bottle of wine. Then Roquefort the mouse spied the cats.

Unnoticed by Edgar, Roquefort had posted himself on the windowsill and was keeping watch. He saw Duchess and the kittens and a tough-looking orange and black cat come into the courtyard.

"Duchess!" squeaked Roquefort.

It was almost too good to be true.

"Hallelujah!" cried Roquefort, and he hopped down off the windowsill.

And there sat the villain! There sat Edgar, who had caused all the trouble in the first place. There sat Edgar with his feet up on the piano and with Madame's wine glass in his hand.

Edgar had locked the little cat door. Roquefort knew that. In a moment Duchess would be meowing on the doorstep. What would Edgar do then? Something dreadful, no doubt. Roquefort had to stop the butler!

The mouse got a running start across the salon, scurried up the leg of the piano, and, while Edgar was still totally involved with his wine, Roquefort tied his shoelaces together.

Then the cats *were* meowing at the door.

"Wait for me! Wait for me!" cried Berlioz, as he always did when the others got ahead of him.

"Me first! Me first!" It was Marie, claiming a lady's privilege.

Edgar heard them and choked on his wine. He leaped up, dropped glass and bottle on the carpet and tried to run.

The shoelaces hobbled him, as Roquefort had planned. Edgar went down flat on his face.

Edgar didn't stop to wonder how his shoelaces came to be tied together. He kicked off his shoes and raced unsteadily to the door in his stocking feet.

Edgar's face was flushed with wine when he opened the door, and there was a ringing in his ears. Just the same, he managed to summon up a look of mock delight. "Duchess! Kittens!" he gurgled. "Thank goodness! You're back safe and sound!"

The kittens scampered into the hall. Duchess waited long enough to say a last goodbye to O'Malley. Then she followed her children into the house. The door closed, shutting her from O'Malley's sight.

"Well," said O'Malley to himself, "it looks like I was wrong. That guy sure seemed glad to see them."

O'Malley waited around for a bit, but all within the house was quiet and serene.

"I guess they don't need me any more," O'Malley concluded. He turned and started away from the faded elegance of the Bonfamille mansion, back to his own humble, dusty, dingy pad.

The kittens swarmed around Edgar's feet and rubbed against his ankles and purred with delight at being home.

"Where have you been?" Edgar asked. He still had his false, welcoming smile carefully in place, and he was slipping out of his coat.

"Duchess! Watch out!"

Roquefort had abandoned all caution. He stood in the doorway of the salon and squealed at the top of his small lungs.

The warning came too late. Edgar's coat suddenly covered the cat and her kittens. The butler gathered them up in one squirming, mewing mass and glared.

"You came back!" Edgar snarled. "You dared to come back!"

Edgar rushed into the kitchen and thrust the cats, coat and all, into the cold oven. He slammed the door on them, cutting off their cries of bewilderment and outrage.

For a horrible moment Roquefort was afraid the fiendish butler might be about to light the oven. But he didn't, for Madame was calling. She had heard the kittens cry at the front door.

"Edgar, they're back!" She came down the stairs as quickly as she could, holding up the skirt of her dressing gown. "Let them in, Edgar. They're back!"

Edgar sped out into the hall and swung the front door wide.

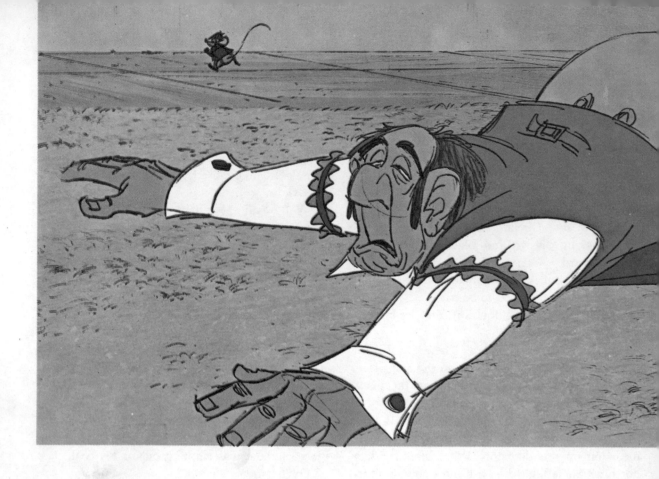

"Duchess?" called Madame. She reached the door and looked out into the empty courtyard. "Kittens? Where are you?"

But they were not there.

A tear made its way down Madame's cheek. "I thought I heard them," she said softly. "I was sure I heard them."

She turned and started slowly, slowly toward the stairs. "I guess it was just the imagination of a tired old woman," she said.

Roquefort scurried into the kitchen. He climbed up onto the stool which Edgar used when he sat and prepared vegetables. From the stool he jumped to the stove. There was a vent in the door of the oven and Roquefort put his mouth to this.

"Duchess!" he called. "It's me! Roquefort!"

"Oh, thank goodness, Monsieur Roquefort!" exclaimed Duchess from inside the oven. "You must run and get help."

"Help? From who?"

"My friend Monsieur O'Malley," Duchess told him. "He will know what to do. He is the cat who came here with us this morning. He is a large, orange and black cat with . . ."

"I saw him." Roquefort cut her short. There wasn't a moment to lose. "I'm on my way," promised the mouse, and he ran off as if his life depended on it.

O'Malley had not gone two blocks before Roquefort caught up with him. The cat was stunned at being confronted by a very excited little mouse—a mouse who talked fast, and who talked about Duchess.

Had this been an ordinary day, O'Malley would simply have put a paw down and silenced this saucy mouse forever. But there was nothing ordinary about the day, or the mouse. The little creature seemed to be a friend of Duchess, and he reported that Duchess was in terrible trouble. The butler—that evil man who had opened the door for the kittens—had locked the cats in the oven. Unless Monsieur O'Malley took steps immediately, the butler would surely murder Duchess and her family.

A plan of battle formed in O'Malley's agile brain. But he would need help.

"Look, little friend," he said to Roquefort, "you get yourself over to the Left Bank and get Scat Cat and his gang. They're alley cats."

"Alley cats?" The hair on Roquefort's head stood up straight with horror. "Monsieur, I am a mouse," he reminded O'Malley.

"Tell them O'Malley sent you and you won't have a bit of trouble," said the cat. "Now get going. Move!"

Roquefort moved as only a terrified mouse can, and in no time he was on the Left Bank.

He found Scat Cat easily enough. The big, tough Tom was lolling in a garbage can in a narrow alley that was strewn with refuse. The gang was with Scat Cat.

The alley cats thought Roquefort was extremely funny. They had been hunted all their lives. They had been chased by dogs. They had had shoes and clocks and other things too numerous to mention thrown at them by humans. But they had never before been pursued by a mouse.

Poor little Roquefort was stiff with fright. It did nothing for his peace of mind when Scat Cat held him up by his tail and swung him back and forth, pretending he was the pendulum of a clock.

"I was sent here by . . . by a friend . . . a friend of yours," Roquefort managed to gasp.

The alley cats howled with laughter. What friend of theirs would hob-nob with a mouse?

"His name is O'Brien," squeaked the mouse.

"Who are you kidding?" Scat Cat wanted to know. He tossed Roquefort roughly from one paw to another.

Roquefort realized that O'Brien wasn't the name at all. "O'Leary?" he cried.

That wasn't it, either.

"O'Flannigan? O'Toole? No! No! It was O'Malley!"

Scat Cat stopped tossing Roquefort around and paid attention.

"That's it! O'Malley!" By now Roquefort was trembling so that he could hardly speak. "Trouble!" he said.

Scat Cat put him gently on the ground.

"O'Malley said to come," Roquefort pleaded. "Duchess and the kittens! They're in the oven!"

In a flash, every cat in the alley was bristling and ready for battle. With Scat Cat in the lead, they started to run.

"Wait for me!" cried Roquefort. "I'll show you the way!"

There was an old trunk in the carriage house. It had a good stout lock, and the corners were reinforced with brass. Edgar dragged it out into the middle of the floor. It would do. It exactly suited his purpose.

He opened the trunk. Then he returned to the house and put on a thick pair of leather gloves. Going into the kitchen, he removed the aristocats from the oven. His coat muffled their cries as he carried them to the carriage house and locked them in the trunk.

When this was done, Edgar went to the telephone, called the express office and arranged for a driver to call and pick up a trunk which was to be shipped to General Delivery, Timbuktu, Africa.

Edgar wrote out the labels for the trunk with great care. This shipment must not go astray. When the tags were ready, he went back to the carriage house and sat down to await the arrival of the express wagon.

Duchess cried plaintively inside the trunk.

"Now, now, my pesky little pet," said Edgar. "Don't complain. You're going to travel first class, in your own little private compartment. And I dare you to come back from Timbuktu!"

Edgar opened the door of the carriage house. The express man should arrive at any moment. The butler was just pushing the trunk toward the door when O'Malley leaped from the rafters and landed on Edgar's shoulders. The cat dug in his claws to get a good firm footing.

Edgar screamed.

Inside the trunk, Duchess realized that O'Malley had come to her aid once more.

The alley cat jumped from Edgar's shoulders and slammed into the open door. It swung shut.

"You mangy meddler!" shouted Edgar. He snatched up a pitchfork and went at O'Malley with the wicked thing. O'Malley danced aside and the pitchfork thunked into the wall.

Mlle. Frou-Frou had been standing quietly, as befits a well-trained mare. Now she entered the contest between Edgar and the cats. And she was on the side of the cats. When Edgar opened the door again, she kicked it closed.

"Stay out of this, Frou-Frou!" yelled the butler.

O'Malley circled the butler, looking for an opening, while Edgar had another go at getting that door open. This time, when the door swung back, the butler was suddenly swarming with very excited, very tough cats from the Left Bank of the Seine. Scat Cat and his friends had moved in, in full battle formation.

There were only five of the alley cats, but they were so lively that it seemed to Edgar that he was under attack by at least fifty mewing, spitting, clawing feline fiends.

Frou-Frou had never seen anything like it. She wanted to do her bit, too, so she kicked at the butler several times. And while this was going on, Roquefort slipped in and efficiently picked the lock of the trunk, freeing Duchess and the kittens.

The aristocats began a dash for freedom.

"Oh, no you don't!" howled Edgar. He grabbed for Duchess.

From the rafters above, O'Malley dropped part of a harness over Edgar's shoulders. The butler's arms were pinned to his sides. Scat Cat discovered a gunny sack in a corner, and he draped this around Edgar's head.

It was Frou-Frou, the gentle mare, who put the finishing touch to Edgar's ruin. She aimed her kick very precisely. And Edgar sailed into the trunk.

The alley cats slammed the lid of the trunk shut.

Roquefort closed the lock and listened to it click. It would take an expert locksmith, or an especially clever mouse, to open it again.

Another kick from Frou-Frou sent the trunk sliding out through the door and into the lane behind the garden. All the labels were still in place. The express wagon appeared a few minutes later and the express man knew what to do. He loaded the trunk aboard his wagon and clip-clopped away down the lane.

Edgar had started the first lap of his long journey to Timbuktu, Africa.

Madame had some trouble replacing Edgar. The butler had been with her for many years, and good servants are difficult to find. But Madame managed. With Duchess and the kittens back in the house, Madame was again full of joy and vigor and vanity. She was equal to anything.

Often she wondered why Edgar had left her so suddenly without giving any notice. But even the best of servants had their irresponsible moments.

In time the household was arranged and running smoothly. And, since Edgar had disappeared, Madame sent for Monsieur Hautcourt. She had to change her will.

"Very good, very good!" said Monsieur when he heard about it. He sat down at the little desk in Madame's sitting room. "Now we scratch one butler, I suppose," he began.

"A pity," said Madame, "but it seems that we must do that. I am sure if Edgar had known about the will he would not have gone away so suddenly and left me alone."

"I am sure he would not," agreed Monsieur Hautcourt. "Now, Adelaide, about your cats. "There is Duchess and Marie and Berlioz and Toulouse . . ."

". . . and O'Malley and Scat Cat and—oh there are many, many more!" exclaimed Madame happily.

"Eh?" Monsieur Hautcourt was sure that his old ears were deceiving him.

"Yes, Georges," said Madame. "You see, I have decided that I can do a great deal more with my fortune that I ever dreamed possible."

Madame stroked Duchess, who was sitting next to her on the rose velvet sofa. "Duchess and I worked out the plan together," Madame told the lawyer. "I am establishing a foundation to provide shelter and comfort for all of the homeless alley cats of Paris."

Monsieur Hautcourt stared at Madame without speaking.

"There is also a mouse," said Madame. "I wish to remember him in my will."

Madame's smile twinkled. "I think one cannot forget the mouse, Georges," said Madame. "Duchess is very fond of him."

Duchess looked into the face of Monsieur Hautcourt. Then the cat got down from the sofa and went out of the room. She was afraid that Monsieur Hautcourt might have some sort of seizure, and she did not wish to see this happen.

Besides, down in the salon, O'Malley and the kittens were about to join Scat Cat and his group in a real swinging session.

Duchess planned to be among those present.

53

Blackbeard's Ghost

BLACKBEARD'S INN was something of a shock to Steve Walker. Of course, Blackbeard's Inn was apt to be a shock to almost anyone. It was startling enough when seen for the first time in broad daylight. Steve came to it in the soft April dusk, after having driven for more than five hundred miles. He braked his small convertible to a stop in the parking lot and stared up at the old building.

"Fantastic!" said Steve.

He said it to no one in particular, but a very thin boy in a sport shirt happened to be wandering through the lot and heard him.

"Pretty wild, huh?" said the boy.

Steve had to agree. The inn was wild. It looked as if it had been put together by a committee of pixilated sea captains. Weathered beams stuck out at odd angles. Windows were all sizes and all shapes. One side of the roof appeared to be made from the poop deck of a sailing ship. Across the front of the porch four carved figureheads smiled wooden smiles as they gazed at the bay. To make the scene even more fantastic, torches burned on the lawn and crowds of people milled around in the glow of a bonfire.

"Blackbeard the pirate built this place," said the thin boy. He seemed very proud of it. "This was his home base. It's mostly odds and ends— old timbers and stuff from ships that were wrecked out in the bay. Lots of ships had accidents while Blackbeard was building."

Steve got out of the car rather stiffly.

"You staying at the inn?" asked the boy.

Steve nodded.

The boy looked doubtful. "Mostly old ladies live here. Salesman going through like to stay over in Godolphin at the Jolly Roger."

"I'm not a salesman," said Steve. "I'm the new track coach at Godolphin College."

The boy looked Steve up and down, taking in the rumpled tweed jacket, the tanned face above the open collar, the sandy hair, now mussed and windblown. Then he grinned and stuck out a skinny hand. "Glad to know you, Coach! My name's Larkin—Gudger Larkin. I'm on your track squad."

Steve shook Gudger's hand and murmured his own name.

"You'd better see Mrs. Stowecroft," Gudger advised him.

"Who's Mrs. Stowecroft?"

"She's one of the old ladies who run the inn. They're all descendants of Blackbeard's crew. They call themselves the Daughters of the Buccaneers."

"Now I've heard everything," laughed Steve. He pointed to a sign on the lawn of the inn:

BUCCANEER BAZAAR TONIGHT
HELP SAVE BLACKBEARD'S INN!

"What's that all about?" he asked Gudger. Gudger nodded toward a dark-haired man who stood alone on the edge of the crowd. The man was very pale. He wore a too-sharp dark suit and a black hat pulled down over his eyes.

"That's Silky Seymour," said Gudger. "He runs the gambling around here. He wants this place real bad. It's mortgaged to the hilt and the debt's got to be paid by the first. If the nice little old ladies don't come up with the loot to pay off the bank, out they go, and Silky will buy the inn."

"So they're trying to raise money with this bazaar?" asked Steve.

"Right."

"I wish them luck," said the track coach. "I also wish I could meet this Mrs. Stowecroft—if

she's the nice little old lady in charge of rooms. I've been driving ever since five this morning."

"You bet, Coach!" Gudger led Steve toward a fussed and fussy little woman who was wearing a silk ribbon which proclaimed her to be one of the Daughters of the Buccaneers.

"Miss Jeffrey," said Gudger, "have you seen Mrs. Stowecroft? This is Mr. Walker. He wants a room."

"She's in the tent over there," said Miss Jeffrey. Her pink, wrinkled little face glowed with excitement. "She's telling fortunes." And Miss Jeffrey scurried on toward a booth where another ancient lady presided over a game of hoop-la.

"Miss Jeffrey's great-great-great-grandfather was Red Dog Jeffrey," whispered Gudger. "He was Blackbeard's second mate."

"Imagine that!" Steve was too tired to care very much. "Well, I'll go find my little old room clerk now."

"Sure," said Gudger. "See you later."

Steve went toward the tent which was pitched at the edge of the lawn. "Granny Woman," a sign announced. "Fortunes! Incantations! Love Potions!"

Rooms to rent, I hope, thought Steve. "Mrs. Stowecroft?" he called.

The tent flap lifted and an elderly lady looked

out. Her head was covered with what appeared to be an old window curtain. Doubtless she believed that fortune tellers should go veiled at all times.

"Yes?" she said.

"I'm Steve Walker," explained the track coach. "The college arranged a room for me."

"Ah, yes." She beckoned him closer. "Give me your hand, please."

"But I don't want my fortune told, Mrs. Stowecroft," protested Steve. "Just a room."

She sighed and emerged from the tent, taking off her veil and patting her gray curls into place.

"Good," said Steve. "Now, if I could have the key to my room, I'll just. . . ."

He was interrupted by a ship's bell being lustily clanged.

"How fortunate," said Mrs. Stowecroft. "You're just in time for the auction."

"Auction?" Steve echoed. "Look, I don't care about any auction. I just want to get to bed!"

The bell clanged again. A remarkably pretty girl stood on the porch. "Ladies and gentlemen!" she called.

The crowd began to move toward her. Interested in spite of himself, Steve moved with them.

"Ladies and gentlemen of Godolphin," she cried. "You all know the purpose of this bazaar." Several people nodded.

"Unless we raise enough money," the girl went

on, "this historic old inn will be taken from our good friends, the Daughters of the Buccaneers. It will pass into the hands of strangers." She glared across the crowd at Silky Seymour, the gambler. He looked back with cold indifference.

"When Mrs. Stowecroft auctions the treasured antiques that she and others have donated, I beg you to bid generously." The girl finished and stepped aside. Mrs. Stowecroft bobbed up onto the porch holding an ancient pistol.

"That's Professor Baker," said a voice close to Steve. It was Gudger Larkin, back to fill Steve in on the local color.

"Professor Baker?" questioned Steve. "You mean that pretty girl?"

"She teaches psychology at the college," Gudger told Steve. "Her name's Jo Anne, but to her face you call her Professor Baker."

"Lot Number One!" cried Mrs. Stowecroft. "A fine antique pistol which has been in the Jeffrey family for many years. What am I bid?"

"One dollar!" called a white-haired gentleman.

"Oh, Mr. Harrison!" Mrs. Stowecroft was crushed. "One dollar? Can't we do better than that? Who'll bid twenty?"

There was silence. Then Steve noticed Silky Seymour staring hard at the man who had bid on the pistol. He saw, too, that several tough-

looking characters were circulating through the crowd. Every so often one of them would look at Seymour and grin. The gambler didn't want the crowd to bid, and he was making sure they knew it.

"Tell me," said Steve to Gudger, "does Silky Seymour always get what he wants?"

"Most always," Gudger admitted.

"We'll see about that!" Steve's hand shot up. "I bid twenty dollars on the pistol!"

Professor Baker rewarded him with an enchanting smile.

"Twenty dollars!" cried Mrs. Stowecroft. "Do I hear thirty?"

Now Mr. Harrison looked at Silky Seymour, reddened, and defiantly raised his bid to thirty.

Excitement began to spread through the crowd. "Thirty-five!" called a large lady in a red dress.

"Forty dollars!" It was a small man standing near the porch of the inn.

"Fifty dollars!" Mr. Harrison had a new burst of courage.

"Sixty dollars!"

"Seventy!"

"Eighty!"

"One hundred!" Mr. Harrison was now determined that he would have the pistol at any cost.

There was no higher bid, and Mrs. Stowecroft happily handed the pistol over to Mr. Harrison.

One of Silky Seymour's thugs edged close to Harrison. "You got taken, buddy," he said. "That gun's a fake. Take my advice. Don't bid again."

"Lot Number Two," announced Mrs. Stowecroft. "A genuine antique bed warmer."

Another of Seymour's men approached Steve. "Tourist junk!" he said. "Mr. Seymour don't like to see you throw money away." Then he moved on to spread the word through the crowd.

Mrs. Stowecroft continued her spiel. "Ladies and gentlemen, this bed warmer is believed to have been the property of Aldetha Teach, wife of the great Captain Blackbeard! What am I bid?"

The crowd was nervously silent.

Mrs. Stowecroft beamed at the large lady in the red dress. "Mrs. Starkey, will you start the bidding?"

Mrs. Starkey, flustered, didn't think she would.

A birdlike person named Finch also decided that he wouldn't bid, and Mr. Harrison announced that the pistol was enough for him. Steve felt himself growing hot under the collar. Could four thugs really frighten a crowd of at least two hundred people?

"Five dollars!" shouted Steve.

Professor Baker smiled again. "Thank you!"

It was a beginning. A man named Purvis raised the bid to ten. Steve, warmed by the professor's admiration, went to twenty. Again the crowd became excited. Despite the jostling by Seymour's men, the bids on the bed warmer went up and up until they reached a hundred dollars.

Seymour moved quietly to Steve's side. "It's just an opinion, friend," he said softly, "but I wouldn't bid anymore if I were you."

"Now, why is that?" Steve asked, just as softly.

"No reason. I just don't want you to."

Steve grinned. Then, not at all softly, he shouted, *"Two hundred dollars!"*

Instantly, Steve wished he'd kept his mouth shut. Two hundred dollars was almost all he had in the world! And what on earth would he do with an antique bed warmer?

"You're new around here, aren't you?" asked Silky Seymour.

Steve answered in a daze. "That's right."

"Just passing through?" Silky wanted to know.

"No," said Steve.

"Might stay around for a while, eh?" Silky seemed pleased. "Fine! We'll see each other again." And he melted into the crowd.

Aldetha's Curse

FOR A TIME, Steve forgot all about going to bed. Holding fast to his bed warmer, he waited in the lobby of the inn. It was a strange place, with its salty old timbers and its bulkhead walls. In the exact center of the room was a ship's helm, with a binnacle and compass. To one side, through a doorway, was a small bar lit by ancient lanterns. Instead of ordinary stairs, a companionway led up to what had once been a quarterdeck. Everything was immaculately clean, and here and there brass fittings shone in the best nautical tradition.

It was past midnight when the last visitor to the bazaar straggled off into the night. Mrs. Stowecroft and Professor Baker came in from the porch. The professor was carrying a tin money box. Her dark hair swung as she turned to Steve and smiled.

"Thanks, Mr. Walker," she said. "We'd never have gotten that auction off the ground if it hadn't been for you."

"How'd you know my name?" asked Steve.

"Gudger told me."

"That boy's handy to have around," said Steve. "How'd you make out on the bazaar?"

"Much better than we had hoped."

"No problem then?"

"I wish *that* were true."

Mrs. Stowecroft drifted away toward some hidden room at the back of the inn. Professor Baker lowered her voice. "We still have to get another thirty-seven thousand dollars for Mr. Seymour before the first of the month. I haven't told the ladies how bad the situation is. They've all been so brave and cheerful. Besides, there's al-

ways the chance that something may still turn up."

Steve frowned. "Why is Silky Seymour so anxious to get his hooks on this place?" he wanted to know.

Professor Baker went to a map on the wall near the bar. "You can see the reason here," she told Steve. "The inn's on a little island. In Blackbeard's time it wasn't an island; it was part of the mainland. Then, about eighty years ago, there was a terrible storm and a flood. The river changed course and cut the inn off from the mainland. Since then, no one's been able to decide just who has legal jurisdiction over the island.

If he owned it, Silky Seymour could tear down this old inn and build a gambling casino and the law couldn't bother him."

"Nice setup," commented Steve.

"If you're a gambler, it's a beautiful setup. Well, I have to get home now." The professor held out her hand and smiled that flashing smile again. "I'm so grateful for what you did, Mr. Walker."

"Call me Steve, please. And can't I drive you home?"

"No, I have my car. Good night, Steve."

"Good night, Jo Anne."

One eyebrow shot up in surprise. "Oh, how did you . . . ?" she began.

"Gudger told me."

"Of course. I should have known."

She went then, and Mrs. Stowecroft pattered back into the lobby. "Now, Mr. Walker, I'll show you to your room," she said briskly. "I do hope we haven't kept you waiting."

She had, of course. She had kept him waiting for hours. At the moment, however, he didn't mind. With his suitcase in one hand and the warming pan in the other, he followed her up the companionway and across the quarterdeck.

"I'm going to put you in his room," said Mrs. Stowecroft. "You were so nice at the auction, and I'm sure he won't mind."

"He?" queried Steve.

"Captain Blackbeard," explained Mrs. Stowecroft. She opened a door and stepped aside so that Steve could go through ahead of her.

Like the lobby of the inn, Captain Blackbeard's room was unusual. The ceiling was low and beamed. On one side was a huge bay window, heavily carved, and obviously from the captain's cabin of some old ship. There was a massive four-poster bed, several ship's chests, and a round table with two chairs.

Mrs. Stowecroft crossed to the window and pulled back the curtain. "This looks out on the river and the upper bay," she told Steve. "The captain used to stand here with his glass and watch the ships. Then he'd pick out the one he

liked. Merchant ship, treasure ship, warship—it was all the same to the captain. I hope you'll sleep well."

"I usually do. I. . . ."

"Sometimes," interrupted Mrs. Stowecroft, "sometimes, when he's in a bad mood, or feeling lonely, we can hear him."

"Him? You mean . . . ?"

She nodded. "Blackbeard. He thumps around. I think he's trying to communicate with us."

Steve wondered whether his new landlady might not be missing a few marbles.

"I suppose we should be angry with him," she said gently, "but it really isn't his fault, poor man!"

"Oh, no?" questioned Steve. "Whose fault is it?"

"Aldetha's. His wife. The one your warming pan belonged to. She was a witch, you know."

Steve hastily put the pan down on the bed.

Mrs. Stowecroft gazed up at a painting that hung on the wall opposite the window. It was a portrait of a woman, a dark-haired woman with high cheekbones, pale skin, and a mouth that seemed tight and thin. The eyes in the portrait were most arresting. They were large, and of a peculiar light green color.

"The authorities arrested Aldetha for witchcraft," said Mrs. Stowecroft.

Looking at the picture, Steve believed this was quite possible. If there was any witchcraft going on around Godolphin, a woman who looked like Aldetha would automatically be a prime suspect.

"Aldetha thought that Captain Blackbeard had informed on her," explained Mrs. Stowecroft. "I don't suppose it was the kind of thing he would do, actually. But she was furious, and she put a terrible curse on him. When they came to take her away, she screeched, 'Edward Teach, sometimes known as Captain Blackbeard, when you come to die, may your soul be racked between this world and the next! May you never find rest! May you always be alone! May this curse hold fast and true, and may you dwell forevermore in limbo until such time as there be found in you, most wicked of all villains, some spark of human goodness!' "

Mrs. Stowecroft's voice had risen as she recited the terrible words. The curse seemed to echo through the inn, and somewhere, Steve thought, he could hear something rustle and something else go bump.

Mrs. Stowecroft smiled her dreamy smile. "So you see, Mr. Walker, it really isn't the captain's fault if he walks here to this day. It was all Aldetha's doing—she and her curse."

"I see," said Steve weakly.

"Good night, Mr. Walker. Sleep well." And Mrs. Stowecroft trotted out.

Gratefully, Steve closed the door after her. Then, just to make sure she wouldn't pop back in with any additional bit of ghostly lore, he turned the big brass key in the lock.

"Nuts!" he said loudly. "This place is nuts!"

Too weary to stand up another second, he slipped out of his jacket and fell back onto the bed.

There was a sharp crack!

"Oh, no!" moaned Steve. He rolled over and stared at his bed warmer—his fine, copper-bottomed, two-hundred-dollar bed warmer. He had snapped the handle in half.

Steve was horribly tired now. Even so, he saw right away that there was something odd about the broken bed warmer. Bed warmers weren't supposed to have hollow handles. And if they did have hollow handles, were the handles supposed to be stuffed with paper?

Steve gingerly touched the roll of yellowed parchment that poked from the broken handle. Then he drew it out and unrolled it. It was a book—a thin old book made up of half a dozen sheets of paper carefully stitched together.

Steve bent to the light on the table and read the faded lettering on the book's cover. "Aldetha Teach—Her Booke of Spells and Conjurations."

So the bed warmer really had belonged to the old pirate's wife!

On the second page of the book, written in a fine, spidery script, there was a spell for turning an enemy into a spotted toad. Steve wondered whether there was anyone he'd particularly like to see as a toad. Silky Seymour, perhaps? But, no, it wouldn't do a bit of good. Silky would be every bit as repulsive as a toad—probably even more so.

The next spell was guaranteed to turn mercury into gold. Since there wasn't any mercury close at hand, Steve went on to the third spell, which promised to bring to sight one who is bound in limbo.

"KREE KRUH VERGO," read Steve aloud. "GEBBA KALTO KREE!"

It didn't make any sense at all!

Just then, Steve was startled almost out of his skin by a mighty clap of thunder. Lightning flashed and a gale burst the windows open and sent the curtains streaming straight out into the room.

Steve leaped to slam the windows. Then, as suddenly as it had come up, the gale died away.

"Crazy!" said Steve. He had heard of sudden storms along the Atlantic coast, but this was ridiculous. "I just don't believe it!" he announced.

"Don't believe what, lad?" said a voice behind Steve.

The track coach turned.

He was there. There was no mistaking him. He looked just as he did in the history books, with his coat laced with gold braid, his wide, sweeping hat, his red face, his dark, glinting eyes, his cutlass and his pistols and his dirk, and, above all, his great, bristling black beard.

"What don't you believe?" asked Blackbeard the pirate.

Steve Walker closed his eyes.

"I know exactly what's wrong," he said aloud. "I've been up since five this morning. I'm tired, that's all."

He opened his eyes. The ghost of Captain Blackbeard was still there, regarding him with mild interest.

"Oh, boy, am I tired!" groaned Steve.

The ghost remained. Steve blinked and tried

to pull himself together. "You're not real!" he said firmly.

Blackbeard didn't answer, but he drew his cutlass from its scabbard. There was the very definite sound of steel sliding on steel.

"That sword's not real," insisted Steve.

Captain Blackbeard smiled and extended the cutlass so that the point was just under Steve's chin.

"It's not real," said Steve. "I'm going to walk

right through it. I'm going to walk right through *you* and go to bed."

"Try it, mate," invited the ghost.

Steve started forward. The very real point of a very real cutlass pricked at his throat.

"It *is* real!" Steve shrank back against the windows.

Blackbeard laughed. It was, Steve thought, a dirty sort of laugh. "Many's the brave lad whose brisket I clove in twain with this here cutlass," chortled the ghost.

Steve wondered foggily just what a brisket might be, but he didn't ask. The insane notion came into his head that the ghost might want to show him—with the cutlass!

But Blackbeard seemed to have lost interest in Steve. The pirate's eye had fallen on the broken warming pan on the bed, and on the old booklet that had been hidden in it.

"Aldetha's writing!" exclaimed the ghost. He picked up the book and leafed through it. Then he looked at the portrait on the wall. "So it were true," he said softly. "She were a witch! It was she what kept me from my rest these mortal years. And me her own legal-spoken husband!"

In spite of his own fright, Steve felt a twinge of pity for the pirate. "She said you turned her in," he told Blackbeard.

"Never!" cried the ghost. "Never did I harm Aldetha, nor peach on her to the magistrates. Oh, my mateys warned me of her. 'Beware, Cap'n!' they said. 'Sheer off. That girl be a true witch!' But I wouldn't listen. And here I am with this terrible curse on me. All these years I have dwelled in limbo. All these years I walked this house unseen. No one has heard my voice."

Steve now was edging around the ghost. He had one desperate hope. If he could get into bed —just get into bed and shut his eyes and sleep— the morning would come eventually. And when it was morning, the ghost would be gone.

Steve gained the bed safely, stretched out, and punched up the pillows.

Blackbeard began to chuckle.

"Huh?" Steve looked around.

"*You* see me," Blackbeard said. "*You* hear

me. You're the first in all these long ages." He looked again at Aldetha's book. "Poor lad! Now *you're* tied up with a witch's curse."

Steve pulled himself up, his scalp prickling. "Are you kidding? It's got nothing to do with me!"

Blackbeard shook the book under his nose. "You're the one who read Aldetha's spell," he

reminded Steve. "You brought me to your sight. Now you're caught in this, just like me."

Steve stretched out again. "Malarkey! I'm going to sleep, and when I wake up in the morning you will be gone and forgotten. And good riddance!"

"Belay that talk!" roared Blackbeard. "Now, I've a great thirst. Where do you stow your rum?"

"I don't drink," snapped Steve.

"Don't drink?" The ghost looked at Steve in astonishment, as if he were some strange bug. Then he snorted once into his beard, stomped to the door, unlocked it, and went out.

Steve intended only to lock the door after the pirate, but his curiosity got the better of him. He followed the ghost out onto the quarterdeck.

On the first floor of the inn, several old lanterns still burned. Steve watched Blackbeard stump down the companionway and through the lobby into the little bar. There was the faint sound of glass clattering against glass before the pirate appeared again, holding a bottle by the neck.

Just then, Mrs. Stowecroft came in from the porch. The ghost turned toward her. "Madam! Your most obedient servant!" He took off his hat and bowed a very low bow.

Mrs. Stowecroft passed him without a glance.

The ghost looked after her, sighed, then started up the companionway. Steve retreated to his room.

"She didn't see you!" said Steve when Blackbeard loomed through the door carrying his bottle. "She didn't see you, and she didn't hear you, either."

Blackbeard uncorked the bottle, took a mighty swig, rubbed his lips with his lace cuff, and sat down on the edge of the bed. The sharp-sweet smell of rum wafted through the room.

"No," said the pirate, "she didn't see me." Again he picked up Aldetha's book and looked at it. "A spell to bring to sight one who is bound in limbo," he read. "I'm beholden to that spell," he told Steve, "and it brought me to *your* eyes only.'"

Steve gulped miserably. "You mean, no one can see you except me?"

Blackbeard took a long pull at his bottle. "It looks as if that's about the shape of it, matey," he admitted, "so I'll just sail alongside you. Whither thou goest, I will go. Let's drink to it." In what was obviously meant to be a gesture of great friendliness, he offered his bottle to Steve. "Won't you freshen your hawse?" he asked.

"I don't drink," Steve reminded the ghost. "And let's get one thing straight right now. I want nothing to do with you."

Steve made for the bed. "I'm going to sleep," he told the ghost, "and you can crawl back into the woodwork, or wherever you came from."

Instantly Blackbeard was on his feet. The cutlass flashed a scant inch from Steve's ear. "Belay that tongue, boy!" warned the pirate. "Captain Blackbeard don't take kindly to insults. To speak plain, I don't favor the cut of *your* jib, neither."

But then the pirate calmed a bit. "We're stuck with each other, lad," he said, not unkindly. "It may be a long cruise. Let's make the best of it."

And, to Steve's horror, Blackbeard replaced his cutlass in its scabbard, took another tremendous swig of rum, and crept into the big four-poster bed, still holding firmly to his bottle.

"Get out of my bed!" shouted Steve.

"Your bed?" Blackbeard was outraged. "It's my bed, boy. I took it personal from a Portugee trader at the sack of Portobello. Spitted that poor soul clean against the headboard with my poniard! See! There's the mark still!"

The ghost pointed to a scar which showed on the wood of the four-poster.

Steve was not impressed. "If you think I'm going to sleep on the floor, you've got another think coming!" he yelled.

Blackbeard cheerfully inched over in the bed. "Devil a man who ever said old Teach was inhospitable," he told Steve. "Climb aboard, lad."

There seemed no help for it, so Steve climbed aboard, just managing to fit himself into the narrow space the ghost had left for him.

"That's right, lad," encouraged the pirate. "Make yourself comfortable."

Steve clung to the edge of the bed and gritted his teeth. "All I ask is to be able to get to sleep," he said. "When I wake up, I know none of this will ever have happened."

Blackbeard took another drink. "Whatever you say, shipmate," he mumbled. Then, after a moment, he began to snore.

"Oh, blast!" Steve exploded. Of all the ghosts who walk the world, why did he have to draw one who snored?

There was a soft rap at the door. "Mr. Walker?" called Mrs. Stowecroft. "Mr. Walker, are you all right? I thought I heard you call out."

Steve got up and padded to the door. "I'm fine, Mrs. Stowecroft," he told her. "I'm just having a nightmare, that's all."

Welcome to Godolphin

Steve did sleep at last, and when he awoke the sun was streaming in through the big window and gulls were screaming above the bay outside. The ghost of Captain Blackbeard, if it ever had existed, was nowhere to be seen.

Steve grinned. Funny the way your mind played tricks on you when you got too tired. He showered, shaved, and dressed, then went down to greet Mrs. Stowecroft, who was hovering in the doorway of the dining room. He wolfed down the enormous breakfast which had been prepared for him by old Mrs. Soames and which was served to him by the great-great-great-granddaughter of Red Dog Jeffrey. After breakfast, Mrs. Stowecroft gave him careful instructions on the best route to Godolphin College. She even

drew a little map for him on the back of a paper napkin. Whistling, he went outside to the car.

And there, sitting in the backseat of the neat blue convertible, was the ghost of Captain Blackbeard.

"Oh, no!" cried Steve.

Blackbeard lowered the glass with which he had been scanning the bay. "It's a fine morning, mate!" he said, with a good deal of cheer. "Where are we off to?"

Steve opened the car door and motioned for Blackbeard to get out. "*I* am off to Godolphin College," he said firmly. "*You* are going to stay right here."

The ghost put his glass down on the seat and laughed. "Not on your life, lad. I've not been away from this house these two hundred years. It's a new day for me now. I'm going alongside you."

"You are not!"

"Oh, come on, boy," coaxed the pirate. "Don't stand there like a booby. There's things to be seen beyond the bridge. Besides, you can't get away from old Teach, you know." The pirate's wicked little black eyes sparkled with glee.

It was true and Steve knew it. There simply wasn't any practical way to dump the pirate. With a fierce scowl, Steve climbed into the car.

"I've long wanted a cruise in one of these craft," said Blackbeard as he stroked the upholstery.

Steve was suddenly aware that the pirate had laid in provisions for his voyage. There was the sound of a cork popping out of a bottle, followed by a hearty gulping from the backseat.

"Great!" said Steve bitterly. "I couldn't have an ordinary ghost on my hands. I had to get a big, ugly, booze-soaked rummy!"

Steve gunned the car, backed out of the parking lot, and headed toward the bridge that crossed from the inn to the mainland. Behind him, the cork thunked back into the bottle.

"There's no call to put the fuddler's name on old Teach," said the pirate sullenly. "I been lonely, lad. My shipmates have all gone off without me. Till now, I've had no one to talk to." The ghost sniffed. "You don't like me," he accused. "I see it plain as print."

Steve couldn't really deny this. He kept still.

Soon Blackbeard became far too busy to worry about whether or not Steve liked him. Beyond the bridge was the town of Godolphin, and there was much to be seen. The ghost was fascinated. There were tall poles along the street with wires strung between them. There was the traffic signal clicking from red to green at the corner of Magnolia and Main. There was the five and ten cent store with its windows aglitter with tiny items made of plastic and paper and tin. There was the supermarket, surrounded by a small sea of cars, and the theater, quiet and dark at this hour. There were the girls strolling along the sidewalk in capris or summer dresses, and the older women juggling purses and shopping lists, and men,

sober-suited and serious, hurrying to their work. Most of all, there were the cars and trucks crowding the narrow streets. It seemed to Blackbeard that they would be run down and sunk at any moment. "Easy!" he said to Steve. "Steady as she goes!" And once, when a huge refrigerator truck loomed up beside them, he leaped for the wheel shouting, "Hard aport!"

Steve elbowed him aside and drove on. "You keep your hands off the wheel!" he warned.

"She was bearing down on us!" gasped Blackbeard.

"Let me worry about that," Steve ordered, and he drove on beyond the town and up the hill to the college. The ghost breathed easier then.

In front of Godolphin's administration building Steve parked his car and looked around. He liked what he saw. There was a row of rosy old brick buildings fronting on a smooth lawn. Beyond these were some newer buildings of poured concrete. Huge old trees cast shadows across well-kept flower beds. And, to Steve's great relief, there wasn't a student in sight.

Steve slid out of the car. "You wait for me right here," he told Blackbeard. "I won't be long."

But the pirate was already clambering out of the backseat. "I'll come along with you," he volunteered.

"No, no!" protested Steve. "Look, you wouldn't want somebody to pirate my . . . er, my craft."

Blackbeard looked at the car. "No," he admitted.

"You stay and watch it . . . er, her," suggested Steve. And to make sure the ghost didn't try a cruise on his own, he leaned over and took the keys from the ignition. Before Blackbeard could question this, he hurried up the walk to the building.

In the doorway of the building there was a man with a broom. He stared curiously at Steve. The man must have seen him talking to Blackbeard. He probably thought Steve was nuts.

"Where is Dean Wheaton's office?" Steve asked.

The one with the broom pointed down a corridor. Steve mumbled his thanks and went on.

Dean Wheaton turned out to be a sad-faced individual with a bald head and the habitual squint of the nearsighted person who refuses to wear his glasses. He greeted Steve with all the enthusiasm of a picnicker welcoming a swarm of ants and waved the coach to a deep leather chair next to his desk.

"I must be frank with you, Mr. Walker," he said to Steve.

Somehow this didn't sound like a promising beginning. "Oh?" said Steve.

"I don't wish to seem negative," said the dean.

Steve wondered fearfully what could be wrong. The alumni committee which had interviewed him at East Heymouth High School had been very, very eager to have Steve sign on as coach. They had gone on at great length about the fine faculty at Godolphin, and the beauty of the Carolina countryside. They had stressed the importance of the track team.

"To be truthful," said Dean Wheaton, "I wasn't in favor of replacing our former track coach when he left so informally."

"Informally?" questioned Steve.

"He . . . er . . . he began to behave oddly during the fall semester. He began to talk to himself."

Steve jumped slightly, thinking of the watcher with the broom.

"Then one day he simply disappeared," said Dean Wheaton. "You see, Mr. Walker, our alumni committee may not have told you everything. For some years now, the track team has done precious little to add luster to the name of Godolphin. To me, there doesn't seem to be much point in going on with it."

Steve's heart sank at the words. Was he getting the glove?

Dean Wheaton cleared his throat. "We have competed in the Broxton Relays for sixty-three years," he told Steve. "The alumni insist that we try once more. That's why they went to East Heymouth to talk with you."

"I see." Steve tried to look as brisk and competent as possible. "The relays are in three weeks, aren't they?" he asked. "And in three weeks I can—"

"Two," said the dean shortly.

"Two. Well, I hope I can restore your confidence in the boys by . . . uh . . . before the relays and. . . ."

"I never had any confidence in the boys," said the dean.

"You never had any? But it can't be that bad. I met one of them last night at the inn. He seemed like a nice kid. Name's Gudger Larkin."

Dean Wheaton looked unspeakably pained. "Gudger Larkin is our star shot-putter," he told Steve. "Of course, he sprints, too."

"Shot-putter? That skinny little . . . ?"

Dean Wheaton nodded a mournful nod.

Steve gulped. "Then things *are* that bad."

Dean Wheaton stood up. "I am sure you'll do your best, Mr. Walker. Good luck!"

Stunned and deeply depressed, Steve fumbled his way out of the office and back to his car. There he found Blackbeard drinking rum and playing the radio. The man with the broom was standing on the sidewalk beside the car watching with fascination as the rum bottle tilted itself in the air and the liquid vanished out of it with a loud glugging.

"Put that away!" yelled Steve.

The bottle vanished under the backseat. Steve brushed past the man with the broom, got in, and started away from the curb with a spurt.

"You're troubled, lad," said Blackbeard.

"You might say that." Steve sounded like a man trying very hard to control himself. "I was not exactly overcome with the warmth of the dean's welcome. Also, I would really appreciate it if you wouldn't play the radio when the car's parked. It runs down the battery. And keep that rum out of sight! There happen to be laws about cars and liquor."

There was a long silence. Then the ghost sniffed. "You be studying some way to get rid of old Teach."

"How'd you guess?" Steve said evenly.

And not another word passed between them all the way back to the inn.

Blackbeard's Treasure

IF MRS. STOWECROFT was surprised when Steve asked her to repeat the words of Aldetha Teach's curse, she didn't show it. She behaved as if every visitor to the inn would naturally wish to commit such an historic bit of magic to memory.

She stood in the bar of the inn, her hands folded and her eyes closed in concentration, and sang out in her most eerie voice, "Edward Teach, sometimes known as Captain Blackbeard, when you come to die, may your soul be racked between this world and the next! May you never find rest! May you always be alone! May this curse hold fast and true, and may you dwell forevermore in limbo until such time as there be found in you, most wicked of all villains, some spark of human goodness!"

Steve thanked Mrs. Stowecroft and she fluttered away, quite pleased.

"She does that good," said Blackbeard as they went upstairs. "For a minute there she almost put me in mind of Aldetha."

"Some spark of human goodness!" Steve was quite excited. "That's the answer!"

"Eh? What are you saying, matey?" Blackbeard marched ahead of Steve into his room.

"Weren't you listening to her? The curse is that you dwell forevermore in limbo until there can be found in you some spark of human goodness."

Blackbeard looked at the portrait on the wall. "Smart as brass, that Aldetha," he told Steve. "Knew me like a book, and that's a fact."

"But you must have done something good."

The ghost searched his memory and found not a worthy deed stored there.

"Didn't you ever pat a dog?" asked Steve. "Or walk an old lady across the street?"

The ghost just laughed a short, miserable laugh. "We're sunk, boy," he told Steve. "Face up to it."

Steve sat down next to the table and began to tap his fingers on the arm of his chair. Then, suddenly, a perfectly brilliant idea flashed into his mind.

"I've got it!" he told Blackbeard. "The old ladies! The Daughters of the Buccaneers! They're your own kith and kin, some of them."

Blackbeard wasn't much interested. He'd known this all along. It was nothing to get excited about.

"Give them your treasure!" cried Steve.

"Treasure?" Blackbeard looked puzzled. "What treasure?"

"*Your* treasure!" It was all so simple. Surely the old coot didn't want that treasure now. It wouldn't do him a lick of good. "Don't think I haven't heard about Blackbeard's treasure," he told the pirate. "It's hidden someplace around here, isn't it? You can show me where and I. . . ."

"Why should I give away my treasure?"

"Why? Because you can do some good with it, that's why. You can help the old ladies, and maybe, that way, you can break Aldetha's curse!"

"You think so, do you?"

Steve was certain of it. "Help the old girls save their home," he urged Blackbeard. "They'll be so grateful. They'll name schools after you. They'll put the name of Teach on bridges, branch libraries, parks, highways! I can see it now—the Edward Teach Free Day Nursery for Babies!"

Blackbeard seemed pleased. "Named for me? A wicked old pirate? Just for a few miserable chests of doubloons and strands of precious jewels?"

"You bet!"

"Me, what has the blood of a thousand brave lads on my hands?" questioned the ghost.

"Don't think about blood," begged Steve. "*I'm* trying not to. Think positive! Come on! Crack loose with the treasure!"

Blackbeard hesitated. "It don't sound right to me," he declared.

"Of course it doesn't!" stormed Steve. "How would a creep like you know the difference between right and wrong? That's why the curse held on so long. Where's your treasure? *Where is it?*"

The ghost regarded Steve with great sadness. "There isn't any," he said.

He sighed. "There isn't any treasure. Not a doubloon. Not a farthing. Not a penny."

Steve almost choked with anger. "That's outrageous!" he yelled. "Do you know that people have been looking for that treasure of yours for centuries?"

The ghost nodded.

"Those poor, deluded souls," shouted Steve. "You . . . you phony!"

Blackbeard sniffed. "You see? Aldetha was smart. I'm no good. No good for anything, lad."

"Stop that and try to think," Steve commanded.

"There must be a few coins you put away somewhere."

"No. I had a treasure once. It was a big one. But it all went in one week in the gambling halls of Port Royal. Ah, that was a glorious week!" He forgot to feel sad, and his eyes sparkled at the memory.

Steve was disgusted. "You're a total loss!" he told the pirate. "You're not even a respectable ghost. You're a big noisy hole in the middle of nothing!"

Blackbeard agreed. "I've run aground."

The Captain's Plan

In the days that followed, Captain Blackbeard learned a great deal about track teams. He learned that a discus thrower is supposed to throw a four-pound disc after spinning around several times. Unfortunately, the discus thrower on the Godolphin team, a slender youth named Bud Bagwell, either dropped his discus on his own feet or didn't let go of at all. In addition, he had an unhappy talent for throwing himself on his head.

Sprinters, Blackbeard learned, are athletes who dash around a cinder course at great speed after a starter fires a gun. One of Godolphin's sprinters, a timid boy named Fellspahr, was afraid of guns. He always stuck his fingers in his ears when he crouched to begin a race. He seldom heard the gun and was always last away from the starting line.

Wisby, another member of Steve's track team, was a chunky lad who couldn't quite clear the hurdles, and Gudger Larkin, team captain and star shot-putter, was unable to put his shot, a heavy ball, much more than four feet from his own toes no matter how he tried. At times it seemed to Blackbeard that Gudger could hardly lift the shot.

All of this physical activity was rather a bore to Blackbeard. He couldn't see much sense in straining to throw a discus just so, or racing around a track without rhyme or reason. But it was, Blackbeard could see, terribly important to Steve. And Steve might be a water-drinking prig, but he had his good side. After the first few nights at the inn, Steve had asked Mrs. Stowecroft to put a cot in his room.

"A cot?" Mrs. Stowecroft had been astonished. Why would anyone want to sleep on a cot when there was a beautiful big four-poster in the room?

"A cot," Steve had repeated. "You see, Mrs. Stowecroft, I'm not used to such a big bed and I . . . er . . . I feel as if I'm getting soft. I have to keep in condition, you know, and I think a cot would be best. Don't you?"

Mrs. Stowecroft didn't, but she did not argue. If Mr. Walker wanted a cot, a cot he would have. He was a strange young man, given to having fierce arguments with himself, but she liked him.

So from that day on, Captain Blackbeard occupied his elegant four-poster alone, and Steve spent his nights on a narrow, hard little bed that Mrs. Stowecroft and Mrs. Soames had resurrected from the attic of the inn. Blackbeard appreciated the courtesy and the respect paid to his rank. To return the favor, the ghost gave up rum, except for a dram now and then when Steve wasn't about, and he tried to take an interest in the coach's track team.

Blackbeard wasn't the only one taking an interest. Jo Anne Baker often showed up to watch the practice on sunny afternoons. Blackbeard had always had an eye for a trim lass. He very much approved of Jo Anne. The young psychology professor knew when to talk and when to be silent—a rare thing in a woman. And her concern when Bagwell dropped his discus or Wisby fell on a hurdle was plain to see.

"You need time," she told Steve on the afternoon before the Broxton Relays. Gudger had just put his shot a wretched four feet three inches. "With a little more time, you could really whip these boys into shape."

Steve shook his head. "There isn't that much time in the world. We're sunk."

"I know it sounds silly," said Jo Anne, "but if there's anything I can do to help. . . ."

Steve looked at Blackbeard, who was sitting on a bench nearby, gazing out over the field.

"As a matter of fact," said Steve, "there *is* something you can do. You see, I have a problem."

Jo Anne nodded, all sympathetic attention. She knew about Steve's problem. The track coach talked to himself. Everyone on campus knew it. Usually it was six months or more before a Godolphin track coach actually began talking to himself. Steve had arrived at the school with the habit full-blown.

"I'd like to discuss it with you," Steve said. "Maybe you'd be able to give me some advice. Would you be free for dinner tonight?"

Jo Anne smiled. "Pick me up at seven." And she went swinging down the walk toward the parking lot.

"Okay, boys!" called Steve. "Hit the showers. That's enough for today."

Gudger and his teammates went off, stumbling over their own feet, and the ghost of Captain Blackbeard left his bench and came to stand beside Steve.

"How fares your day today?" asked Blackbeard, kindly enough.

"Terrible! You saw it."

The ghost sighed. "Not a likely bunch of lads."

The track coach didn't answer.

"I took a walk today," said the ghost.

"Is that so?" Steve said. "I knew you were gone. For a short, wonderful while there I thought I'd lost you."

"You know where I went, my boy?" asked Blackbeard. "I went to Godolphin town and roamed the streets. And by chance I happened to find myself in a gaming establishment by the name of Silky's Place."

"That hood!" snorted Steve.

"I came upon some of the natives there," continued Blackbeard, ignoring the interruption. "They were discussing a matter of gambling. Now, I love to risk a bit of gold or silver on a wager, so when I heard we could get forty or fifty to one on some forthcoming enterprise with these little rabbits you're working with. . . ."

Steve reared back. "Now, just a minute!"

Blackbeard smiled a cunning smile and leaned close to Steve. "Don't you want your lads to win?" he whispered. "I can teach you how."

Steve angrily pulled away from the pirate.

"Why not?" Blackbeard wanted to know. "I was not a bad hand at training young crews. 'Twas not by accident they hailed me the greatest pirate ever to sail the Spanish Main! My lads were taught to win. Always to *win*! By hook and by crook, by fair means and foul, they always won!"

"Now, wait!" shouted Steve. "Now, listen to me!"

Blackbeard went on as if Steve hadn't said a word. "It's not for myself I'm asking, boy," he explained. "It's for those dear, sweet old ladies. They look upon disaster, do they not?"

"Yes," Steve admitted, "but. . . ."

"Then we shall snatch them from the jaws of that monster, Silky Seymour. We shall keep those dear, frail little souls from being hurled into a cold, vicious world! Doesn't this suit you?"

"Hold it!" yelled Steve. "Forget the snow job. I feel as sorry for those ladies as anyone, but that doesn't mean you're going to put your bloody paws on my team! I don't want you near those boys. If we win anything at all—which we won't —we're going to do it honestly!"

"Listen," cried the ghost, "there's a thousand tricks I could show you, lad. I know them all."

"You keep away from my team, you hear?"

"I hear, Mr. Walker," said a deadly calm voice behind Steve.

Aghast, Steve turned to face Dean Wheaton. The dean was looking at him with a mixture of sadness and curiosity.

"I realize, Mr. Walker, that you are under great

pressure," said Dean Wheaton. His eyes swept the field beyond Steve—a field on which not a living being could be seen. "I think, however, that you are imagining things when you believe someone is trying to tamper with the Godolphin track team. The team, you must be aware, doesn't require tampering with. They will no doubt lose at the Broxton Relays. Good afternoon, Mr. Walker."

"Yes, sir," said Steve, and the dean walked on.

"I don't much fancy the cut of *his* jib," said the ghost of Captain Blackbeard.

"Oh, go maroon yourself somewhere!" growled Steve.

Silky's Place

I<small>T WAS</small> J<small>O</small> A<small>NNE</small> who suggested Silky's Place for dinner. "I know there's gambling in Silky's back rooms," she told Steve, "but Silky's *is* the best restaurant in town. And we don't need to go into the back rooms."

"I think we'd better *not* go into the back rooms," said Steve. He remembered Silky's threatening manner at the Buccaneer's Bazaar.

Surprisingly, Silky was more than cordial when Jo Anne and Steve appeared at his restaurant. It was a snug little place perched out on the end of a pier, and from the big windows in the dining room there was a magnificent view of the bay. Silky himself showed them to a booth near a tank filled with colorful tropical fish. The gambler suggested a good lobster dinner and invited them to drop into his back rooms afterward.

"I hardly think that's likely," said Jo Anne. And out of feminine stubbornness, she ordered the shore dinner instead of the lobster.

"I can't tell you how much I appreciate this," said Steve warmly, after the waiter had gone off with their order.

"Appreciate what?"

"Your having dinner with me," Steve told her. "I really need someone I can talk to. You see, there's this problem I've been having for the past couple of weeks."

Jo Anne assumed her best psychologist manner. "Yes?" she encouraged. "Please go on."

"It started the night of the auction," said Steve. "I was tired and not really noticing what I was doing. I sat on the handle of that antique bed warmer I bought and I broke it off."

Jo Anne smiled. If this was the problem, things were going to be simpler than she had hoped. "You mustn't let that upset you," she told Steve. "I'm sure the bed warmer can be fixed. There's a man in a little shop on Fourth Street who does wonders with antiques. I have his name right here." She rummaged in her bag, looking for her address book.

"Wow!" said Steve.

She looked up, puzzled. "Wow?"

"All that money." Steve pointed to a thick roll of bills clearly visible in Jo Anne's purse. "Aren't you afraid to carry that much around?"

"Oh, that." She picked up the bills and riffled through them. "This has all been donated to the Daughters of the Buccanners. I didn't want to leave it in my apartment."

She put the bills back into her bag.

Beyond the tank of tropical fish, the ghost of Captain Blackbeard watched. Paper money, he knew, was as good as gold. The lass was a fool to carry a treasure about like that.

"I hope those little old ladies are going to make their mortgage payment," said Steve. "I hope—"

Jo Anne shook her head. "I have nine hundred dollars here," she told him, patting the purse. "There's a bit more in the bank—the proceeds of the bazaar. I'm sorry to say that unless almost thirty-six thousand dollars turn up by midnight tomorrow, the ladies lose their home."

Blackbeard leaned against the fish tank and did a quick bit of arithmetic. Nine hundred dollars wisely bet—say at fifty to one odds—could produce the very handsome sum of forty-five thousand. Carefully keeping out of Steve's line of vision, the pirate began inching around behind the booth where Steve and Jo Anne sat.

Steve, suddenly worried about his ghostly companion, looked over his shoulder.

"Steve, are we looking for someone?" asked Jo Anne.

"Yes," admitted Steve. "For my problem. You see, on the night of the auction, when I sat on the bed warmer, he appeared."

"He?"

Steve nodded. "I haven't been able to get him off my back since."

Blackbeard went down on his knees and crept around behind Jo Anne. He had never been much of a pickpocket. He had always preferred a more direct approach. Still, he knew, one had to do what appeared to be best.

"Is he here now?" Jo Anne asked Steve.

"I don't see him, but he's probably here somewhere. He's latched on to me."

"Does he have a name?"

Steve leaned forward and said in a very low voice, "Blackbeard!"

"Blackbeard?"

"Well, Blackbeard's ghost."

Jo Anne instantly felt that she should be very, very careful here. She shifted in her seat, moving her bag onto the table. "But . . . but how do you know he's Blackbeard's ghost? I mean, is he really the ghost of Captain Teach?"

"No question about it," declared Steve. "You should see him—whiskers, cutlass, the whole bit!"

"Then he's the person you talk to? Is that it?"

Steve looked miserable. "I know. Everybody thinks I'm nuts!"

"Oh, I wouldn't go so far as to say that," said Jo Anne firmly. "But you *do* seem to have a problem."

At that, the waiter came scurrying up with their salads. Blackbeard dodged out of the way. Jo Anne smiled at the waiter and obligingly moved her bag from the table to the seat of the booth. Blackbeard grinned. It would be very easy now.

"Please go on," Jo Anne urged Steve when the waiter had departed. "You were telling me how you met Captain Blackbeard. You were sitting on your antique bed warmer."

"Oh, yes." Steve picked up his fork and launched into the tale of Aldetha's book and how he had read the spell aloud. Blackbeard didn't bother to listen. He knew what had happened. He reached around from behind the booth, touched the purse, and, after fumbling for a moment, got it open. His fingers closed around the roll of bills. Then, still on his hands and knees and well out of Steve's sight, he scuttled for the door to the back rooms.

Naturally, Silky Seymour's back rooms were guarded by one of Silky's toughest and most reliable men. This didn't worry Captain Blackbeard a whit. The ghost just waited until one of Silky's regular customers showed up. Then he slipped through the door behind the man.

What did worry Blackbeard was how he could place his bet. Certainly the teller at the bettor's window couldn't see him. Several men were watching the races on a big color TV, but they were no use. They couldn't see him or hear him, and there wasn't one in the bunch Blackbeard would trust with a farthing, let alone nine hundred dollars.

Still, one thing at a time. Blackbeard took himself to a counter on one side of the room, picked a piece of paper from a pigeonhole, and, with a ball-point pen that was chained to the counter, he began to express his faith in Steve's track team.

"Godolphin to victory at Broxton!" he wrote in a large, clumsy hand. There! That was simple enough. Anyone would know what he wanted.

Blackbeard surveyed the room. It was the routine at the betting window that interested him. Every few minutes one of the racing fans would go up to the window and shove a note and some money at the sour little man who sat behind the grill. The man would take the money,

make out a slip, and then give the slip to the bettor. That was all there was to it.

The ghost waited until a lean, pasty-faced individual went to the window, put down a bet, covered it with a ten-dollar bill, then turned to watch the glowing screen of the televison set.

Blackbeard could be remarkably quick on his feet for a ghost of his size. Before the teller could look up, the pirate was at the window and had snatched the gambler's ten and his bet. In their place the ghost plunked down the nine hundred dollars and his own carefully composed wager.

The teller scooped up the wad of bills and the note. "Godolphin to victory at Broxton," he read.

"A sucker bet!" was his first thought. He looked out through the grill. Danny Oley stood there. What was Danny doing putting down a bet like this? And for nine hundred dollars!

"This your bet?" he asked.

Danny didn't look around. "What do you think I'm standing here for?" he wanted to know.

"I hope you know what you're doing," cautioned the teller.

"Blast the sum!" thought Blackbeard. "Can't he make out his chit and be done with it?"

To the pirate's annoyance, the teller carried the money and the bet away from the window and into a room beyond. In a few minutes he was back, sorting Jo Anne's bills into his cash drawer. "Okay, Danny," he said, pushing a betting slip through the grill.

Blackbeard seized the slip and slid Danny Oley's bet onto the ledge in front of the window. Then the ghost paused to read the slip. It was beautiful! It acknowledged the receipt of nine hundred placed for Godolphin in the Broxton Relays, and at fifty to one odds. Best of all, it was signed by Silky Seymour himself! Doubtless that pale worm behind the window had gone to the gambler to get the bet approved. Well and good. Blackbeard had Seymour's word, pledged in his own hand.

Ignoring the quarrel which had suddenly sprung up between the teller and Danny Oley, the ghost sauntered back to the restaurant. Jo Anne and Steve were just finishing their dinner. Steve saw the pirate and flinched slightly. Blackbeard paid no heed. Jo Anne's purse was open on the seat beside her. As he passed the table the pirate bent slightly and tucked the betting slip into the bag.

Steve and the learned lass seemed to be getting on well. She was telling him, very calmly, that he must try to understand his problem—and also that if he just ignored Blackbeard, the ghost would go away.

"Well, lad," said Blackbeard, "if that's the shape of it, I *will* go. I'll wait for you in the car." And, highly pleased with his evening's activity, the ghost wandered out to the parking lot. Yes, it had been an interesting evening.

Up the Jolly Roger!

ON THE DAY of the Broxton Relays, Steve drove to Broxton with Gudger and Wisby in his car; Captain Blackbeard rode cheerfully on the lid of the trunk. The other members of the Godolphin team followed them in Fellspahr's ancient station wagon.

The Broxton coach welcomed them gently, rather like someone greeting a collection of doddering great-aunts. Gudger gulped when the Tidewater and State teams arrived—lean, muscular youths, every one of them.

"We're dead!" was Gudger's verdict.

Steve tried to think of some comforting remark, but nothing occurred to him. He led the way to the Godolphin dressing room, where the boys changed to their track suits in almost total silence. When they were ready, and the stirring music of the Broxton band floated down to them, they faced Steve.

He cleared his throat.

"It's okay, Coach," said Fellspahr. "We know."

"No," protested Steve. "Wait! You've got to get this thing in proportion. Don't look at it as a track meet. Look at it as a preparation for life."

Wisby groaned. Somebody was always telling him to prepare for life.

"Some of you will graduate soon," Steve told them. "You'll find the world outside full of nothing but trouble, frustration, and strife. Just remember, there could be no better preparation for that world than to be on the Godolphin track team!"

"You can say that again!" agreed Wisby.

Steve wet his lips. Somehow that hadn't come out quite as he had intended it.

"All right," he told the boys. "I just want you to know that no matter what happens today, each one of you is a champion!"

Gudger straightened up a bit at that. "Let's go!" he said to his teammates.

The boys clumped out of the room, and Steve followed. In the corridor, Jo Anne was waiting.

"Jo Anne!" Steve was very pleased. "How nice of you to come. We can sure use some good wishes."

Jo Anne's chin went up. "I do wish you and the team the best of luck, but that's *not* why I'm here."

"It's not?"

Jo Anne held up her purse. "As you know, last night I had nine hundred dollars in my bag. This morning, when I opened the bag, I found this!"

She handed Steve a small piece of paper. He took it and read, "Nine hundred dollars. Godolphin. Fifty to one. S. Seymour."

Steve was stunned. The girl must be mad!

"That was a nice gesture of confidence," he told her, as gently as he could, "but you know our boys don't have a chance out there today. You shouldn't have done it."

"Mr. Walker!" snapped Jo Anne. "I do not bet. And if I did bet, I certainly wouldn't embezzle other people's money to do it. Last night I put the money in my purse. This morning the money is gone and the betting slip is there."

Suddenly Steve knew exactly what had happened. "It's that rotten pirate!" he cried. "*He* did it! *He* did it!"

"*Someone* did it, Mr. Walker!" There was a nasty edge to Jo Anne's voice.

"Now, hold on there! You don't think *I'd*. . . ."

Gudger popped around a turn in the corridor. "Hurry up, Coach," he called. "It's beginning."

"I won't bother you any longer," said Jo Anne. "I do understand. Your motives are good, but your reasoning is perfectly idiotic!" And she spun around and clicked away.

Blackbeard's ghost loomed up beside Steve. "Is something amiss, lad?" he wanted to know.

Steve turned on him. "You took that money!" he accused.

"Money?" The ghost was completely undisturbed by the charge. "Oh, yes. The odd bit of flimsy I removed from the satchel of your bookish lady. Why should that anger you? Did I not restore a document to her? That selfsame document will certainly procure money for her crew of old ladies. I shall see to the matter personally."

"And just how do you figure to do that?"

Blackbeard put on his most commanding look. "Simply by achieving victory in the event which even now goes on out there. Stand aside. I must take my task in hand."

"What task?" asked Steve, much too softly.

Blackbeard looked at the track coach with some contempt. The boy was slow to understand, and that was the truth. "I shall see to it that your lads win," he told Steve. "At the risk of seeming spoffy, I'd say *you've* made a botch of things so far."

Steve barred the way. "Let's get just one thing

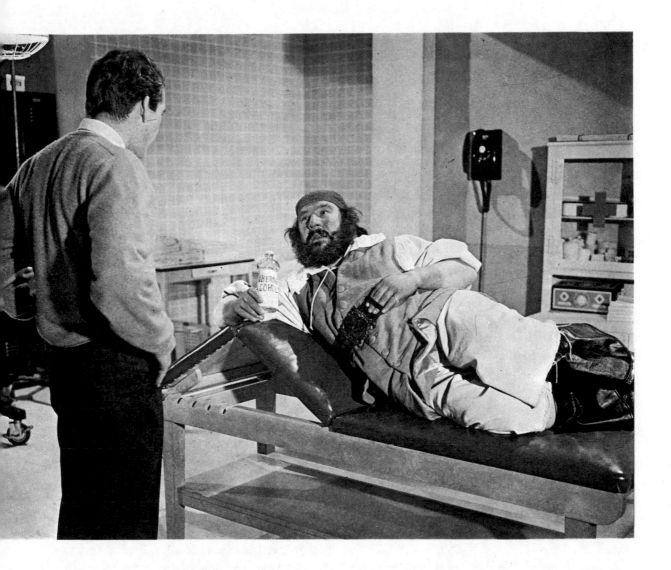

straight," he told the pirate. "You're to keep your grubby mitts off those boys. They may not win, but they're not going to cheat!"

Again Gudger zipped around the turn in the corridor. "Come on, Coach, will you?" he pleaded. "We've come in last in two events already!"

Steve said no more, but he shot a warning look at Blackbeard before he turned and went out toward the field.

"Young puppy!" huffed the ghost. "Sanctimonious pipsqueak! If that's the way you want it, no help shall you get from me!"

And the ghost stomped down the corridor and out onto the field, where the discus throw was just being announced.

The first contestant was a wiry young man named Sewell, of Broxton College. As Steve and Gudger watched glumly, Sewell got off a mighty heave which sent the discus down the field for a stunning one hundred and seventy feet.

Blackbeard glared at Steve. The coach ignored the ghost and turned to spindly Bud Bagwell. "You're up next, Bud," he said. "You'll be all right. Just remember to let go on the second turn."

Bagwell twisted his hands. "Yes, sir," he agreed. "Let go on the second turn. Okay!"

The rooters in the Godolphin section applauded loyally as Bagwell ambled out to the circle, seized the discus, and began to turn.

He turned.

And he turned. . . . And he turned again. . . .

"Let go!" yelled Steve. "Bagwell! Let go of the discus!"

Now spinning furiously, Bagwell tried. It wasn't easy. It took three more turns before he finally released his frenzied grip on the discus. When he did, the thing came whizzing across the field, narrowly missed Steve's head, then zoomed on into the stands to crash into the tray of a popcorn vendor. Popcorn exploded in every direction.

The Broxton, State, and Tidewater rooters howled with laughter. Poor Bagwell drooped, and Steve covered his eyes.

"Serves you right!" snarled Blackbeard.

Just then a movement near the stairway to the stands caught Blackbeard's eye. Silky Seymour and two of his men came striding in. Jo Anne, catching sight of the gambler, scampered down the stairs to intercept him. An interesting occurrence, thought Blackbeard. He moved closer to listen.

"Mr. Seymour! Just a moment!" called Jo Anne.

Seymour stopped and waited.

Jo Anne dived into her purse and came up with the betting slip. "Yesterday, I can't explain how, nine hundred dollars belonging to the Daughters of the Buccaneers was bet on Godolphin."

Seymour smiled. "So that bet was your doing?"

Jo Anne didn't trouble to deny it. "It was a very foolish thing to do," she told Silky. "Would you be kind enough to call it off and return the money?"

Silky was enjoying the situation. "Now, you know I'm a man of principle," he told Jo Anne. "And my guiding principle has always been that a bet's a bet."

"You mean you won't give back the money?"

"No, sweetness, I won't. But look at it this way. Suppose Godolphin wins. I stand to lose forty-five thousand dollars. That's pretty good bread."

"But you know very well that Godolphin can't win."

Silky just shrugged.

"What's to become of the old ladies?" Jo Anne asked. She pointed into the stands, to the place where the Daughters of the Buccaneers had gathered to cheer Godolphin on to victory—or whatever fate might await them. "Look at them," said Jo Anne. "You know they don't have anywhere to go."

And she glared at the gambler.

Seymour made a concerned, clucking sound. "I've been thinking about those dear old girls," he told Jo Anne. "They live in that drafty old inn, working their fingers to the bone. It's too bad!"

Jo Anne began to wonder whether he mightn't have a heart after all.

"They're also cluttering up a valuable piece of real estate," Silky finished.

Jo Anne gasped with anger. He had a heart, all right. It was pure, solid flint.

"Do the ladies know about the bet?" Silky asked.

"Of course not. I wouldn't dare raise a lot of false hopes. Won't you return the money?"

"No, sweetie, I won't!" Silky walked on.

Blackbeard, watching, could see that Jo Anne was about to cry.

"Snaky, scavenging sea rat!" thundered the ghost. No one could hear him, of course, but it relieved his feelings a bit.

Jo Anne put the betting slip into her purse and started toward the Daughters of the Buccaneers. Her head was down, but tears showed on her cheeks. The old ladies, wrapped in their scarves and busy with their knitting, gently welcomed her back to the group without really looking at her.

The sight of Jo Anne's tears, and of the elderly gentlewomen—descendants of his own loyal shipmates—waiting like so many lambs for the slaughter, was too much for Blackbeard. "By thunder!" he raged. "There be a time to stow the puling and the blib-blab. There be a time for action!"

With a mighty sweep, he drew his cutlass and leaped to the roof of the ticket booth that stood

next to the stands. The booth fairly rocked on its foundations, sending the wizened little ticket seller inside into a spasm of fright.

"Curses!" shouted the ghost. "I've got the devil's own dust gathered in my sinews these two hundred years, but there's an end to that now!" He jabbed the cutlass into the roof of the booth, stripped off his coat, and began flailing his arms and jouncing up and down, as he had seen Steve's team do during warm-ups.

The little booth shuddered and shook. The ticket seller clutched at his piles of quarters and dimes and half-dollars and prayed that the earthquake, or whatever it was, would subside quickly.

It did. For, "Up the Jolly Roger!" roared Blackbeard, and he charged out onto the field.

The Broxton Relays

It was Ted Shockley, Godolphin's bumble-footed high jumper, who first became aware that Blackbeard had entered the relays. Of course, Shockley had no way of knowing that it was Blackbeard. He only knew that as he began his run-up toward the jump, something took hold of the seat of his pants and tossed him forward and up. He cleared the bar at six feet, seven inches.

Slightly puzzled by Shockley's performance, the officials made way for Higgins, Broxton's long-legged jumper. Supremely confident, Higgins began his run-up. Blackbeard considered tripping him, but decided that this might be too obvious. Instead, the ghost waited until Higgins was in the air. Then, just as Higgins cleared the bar, Blackbeard reached up and knocked the thing off so that it tumbled down into the pit on top of Higgins.

The officials began to raise the bar, and the field announcer cried, "Shockley of Godolphin is ready for his try at six-ten."

On the sidelines, Steve was openmouthed with shock. Blackbeard waved merrily at him.

Hesitantly, Ted Shockley trotted toward the high jump. This time Blackbeard used a little

finesse. He didn't simply hurl Shockley over the jump. He clasped his hands stirrup fashion, got them under one of Shockley's feet, and boosted the boy over.

The effect was elegant. Shockley soared in a rising swan dive, and five first place points were slapped next to Godolphin's name on the scoreboard. The Godolphin rooters screamed.

Steve began elbowing his way through the crowd of sportswriters who had surged up to find out just how Shockley had developed his unusual style. Steve was not about to talk to sportswriters. He wanted a word with the ghost of Captain Blackbeard.

But Blackbeard did not tarry for talk. He made his way quickly to the cinder track where the mile run was in progress. There Burley, the Broxton runner, was holding a comfortable lead over the Tidewater and State men. Little Gudger Larkin was wheezing along in last place.

For Blackbeard, it was the work of a moment to trip the Broxton runner and send him crashing to the ground. He was still shaking his head groggily when Blackbeard picked him up, dusted him off, spun him around a time or two, then sent him jogging back the way he had come.

"You idiot!" shouted Steve. "Get out of there!"

Blackbeard looked around. Steve was trying to get to him, but the way was blocked by a large fellow in uniform. Some kind of official, no doubt. Well and good. The pirate had no time to debate ethics with the coach at the moment. He had to attend to the State runner and the Tidewater man. And he did, sending both of them back along the track.

Gudger Larkin, panting into home stretch, passed the Broxton, Tidewater, and State men going the other way. This puzzled Gudger, but it didn't stop him. If they had changed the rules of the race, no one had told *him* about it.

"Go! Go!" screamed the Godolphin cheerleaders.

Gudger staggered on until he breasted the tape and fell into the arms of his teammates.

Another five points slammed into Godolphin's scoring column.

The Godolphin band blared forth with the victory march that they so rarely used at relays, and the pompon girls leaped in a wild dance. A sprightly bunch, thought Blackbeard, and he went so far as to join them for a few steps.

Steve, looking frightfully purple around the face for one so young, ran toward the pompon girls. "I've told you for the last time, get off the field!" he yelled.

It was plain the girls weren't listening, for they crowded around him screeching and skibbering. Blackbeard disappeared under a flurry of pompons and slipped away. The javelin throw was about to begin, and this would require the pirate's complete attention.

Fellspahr of Godolphin was the first to launch a javelin in the event. Afterward, everyone agreed that Fellspahr's throw was a remarkable thing. It was unique; a javelin throw such as had never before been seen at Broxton—or perhaps anywhere else. For some distance the javelin went straight and true down the field. Then it performed several bounds and leaps. And then it

stopped and bobbled in midair before whistling on with tremendous force to smash into the exact center of the wooden scoreboard.

Later, those in the stands declared that the Godolphin track coach went really berserk during the javelin throw. He actually attempted to chase the javelin down the field. Several sturdy persons restrained him and dragged him to the sidelines.

After the throw, more points appeared next to Godolphin's name on the ruptured scoreboard.

Blackbeard allowed himself the luxury of a glance into the stands. Silky Seymour had just bitten his cigar in two. Steve's bookish lady was joyfully waving a piece of paper at the gambler.

Blackbeard looked back at Steve. He was arguing furiously with some official persons. "What do you mean, you want to enter a protest?" one man was shouting. "You won those last three events!"

"It wasn't us! It was *him!*" Steve pointed toward the pirate. The official persons looked around, looked at each other, then looked at Steve in a very marked manner. The two men

who had dragged him off the field held tight to his arms.

"You just stay here with us, Coach," said one soothingly. "Everything's going to be just fine."

Blackbeard chuckled and walked to the shot-put circle, where the Broxton shot-putter, a giant lad, was strutting up and down displaying his muscles.

Blackbeard studied the fellow for a moment, then moved around in front of him. The boy stepped up to hurl his shot. Blackbeard's hand went out. The shot described a tiny arc and dropped almost at the Broxton man's feet. An embarrassed official measured the throw at exactly three feet, seven inches.

Now Gudger stepped into the shot-putter's circle.

Blackbeard's approach to the problem of Gudger was inspired. The pirate stood behind the boy and a bit to one side. When Gudger started his feeble little toss, the pirate sprinted up, seized the shot, and ran with it.

On the sidelines, Steve was appalled at the sight of Blackbeard racing along, tossing the shot from hand to hand in a playful way.

"Can't you see what he's doing?" yelled Steve.

The officials couldn't see. They were aware, of course, that the Godolphin man seemed to have unusual control over his shot. It was coming downfield in an erratic series of arcs and scallops. But it was a very good shot. So good, in fact, that it completely cleared the field, scattering athletes on all sides. The measurement, when it was over, was eighty-six feet, two inches!

Joyous pandemonium broke out in the Godolphin stands. Jo Anne threw caution to the winds and waved her betting slip in front of Mrs. Stowecroft and the other Daughters of the Buccaneers. They began to smile and wave at Silky Seymour.

It took the pole vault to tie the score between Godolphin and Broxton. Blackbeard managed the pole vault very neatly. When the Broxton vaulter ran up to the stopboard, the pirate simply drew his cutlass and slashed the man's pole in half. The Broxton vaulter, carried on by momentum, put the remains of his pole in the stopboard and managed to get about five feet into the air before turning an awkward cartwheel and falling flat on his back.

Near the stands, the officials began to drag Steve away to the locker room.

Bud Bagwell trotted up to the vault, balancing his pole with some difficulty. Bagwell managed to get the pole set firmly enough into the stopboard. This made things quite easy for Blackbeard. He grabbed the pole. "Hold tight, matey!" he yelled, and he heaved on the pole.

Bagwell was whisked high over the bar. He came down so hard that he bounced. No matter, for he knew that by some miracle he had made the vault of the century.

The last event of the day was the relay race. Blackbeard felt winded after his exertions. He didn't try to tamper with the relay race at first. Let the lads sort themselves out and show what they were made of, and he'd know what to do.

It was immediately apparent that what the Broxton, State, and Tidewater men were made of was grit, muscle, and skill. At the end of the first lap, Broxton was in the lead, with State and Tidewater close behind, and poor Ted Shockley of Godolphin running last.

The baton was passed for the second lap. The second Broxton runner forged ahead, leaving the State and Tidewater men behind. Fellspahr pumped stolidly in the rear for Godolphin.

On the third lap, all of the runners took off with great bursts of speed.

Blackbeard strolled up to the sidelines and laid in a few provisions for his coming battle. A Godolphin pennant might be just the thing, he decided. He also gathered up an empty pop bottle and snitched a hot-dog sandwich from the tray of an unwary vendor. Then he hastened back to the track and took up his station at the passing zone, where the four runners who would race the last lap were waiting to seize the batons from their teammates.

Dewey, the Broxton runner, sped into the zone, his hand outstretched to give his teammate the baton. The Broxton man sprang into the race.

He reached for the baton, grasped something, and streaked down the track.

It took him some time to realize that he was not running with a baton. He was running with a hot-dog sandwich clutched in his fist.

The Tidewater men made their pass, and the runner started on the last lap of the relay proudly bearing a Godolphin pennant.

The State man got away with an empty pop bottle.

Wisby came gasping into the passing zone and handed his baton to Gudger just as the Broxton, State, and Tidewater men got themselves turned around and headed back for their batons.

Blackbeard helped Gudger on his way with a mighty whack from the broadside of his cutlass.

The three other runners hurtled back into the passing zone to get their batons from the third lap men. There was some hurried and hectic debate about the Godolphin pennant, to say nothing of the pop bottle and the hot dog. Blackbeard thoroughly enjoyed this. But at last the runners had their batons straightened out and were off again.

Gudger, meanwhile, had forged ahead for a gain of almost a third of a lap. In the stands, the Daughters of the Buccaneers were in a state of joyful hysteria and Jo Anne was leaping up and down like a pompon girl.

But brave little Gudger couldn't quite do it alone. The day had been too much for the lad. As he came into the straightaway, he began to slow down and weave. The others started closing in.

The Godolphin rooters groaned.

Blackbeard had done a mighty piece of work. He knew it, and he had no intention of letting Gudger botch it at the last minute. Bowling referees and news photographers aside, he charged across the track, lifted Gudger bodily into the air, and began to run with him.

Gudger kept trying. He was determined. His feet pumped furiously a foot above the track. The Broxton man was close behind now. With a last great effort, Blackbeard threw Gudger forward.

Gudger's teeth caught in the tape as he crossed the finish line. When he picked himself up, his lip was bleeding. He didn't care. He had won the Broxton Relays for Godolphin.

Blackbeard, who liked victory above all things, stayed on to enjoy the excitement. And there was quite a bit of it to enjoy. There was, first of all, the exit of that low bilge rat, Silky Seymour, who hurried away in an icy rage. Then there was a nice bit when the pompon girls carried little Gudger off the field, with Jo Anne and the violently happy Daughters of the Buccaneers lending a helping hand. Last of all, there was the spectacle of the entire student body of Godolphin College breaking into the locker room under the stands to free Steve, their imprisoned track coach, and carry him to his car in triumph.

At last it was over. The stands were empty, except for bits of paper and discarded programs. Blackbeard sighed a happy sigh. A most satisfactory encounter. Then the pirate decided that he would walk back to Godolphin. Somehow, he didn't want to hear Steve's opinion of the day's events. Not just yet, that is.

Ready for Duty

THE EVENING was well along when Captain Blackbeard reached Godolphin. Though not much of a one for walking, the ghost had rather enjoyed his saunter from Broxton. It had given him a chance to cool down after the excitement of the relays. And by this time, the worthy captain reflected, Steve would surely have realized that victory, however it was gained, was a very sweet thing indeed.

But when he reached the inn, Blackbeard found Steve packing his suitcase.

Blackbeard liked to get right to the point. He tapped the open bag on the table in Steve's room. "What's this, matey?" he wanted to know.

Steve glared at him and transferred a handful of socks from one of the sea chests to the suitcase.

"You leaving?" asked Blackbeard.

Steve went back to the sea chest for his shirts.

"If it's something I did, I'm sorry," ventured the ghost. "I only wanted to help."

"Help!" cried Steve. "That's a yock!"

Blackbeard wasn't quite sure what a yock was, but he could guess. "Didn't you once say that I might manage my own salvation by helping the old ladies?" he asked Steve.

Steve didn't answer.

The pirate stretched himself on the bed. "I see now that it's no easy matter to commit a good deed in a dirty world," he said sadly. "But in truth I meant no harm. And why should you go away now? What's done is done. Look on the good side of it, lad. Your boys have triumphed. Your long-faced dean is pleased. The wager with that scut of a Seymour is won, and there's money and to spare for the old ladies. Your lass is happy. I fail to divine the purpose in your leaving."

"Don't strain your brain," Steve advised.

"Further," the pirate went on, "before the dawn the old ladies will burn the mortgage. When that happens, perhaps the evil curse may be lifted from my own good self. Is this not mutual joy?"

"I'm happy!" snapped Steve. "I'm so happy!"

"Once I'm gone," Blackbeard pointed out, "you will be able to live a serene life here. Somewhat dull, perhaps, but serene."

Enraged, Steve whirled on the ghost. "Look, frizz-face," he said, "do you think I can stay after what happened at Broxton today? Tomorrow the Godolphin track team will be the same bunch of shambling wrecks they've always been. What am I supposed to do for an encore? I'm getting out—now! I'm going to go somewhere and start over!"

A sharp rap on the door brought Steve up short. When he opened the door, Jo Anne Baker was standing outside. There was hot color burning in her cheeks.

She glanced past Steve and saw the suitcase on the table. "And where do you think you're going?" she demanded.

Blackbeard, who was a nice judge of these things, decided that the lass was very, very angry.

"I'm leaving," Steve told her.

"No, you're not." Jo Anne swept into the room and slammed the door behind her. "You took my money," she accused. "Now you're not running off and leaving us all in the lurch!"

"There's a spunky wench!" Blackbeard applauded.

Steve was bewildered. "What are you talking about? You got your money, didn't you?"

"No, I didn't!"

Blackbeard stirred himself and sat up on the bed. What was the lass saying?

"Silky welshed on the bet," Jo Anne told Steve. "He . . . he laughed at me! He says he won't pay off. And he's throwing Mrs. Stowecroft and the other ladies out as soon as the bank opens in the morning!"

At first Steve said nothing. He just stared at Jo Anne. Then he muttered something that neither Jo Anne nor Blackbeard could quite hear. Then, in a loud, shaky voice, he called Silky Seymour a low-down, scurvy bilge rat.

Jo Anne looked startled.

"Under normal conditions—if I remember correctly—I have a sweet and lovable nature," said Steve.

"If I may offer a suggestion, lad . . ." began Blackbeard.

"Shut up!" yelled Steve.

Jo Anne gasped at him.

Blackbeard tried again. "Now, boy. . . ."

"Be quiet!" roared Steve.

"But . . . but I didn't say a word!" protested Jo Anne. Then, suddenly, she was all concern. "Are you seeing things again?" she asked gently.

"I am not seeing things!" shouted Steve. "What's more, I am getting awfully tired of people fussing over me and giving me a lot of cheap advice. I am now going to see that rat Seymour and I am going to wring that money out of his crooked neck!"

"Steve, you mustn't!" Jo Anne was really alarmed now. "Not in your condition!"

"What do you mean, in my condition?" Steve was struggling into his jacket.

"Why, anyone can see that you're just not yourself. You can't go fight Silky and that gang of his."

Blackbeard patted his cutlass. "The fluff is right, boy. This be a job that takes innards."

At the moment Steve felt that his innards were at least as good as Silky Seymour's. "Innards, is it?" he yelled. "Well, fine! You can just sit there and contemplate yours. I've got things to do."

"Aha!" Blackbeard leaped off the bed and got between Steve and the door. "Now *that* be the sound of a man!" he shouted happily. "You may be a prig, but you've got stuff in you."

He saluted smartly. "Request permission to accompany you, sir," he said.

"No, you don't, buddy boy! I'm calling the shots this time."

Again the ghost saluted. "I'd be proud to serve under you, sir," he told Steve.

Steve looked searchingly at the pirate. "You mean that?" he asked.

Blackbeard drew himself up to his full, bristling height. "My word, lad, is the ultimate

guarantee!" he announced. "And you have it!"

Steve considered this for a moment. Then he nodded. "Right!" he said. "Let's go!"

Jo Anne, hearing only one side of this conversation, was now panic-stricken. She clung to Steve's arm. "No!" she cried. "You're not going! Don't you see? You've really flipped!"

Blackbeard disliked treating ladies roughly, but there had to be exceptions if a man was to remain a man. "Throw the wench aside," he advised. "There's work to do."

Steve was in complete agreement. "Stand aside, wench," he ordered. "Clear the decks for action!"

"Battle stations!" roared Blackbeard.

"Make ready for the boarding party!" yelled Steve.

With that, the track coach and the ghost charged out onto the quarterdeck, and Blackbeard began to sing:

> "Hearts of oak are our ships.
> "Jolly tars are our men.
> "We'll always be ready.
> "Steady, boy, steady.
> "We'll fight and we'll conquer
> "Again and again!"

"Hey, wait!" called Jo Anne. "Wait for me! I'm certainly not letting you go to that place alone!" Her jaw was set and her face mirrored her determination.

And she scampered after Steve, to save him if she could.

The Game

BY THE TIME they reached the pier, and Silky's Place, Steve was also singing of hearts of oak and jolly tars, and Jo Anne had joined in. For some reason which she did not at all understand, Jo Anne had begun to feel that Steve might not be as nutty as he seemed.

And so, when the door to Silky's restaurant swung open all by itself, Jo Anne hardly noticed. She was in a mood to accept anything. She just marched through the door and into the place, with Steve close behind her.

The door to Silky's office was guarded by one of Silky's largest hoods. "You again!" he snarled.

Steve stepped to one side, bowed to his invisible friend, and suggested that it was Blackbeard's turn.

The ghost plucked the thug into the air and tossed him aside, very much as one might toss an old coat. The hoodlum came to rest against a wall. The door to Silky's office opened, and Jo Anne, Steve, and their unseen ally marched in.

Silky Seymour was alone in the office, standing in front of a large safe. There were stacks of money in the safe. Silky turned when they came in, then quickly closed the door of the safe and spun the dial to lock it.

"Well, Professor Baker!" Silky was very cool. "And Mr. Walker! What can I do for you?"

He took himself to the desk and sat down.

Steve began on a nice, positive note. "We're here to pick up all that money you owe Professor Baker."

"Professor Baker's money? You've got to be kidding." Unseen by Steve, Silky's hand touched a button underneath the desk.

Unseen by Silky, Blackbeard was valiantly trying to open the safe. Why waste time talking when such treasure was there, ready at hand? But the safe door wouldn't budge. Doubtless there was a trick to the thing—a trick Blackbeard didn't know.

"Mr. Seymour," said Steve, "you are going to pay the forty-five thousand dollars you owe or—"

"Or what, Mr. Walker?"

"Or we may have to get a little tough."

The door that led to the restaurant opened and four of Silky's hoods drifted into the room.

"I've got to admire your style," laughed Seymour. "Tell you what." He opened his wallet, took out a handful of bills, and put them on the desk. "I'll return the nine hundred you put down on the bet."

Nine hundred, Jo Anne knew, was as good as nothing to the Daughters of the Buccaneers. "No! You know we need *all* the money you owe me!"

Silky shook his head. "I pay that forty-five thousand," he pointed out, "and the old ladies pay off the bank. And there goes my chance to run a real classy gambling joint. Sorry. No dice."

Blackbeard abandoned the stubborn safe and moved to Steve's elbow.

"We run a nice little roulette wheel here," said Silky. "Why don't you forget that phony bet and

97

take the nine hundred? You go out to my wheel and win some money honestly. How about it?"

Blackbeard had glimpsed a roulette wheel on his previous visit to Silky's. It offered some advantages to one who was invisible. "Take the money, lad," the pirate advised Steve.

Steve looked startled. "What?"

"Let the lass try her luck."

"Are you sure you know what you're doing?" Steve wanted to know.

Silky and his men looked amused. They had heard rumors that the track coach talked to himself. Now they knew it was true.

"Suppose she loses?" Steve suggested.

"She won't lose," Blackbeard promised.

"Okay." Steve had faith in his ghost. He took the pile of bills from Silky's desk.

"Steve!" cried Jo Anne. "What are you doing?"

"Mr. Seymour has made a very good suggestion," Steve told her. He glanced at his watch. "We don't have much time. Come on."

He urged her toward the door, but she tried to hang back. "I don't understand you!" she protested. "One minute you're a knight in shining armor and the next you're a . . . a tinhorn chicken-liver."

"We all make mistakes at one time or another," said Steve smoothly.

"Sure," agreed Silky. "It's a smart man knows when to crawfish. Come along. We have a nice, quiet room reserved for our more valued customers."

The affable Silky ushered them out of his office and into a small room which was over-decorated to the point of suffocation. There were walls covered with red damask, a gilded ceiling, and thick, noiseless carpets. A cashier lurked behind a window on one side of the room. And there was a roulette table, guarded by a bored gentleman who looked as if he had never in his life seen the sunlight.

"These are friends of mine, Harry," Silky told the bored one. "Take good care of them."

Harry promised that he would. He took up his post next to the roulette wheel.

"Good luck, folks," murmured Silky, and he left.

And good luck, in extremely large doses, was exactly what Steve and Jo Anne proceeded to have.

Steve began by buying nine hundred dollars' worth of chips. Jo Anne had only the vaguest idea how a roulette game operated, but she bravely put a few chips on number twenty-nine. Harry spun the wheel. A little ivory ball whizzed around and clicked into a slot marked thirty-one. At which point Blackbeard quickly moved Jo Anne's chips to thirty-one.

Harry, who could have sworn that Jo Anne's bet had been twenty-nine, sourly pushed a small stack of chips toward the professor.

"How nice!" said Jo Anne.

"Let it ride," said Steve.

This time Blackbeard varied his technique a bit. Harry, he had noticed, was wearing a toupee. It was child's play to push the toupee down over Harry's eyes just as the wheel spun. By the time the croupier had struggled free of his hairpiece, the roulette wheel had stopped spinning. The little ivory ball was resting in the slot marked nineteen, and Jo Anne's chips had moved to number nineteen.

"Now have the lass change her bet," instructed the ghost.

The growing stack of chips moved to five. The wheel spun. The ivory ball rattled, then came to rest in the number five slot.

Jo Anne didn't understand it at all. She had never won a thing in her life. She didn't understand it, but she didn't question it.

"Hurry it up," Steve told Harry. It was eleven-thirty. If the bank was punctual—as banks often are—there would be someone at the inn to foreclose at midnight, when the mortgage came due.

A white-haired man oozed into the room. "Evening, folks," he said, not unpleasantly. To Harry he whispered, "What goes on here?"

"You tell me," was all Harry could say.

Steve made a few quick calculations on the back of an old envelope. Just one or two more turns of the wheel and they'd be home free. "Put everything on fifteen," he told Jo Anne.

"Everything?"

"Yes. Hurry!"

Something in his tone rankled. Defiant, she moved her stack to number seven. "I have a system," she told Steve.

"System? What system?"

"Woman's intuition, that's what." She turned to the croupier. "Spin the wheel, please."

Harry spun the wheel. His white-haired friend watched intently. The little white ball rattled around, clattered into number fifteen, then hopped across into number seven.

"I win again!" cried Jo Anne.

Harry dived into a drawer for more chips to build up Jo Anne's pile.

"Don't fool with it anymore," muttered the white-haired man. "Go to the gaff!"

The gaff? Blackbeard, standing near the two gamblers, pondered the remark. Now, what might a gaff be? The two were up to no good, that was plain to see.

Harry edged closer to the roulette table. The ghost watched him narrowly. The croupier bent his knee and pressed his leg against a certain spot in the elaborate carving that adorned the table leg. Then the man smiled a very assured little smile.

Blackbeard didn't like that smile. He went down on his knees to finger the table leg. Just as he suspected! There was a contrivance of some kind there. The carving on the table concealed a button which the croupier could press with his knee. The man was going to cheat!

Now, Blackbeard believed in victory, no matter what the means. But he always liked to be on the winning side. It was not to be tolerated if his opponents used foul play like this.

Blackbeard slithered under the table and found the wires that led from the hidden switch to the roulette wheel. So it was done with electricity! The ghost didn't completely understand electricity, but he had seen something of what it could do. He knew that it lighted rooms, and perhaps accomplished other remarkable things. He knew that it was contained in those little copper wires.

It took only a moment to detach the clips that

held the wires to the underside of the roulette wheel. Blackbeard delicately lifted one of the croupier's trouser legs. Good! The man was neat. He wore old-fashioned garters. Nimbly the pirate attached the clips to the metal fastening of the garter. Then he popped back out from under the table, ready to go on winning money for the sweet little old ladies.

Everything Jo Anne had was riding on number seven. Harry spun the wheel. The ivory ball skittered around. Jo Anne grasped at Steve's hand, and the croupier smiled again.

The wheel slowed and the ball hesitated for just a moment at number twelve. Before Harry could draw a breath, however, it danced on to number seven.

With a sly look at Jo Anne, the croupier pressed his knee against the leg of the roulette table.

There was a crisp "Zzzt!" as electricity leaped through the wires to Harry's garter.

"Aaaargh!" screamed Harry. He threw up his hands and leaped away from the table.

Very pleased, Blackbeard bent and pressed the carving on the leg of the table.

"Aaaagh!" shrieked Harry, doing a stiff-legged little dance.

The wheel stopped, with the ball now quietly secure in number seven.

"Ya-hooo!" crowed Jo Anne.

"That'll do it," announced Steve. "Let's go!"

"But we're on a winning streak!"

"It's a quarter to twelve," Steve pointed out. "We can barely make it to the inn."

Harry by now had discovered that he was wired up to 110 volts. He yanked the clips loose and sullenly pushed more chips across the table.

Steve snatched the chips and rushed to the cashier's window. "Pay up!" he demanded.

There seemed no help for it. The cashier paid up with packets of bills totaling more than thirty-eight thousand dollars. At the same time the cashier quietly pressed a button which sounded a buzzer in Silky Seymour's office.

And when Jo Anne and Steve turned to leave the room, with the money stowed in Jo Anne's purse, the door opened and Silky came in. Behind him were his four musclemen.

"You did very well, I hear," said Silky pleasantly. "You took Silky's advice. Now you'd better take Silky's advice again. Let me keep that money for you. This is an extremely rough neighborhood."

101

Bang! Bang!

Steve and Jo Anne simply stared at Silky.

"That's too much bread to be carrying," coaxed Silky. "Come on. Give it to me."

Jo Anne backed off. "No!"

Steve noted that each of Silky's hoods had a bulge in the front of his jacket—a bulge doubtless caused by a gun carried in a shoulder holster. Steve looked around at Blackbeard. The ghost was lounging next to the roulette table, studying the situation. Steve touched a hand to his breast pocket. He nodded to Blackbeard, then jerked his head toward the four thugs.

Blackbeard looked at the men, then looked back at Steve. Again Steve put his hand to his breast pocket.

Blackbeard understood. He winked, then slipped around behind the hoods. He reached over the shoulder of the first one and very carefully slipped his gun out of its holster. He stowed the gun in the roomy pocket of his own coat and moved on to the next thug. In a trice, all four men were disarmed.

Silky, meanwhile, was beginning to lose patience with Jo Anne. And Jo Anne, for her part, was not being a bit gracious about surrendering her thirty-eight thousand dollars.

"Okay!" snarled Silky at last. "I tried to be civilized. Now I'm not fooling around. Let them have it, boys!"

The boys tried. As one man they reached for their shoulder holsters. Then they froze. "My gun!" cried one. "What happened to my gun?"

"So we're getting tough?" said Steve. He pushed Jo Anne behind him.

Blackbeard eased up behind the first hood in Silky's line of offense and held his ancient pistol over the man's head. He pointed invitingly to the thug, then extended a thumb and index finger like a child playing with a make-believe gun.

"Shoot the cur, lad!" he commanded Steve.

Steve extended his right hand, pointed a deadly index finger at the thug, and cried, "Bang!"

Blackbeard's old-fashioned pistol crashed down on the tough one's head and the hoodlum slumped to the floor.

Blackbeard moved on to the second hood.

Again the antique pistol rose into the air.

Again Steve's finger pointed.

"Bang! Bang!" cried the track coach.

The second thug slumped down, moaning.

The third hood was a bit confused, but he prided himself on being the fastest draw on the Carolina coast. He pointed his finger at Steve.

"Bang!" he yelled.

Steve ducked behind the roulette table. "Missed me!" he jeered.

"Bang!" He returned the hood's fire, and the man went down on his face.

"Bang! Bang!" The fourth muscleman bit the dust, and Steve blew imaginary smoke from his fingers, like a Western hero cooling his gun.

The cashier ducked out of sight behind his window. Poor, shocked Harry tried to hide in a corner. Harry's white-haired friend simply zipped out through the door. Silky, who really didn't believe what was happening, cautiously put the roulette table between himself and Steve. As for Jo Anne, she had long since stopped being surprised at anything that happened when Steve was around. She held on to her money and waited to see what would come next.

What came next was that Silky's men began to stir and moan. Then, groggily, they lurched to their feet and all four started toward Steve.

"Fire at their toes, mate!" roared Blackbeard.

Steve obliged, shooting with two hands, and Blackbeard tromped down on the men's feet.

Silky scrambled under the roulette table and tried to decide what to do next. From his vantage point, he could see his men leaping around like a pack of loons, yelling with pain.

"Bang! Bang! P-chowee!" shouted Steve.

The coach had lost his marbles, decided Silky. But then, his own men had lost their marbles, too. Perhaps Silky himself had lost his marbles—but that was no reason to give up thirty-eight G's. And the little old Daughters of the Buccaneers had to be tossed off Blackbeard's Island first

thing in the morning. Whatever the distraction, Silky liked to keep his eye on the ball. And, at the moment, Jo Anne was carrying the ball.

Silky slid to the edge of the table and looked up at the lady professor. She didn't notice him. She was busy watching her boyfriend play cops and robbers with Silky's bodyguards. It would be a snap!

Silky scooted out from under the table and grabbed at Jo Anne's purse.

"Steve!" screamed Jo Anne. "Help!"

Blackbeard rushed toward the girl.

"Shoot!" shouted Steve. "Shoot him!"

Jo Anne let go of her bag and Silky started to back away from her. She closed her eyes and pointed her finger at the gambler.

"Shoot!" ordered Steve.

"Bang!" cried Jo Anne.

Blackbeard's fist came down on Silky's head and the gambler quivered and sank to the floor.

Jo Anne opened her eyes and looked down at Silky. "Good heavens!" she exclaimed.

The four thugs, unencumbered by Blackbeard, now swarmed all over Steve.

"Stop that, you!" shrilled Jo Anne. She pointed her finger at the mobsters.

"Watch out!" warned Steve. "Don't point that thing over here!"

The terrified hoods let go of Steve and scattered.

Steve leaped to Jo Anne's side. "We've got to get out of here right now!"

"All ashore that's going ashore!" sang out the ghost of Captain Blackbeard. He aimed a kick at the door and it smashed open.

Silky Seymour reared up from the floor and tried to get in Jo Anne's way, and Steve had the sweet satisfaction of landing an uppercut right on the point of Silky's chin. Then he and Jo Anne raced out through the door, with Jo Anne steadfastly carrying her treasure.

Silky's hoods regrouped and started to give chase. Blackbeard put a stop to this with one or two well-aimed punches.

"You go ahead!" he cried to Steve. "I'll just tidy up a bit."

Steve would have liked to stay and watch the fun, but the ghost was right. There wasn't time. Pulling Jo Anne with him, Steve raced through the restaurant and out onto the pier. At the end of the pier there was a ramp, and at the end of the ramp a boat was tied. It had an outboard motor.

Steve half-lifted, half-shoved Jo Anne down

the ramp and into the boat. He cast off and started the outboard. Then he and Jo Anne sped away across the bay, bound for Blackbeard's Island. Behind them there sounded a great splash. It was Silky Seymour, who had just been dropped off the pier by an unseen adversary.

After this there were several mighty crashes. Captain Blackbeard was tidying up a bit.

Blackbeard Sets Sail

ON THE BEACH in front of Blackbeard's Inn, Mrs. Stowecroft, Miss Jeffrey, and the other Daughters of the Buccaneers had built an enormous bonfire in their old whale oil cauldron. A bonfire is always nice when one plans to burn a mortgage. But now it looked as if the good ladies might not have use for their fire. Instead of forty-five thousand dollars, dear, pretty Professor Baker had nothing to show after the Godolphin victory at Broxton but a betting slip worth nothing at all.

Of course, that nice Mr. Walker had gone storming out, vowing to get Mr. Seymour, and Professor Baker had run after him. But that had been almost two hours ago, and they hadn't come back. And Mr. Ainsworth, the old pettifogger, was here with his legal papers in one hand and his watch in the other, waiting to foreclose on the inn at the stroke of midnight.

"Can't you give us just a little more time?" Mrs. Stowecroft asked anxiously. Who could tell? Perhaps Mr. Walker could indeed make Mr. Seymour pay off on the bet.

Mr. Ainsworth looked at his watch. "I'm sorry," he said, "but I'm always precise in these matters."

Mrs. Stowecroft made an impatient little sound with her tongue. Precise people, she thought, could be most exasperating.

From out of the bay came the drone of an outboard motor. Mrs. Stowecroft looked toward the sound, but she could see nothing. The fog was coming in.

Mr. Ainsworth brandished the mortgage. "According to the terms of this document, unless you produce the required payment by midnight of this date, I must take possession of the inn."

The outboard sounded nearer, and now Mr. Ainsworth looked toward the bay.

"If you could just wait until morning," pleaded Mrs. Stowecroft.

And a boat came speeding out of the mist and up through the gentle surf. Carried by its momentum, it sped on across the sand to Mr. Ainsworth's side.

Steve Walker let go of the tiller and grinned.

Jo Anne thrust her winnings, handbag and all, into Mr. Ainsworth's arms. "Thank you, Mr. Ainsworth." She favored him with her most brilliant smile. "It's a pleasure to do business with you."

Mr. Ainsworth looked at his watch. It was just a tick before midnight.

He bowed to Jo Anne and, carrying the bag, he trudged off to his car. But not, of course, before he handed the mortgage to Mrs. Stowecroft. Mr. Ainsworth was very precise about these matters.

The Daughters of the Buccaneers crowded around, awash with gratitude and curiosity. How had Steve and Jo Anne done it? How had they made the feared and fearsome Silky Seymour pay up? The ladies asked so many questions that Steve had no chance to answer—which was perhaps just as well.

Then, when Steve and Jo Anne had climbed out of the boat, and the Daughters of the Buccaneers had donned their official Daughters of the Buccaneers ribbons, and Miss Jeffrey had put another couple of logs on the fire, Mrs. Stowecroft called the group to order.

"Mr. Walker," she trilled, "this is a moment most of us have waited for all of our lives."

Around her, the ladies glowed softly, like old lanterns.

"We are proud and grateful to share this moment with you," went on Mrs. Stowecroft. "Mr. Walker, will you burn the mortgage?"

She tried to give him the paper Mr. Ainsworth had left, but Steve waved it aside. "Thank you,

Mrs. Stowecroft," he said, "but that honor isn't for me."

He looked toward the bay. Not knowing why they did it, all of them followed his gaze. But there was nothing to be seen but the fog. Nothing to be seen at all. And nothing to be heard.

But no. There *was* something.

It was very faint at first. Then it came more clearly. Someone was singing. It was a lusty voice and a lusty song.

> "Hearts of oak are our ships.
> "Jolly tars are our men.
> "We'll always be ready.
> "Steady, boy, steady.
> "We'll fight and we'll conquer
> "Again and again!"

106

The song ended and the ladies on the beach heard the noise of oars moving in tholes. Then, out of the mist, came a rowboat.

"Here's the one you should really thank," said Steve warmly.

Mrs. Stowecroft stared at the boat. The oars moved in a steady rhythm, but no one was rowing!

Jo Anne shivered and put her arm through Steve's.

The boat scraped on the beach and the oars shipped themselves. Footprints appeared on the sand next to the boat and marched steadily toward the bonfire.

"Gracious!" exclaimed Mrs. Stowecroft.

Steve reached into his pocket and took out a book—an old, thin, yellowed book. He moved close to the fire, opened the book, and turned a couple of pages until he found what he was looking for.

"Jo Anne!" he said. "Ladies! Will you please repeat after me: KREE KRUH VERGO!"

The footprints stopped near the fire.

"KREE KRUH VERGO!" chorused the ladies, very uncertainly.

Beyond the inn, the wind stirred.

"GEBBA KALTO KREE!" chanted Steve.

"GEBBA KALTO KREE!" repeated the ladies, more strongly now.

Thunder crashed, and the bea   'enly white with lightning.

"Ladies!" announced Steve. "Allow me to present your real ba   "

Captain Blackbeard

No one needed to tell Mrs. Stowecroft who it was. She knew right away. So did Emily Jeffrey. So did all the other ladies. Even Jo Anne, who was *not* a descendant of Blackbeard's bloody crew, knew immediately that she was gazing upon the ghost of Captain Edward Teach.

"My respects, ma'am," said the captain to Mrs. Stowecroft.

A patter of applause broke out and Mrs. Stowecroft dropped a curtsy to the captain.

"So handsome!" gasped little Miss Jeffrey.

"Very dashing!" was Miss Peabody's only comment.

"Much better looking than his portraits!" decided old Mrs. Soames.

Jo Anne said nothing. She held tight to Steve's arm and smiled the happy smile of a girl who has just discovered that the man she loves does not really have bats in his belfry.

Captain Blackbeard swaggered a bit then. He loved nothing better than an audience—and he'd been denied one all these many years.

"Good ladies," he said, "your welcome has touched me deeply. Loath as I am to play the gallant, I am bound to say that never have I beheld creatures that stirred me more."

The fair creatures giggled.

"You cannot know what it has been like for me," the ghost went on. "I have been alone these two hundred accursed, dusty years. Now I hear again the delicious murmurs of—may I say it?—of admiration from members of your delightful sex."

The murmurs of admiration grew louder.

"I thank you," said the ghost.

There was another burst of applause.

"But stay!" cried Blackbeard. "It isn't my wish to make off with all the glory." He clapped a hand on Steve's shoulder. "This young rooster did a modest part in your delivery from disaster."

Again the ladies applauded.

"Enough!" shouted Blackbeard. He took the mortgage from Mrs. Stowecroft. "Now for this vile paper!" he announced, and he tossed it into the fire.

Afterward, the ladies said that the flames that leaped to consume the mortgage were green. Perhaps they were. It is enough to say that the paper was destroyed. And no sooner had it crinkled to ashes than Captain Blackbeard cocked an ear toward the curtain of fog that was edging nearer the beach.

"The time is here," he said. "I have managed to perform a small service to you. Now I go to a distant and, I hope, hospitable shore."

A little groan went up from the ladies.

"Tut! Tut!" scolded the ghost. "I pray you, only take notice that Captain Teach was not all bad. Remember him with kindness."

He gripped Steve's hand firmly. "Fare you well, lad," he said. "We shall not meet again."

To his own surprise, Steve felt his throat go tight. He could only nod.

Blackbeard strode to his rowboat, shoved the boat off the beach, climbed in, and took the oars in hand. Then, just before he rowed into the mist, he threw a kiss to the ladies. "Share it among you, my loves!" he called.

Then he was swallowed up by the fog. The watchers on the beach glimpsed, just for a moment, the faint outline of an old sailing ship. Quite clearly, the sound of a ship's bell rang across the water, and they heard a boatswain's pipe shrill to welcome a captain aboard.

"Cap'n!" cried a rough voice. "Proud to see you again, sir!"

"What's our course to be, Cap'n?" asked a second voice.

"Stir yourselves, you lazy swabs!" This time it was Blackbeard—unmistakably Blackbeard. "Lift the anchor! Shake out the main! Lively now, or I'll carve your gizzards!"

Then the voices died away and the ship, if it had been there at all, was there no longer.

"You know something?" said Steve. "I think I'm going to miss that old scoundrel!"

Westward Ho the Wagons!

The Promised Land

THE grass is up! The grass is up!" The news spread quickly, passed from one person to another in the wagon camp.

"The grass is up, Dan!" little Myra Thompson said. She was holding a bucket from which her twelve-year-old brother was scooping up a gob of grease.

"Did you hear me, Dan? The grass is up!" Myra repeated.

"I heard you," Dan said, smearing grease on the hub of a wagon wheel.

"But what does it mean?"

"Means that the spring grass is up along the Oregon Trail," Dan said. "Means there'll be plenty of grass to eat for the livestock in the wagon train."

"And what does *that* mean?"

"Don't you ever get tired of asking questions?" Dan said sharply.

His older sister, Laura, looked down at them from the wagon and laughed.

"It means we'll be going on west as soon as Captain Stephen finishes getting the wagon train ready," she said.

"That's right," said another voice—a man's voice. "Better finish greasing those wheels and be ready to travel. Captain Stephen just announced that we're moving out at noon."

Dan glanced over his shoulder. Dr. John Grayson was standing beside them.

Doc was a cheerful man—young, tall, and broad-shouldered. Folks said that he had really studied to be a doctor. But he had never done much doctoring. He was just a fiddle-footed drifter, and seldom touched his medical kit.

"We're moving out at noon?" Laura said. "That's short notice, John."

"Maybe I can help you," Doc said.

Dan spoke up quickly. "No need for that. We'll be ready in time."

"Sure you will, Dan," said Doc, smiling. "Well, I'll see you on the trail."

He nodded and walked off toward one of the other covered wagons.

"You weren't very polite to Doctor Grayson, Dan," Laura said.

"Doctor Grayson! John! Why can't you call him Doc like everyone else?"

"I can be polite, if you can't," Laura said. "He was only trying to be helpful. We all have to help each other if we hope to get to Oregon safely."

"We've been doing all right by ourselves. We got here all the way from Ohio without help, didn't we? And we did all right before that, too."

"Dan," said Laura quietly, "you still think we should have stayed in Ohio, don't you?"

Dan shrugged and went back to greasing the wheels. He didn't want to quarrel with Laura. Although she was only a young girl herself—she had just turned twenty—she had been like a mother to Dan and Myra since their parents had died. Those years had not been easy. But somehow they had managed to stay together, and Dan was proud of the way they had made out alone.

And then one day Laura had told him about Oregon, the far-off land on the shores of the Pacific Ocean.

"It's a new land opening up," Laura said. "Miles and miles of it, just waiting for settlers. The soil is much richer than it is here. The mountains are covered with fine timber, and the rivers are full of fish. And the climate is good, too—not too hot and not too cold. No wonder they call it the Promised Land! Dan, I think we could get together enough money to buy a wagon. We could start a new life out there, a better life. We could grow with America."

Dan had heard talk about Oregon fever—something that got into folks and made them want to move west. Most of them wanted to better themselves. They hoped to find better farm land, or to make their fortune as the country grew. But others had no real reason for moving. They just wanted the adventure of seeing new places, of being part of something big.

And looking at Laura's shining eyes, listening to her eager voice, Dan knew that she had Oregon fever.

"Well, Dan," Laura said, "what do you say? Shall we go to Oregon?"

Dan was silent for a while. Most boys would have jumped at the chance to go west. But Dan's hard life had made him older than his years. It was true that there wasn't much to keep them in the Ohio Valley. But would things be better in Oregon? Laura and Myra were the only family he had. And as the man of the family, he had to protect them.

"Still," thought Dan, "Laura is older than I am. She ought to know what's best."

Then he said aloud, "Guess we're going to Oregon. We'd bettter get that wagon."

And so they had set off, and here they were in Independence, a busy frontier town in Missouri. Already they had traveled many miles, but the worst part of the journey was ahead. In that year of 1844, Independence was the jumping-off point for many wagon trains. Beyond it stretched the trail, winding for two thousand miles through wild, open, untamed country.

Two thousand miles, five months of travel. . . . There would be deep, swiftly-flowing streams to ford. There would be shifting sandhills and scorching deserts to cross. There would be steep mountains to climb. And always there would be the danger of Indians.

But at the end of the trail lay Oregon, the Promised Land.

"It can't be as wonderful as everybody says," Dan thought. "It just can't be."

As he finished greasing the last wheel, he heard Captain Stephen shout:

"Fall in and stretch out!"

Quickly, Dan made a final check of the wagon. He went after his favorite horse, Chieftain, and swung into the saddle. Myra climbed up on the wagon seat beside Laura, who unwound the reins from the brake handle.

"Catch up! Catch up!" Captain Stephen bellowed.

The wagons lumbered and creaked into line. Soon they were formed into a long column.

The herd of livestock was driven into place behind the last wagon.

"Hiyah-up!" cried the drivers. "Hee-yah-ho!"

Whips cracked over the horses, and dust rose as the wagon wheels turned. The emigrants shouted and waved, and some began to sing:

> Westward ho the wagons!
> Westward roll them far!
> Westward ho the wagons
> Toward the western star!

Suddenly, without knowing why, Dan shouted, "On to Oregon!"

Laura threw him a quick look, and he dropped his eyes, ashamed. But he could not help being excited.

For the wagon train was really rolling now, slowly rolling west, carrying people to a new life. And exactly what that new life would be like, no one could say.

"Guess I've got a touch of Oregon fever myself," thought Dan. "Maybe they're right about Oregon being the Promised Land."

All the same, he wasn't sure. And he was silent as the others sang:

> Westward ho the wagons!
> Always westward roll!
> Westward ho the wagons!
> For Oregon's our goal!

Pawnee Trick

FORT UP!" Hank Breckenridge called, riding back along the wagon column. "Circle the wagons tight! This is Pawnee country!"

The old frontier scout was smiling. But his eyes darted about, watching for the smallest sign of danger.

A month had gone by since the wagon train had left Independence. For the last few days it had been following the south bank of the Platte River, in southern Nebraska.

The sandy soil made traveling slow and hard. Most of the emigrants walked beside their wagons, so that their teams of horses would have a little less weight to pull. Slowly the wagons pushed on, past the endless sandhills, past the great herds of buffalo that roamed the prairie.

Dan reined Chieftain up beside the Thompson wagon. "We're making camp for the night, Laura. They say we're on the Pawnee Trail."

Myra poked her blonde, curly head out from under the wagon cover.

"What's the Pawnee Trail?" she said.

"There you go with your everlasting questions," Dan said.

But his voice was kind, and Myra asked her question again.

"It's an Injun trail," Dan told her. "And these Injuns aren't friendly."

"We don't know for sure that they're unfriendly," Laura said.

"Well, we can't take any chances," Dan said. "We got to fort the wagons up tight."

At a signal from Captain Stephen, the wagons strung out in single file. He gave a second signal, and the drivers wheeled them into a circle. The teams were unhitched, and the tongue of each wagon was pushed close to the tailgate of the wagon ahead of it. That way the wagons formed a solid barricade.

By the time the livestock were picketed outside the ring of wagons, darkness had come. The emigrants made small campfires of buffalo chips, and roasted buffalo meat and antelope steaks for their evening meal. When they finished eating, they did their chores and began to settle down for the night.

Dan went out to see that Chieftain was picketed where there was plenty of grass. Then he returned to the wagon circle. He joined some children huddled around a campfire, where Hank Breckenridge was telling one of his tales.

Dan noticed that Doc Grayson was standing nearby, beside the Thompson wagon. He seemed more interested in watching Laura than in listening to the scout. Dan scowled. Why was Doc always hanging around their wagon? Why was he always talking to Laura?

But Dan soon stopped thinking about Doc as Hank went on with his story.

". . . and there I was alone in my camp, mindin' my own business an' everything all peaceful. Suddenly—zip!—in comes a Pawnee arrow within a foot of my head—"

Hank leaned back, resting against a wooden

crate. He paused for a moment—and a real arrow whizzed past his head. It thudded into the crate, its shaft quivering.

"I can almost see it now," Hank said drowsily. "It was . . ." Suddenly, he blinked his eyes and stared at the arrow. Leaping to his feet, he snatched it from the crate and looked at its markings.

At the same time, Doc Grayson sprang forward. He scuffed his boot sideways through the sandy soil, kicking dirt over the small campfire. "Pawnees!"

Doc's shout rang out in the darkness. All around the circle men jumped from their wagons, rifles in their hands.

"Douse all fires!" Hank bellowed. "Everybody to his place!"

Picking up his rifle, he dove under the nearest wagon. He squinted out between the wheel spokes, looking for Indians. Dan quickly followed the scout's example. He picked up his rifle and slid under his own wagon.

Doc Grayson was shouting at the frightened children around the campfire. "Into your wagons! And keep low!"

Dan made no sound, hoping that no one would make him hide in a wagon like the other children. Near him, Doc, Hank, and Captain Stephen peered into the darkness. The camp was silent, waiting for the Indian attack.

Captain Stephen whispered anxiously to Doc, "Where are they? Why don't they start?"

"Reckon one arrow doesn't make an attack," Doc said. "Let's go out and take a look."

Gripping his rifle in trembling hands, Dan followed the men. He kept a few paces behind. If they saw him, they might send him back.

The men moved carefully in the darkness. But there was no sign of Indians. Some distance from the camp they found Obie Foster, who was standing guard over the horses.

"You got no call to come lookin' for me," Obie said angrily. "I'm on the job, if that's what's worryin' you."

"You better be," Doc said. "There's Indians around!"

Dan did not hear the answer. He had spied something on the ground—something quiet and still. It was a man's body, with the shaft of an arrow sticking out from its back.

"Look!" Dan cried, pointing.

Captain Stephen rolled the man over carefully so that they could see his face. "Who do you reckon he is?"

"A present from the Pawnees," Doc said bitterly. "Give me a hand. The poor devil's still alive. Come on. Take his feet. Easy, now!"

They carried the wounded stranger into camp. Mrs. Stephen and Laura hurried to bring sheets and blankets, while Hank ran off to fetch Doc's medical kit. Dan helped push some boxes and crates together to make a table.

"Dan," Laura said, "go back to the wagon and look after Myra."

Dan obeyed. But he found Myra asleep and the wagon well guarded. He went back to the place where Doc was working on the wounded stranger. Dan stayed in the shadows.

An hour later, Doc let out a deep sigh. He shook his head. His shoulders sagged, as though he were very tired. The body on the table lay motionless, a wide-brimmed hat still on its head. Hank had told them not to remove it. A scalped man was not a pleasant sight.

"I . . . I couldn't save him," Doc said quietly, as though talking to himself.

Laura touched his arm gently. "He was too far gone. No one could have saved him, John."

"We'll give him a fittin' burial," Hank said. "Don't you worry, Doc. You done your best. Sometimes—hey! Listen! What's that?"

From the direction of the grazing area came the sound of hoofbeats.

"The horses!" somebody cried. "The Injuns are stealin' our horses!"

"Chieftain!" Dan said.

He ran with the men toward the picket string.

They found that five of the best horses had been driven off. And Chieftain was one of them.

"Shoulda known," Hank said. "Them Pawnees was tradin' that wounded white hostage for a chanst at our horses. Figured we'd leave 'em unguarded—which is exactly what we done."

"Guards back to your posts!" ordered Captain Stephen. "At that," he added, "I reckon we're lucky to lose the horses, instead of more lives."

Turning away from the men, Dan ran back to the camp. Laura started to scold him for leaving Myra alone. Then she noticed the look on his face, and asked, "What is it, Dan?"

"The . . . the horses! They . . . stole five of the best!"

"Chieftain?" asked Laura gently.

Dan nodded.

"But I'll get him back!" he said, sobbing. "You'll see! I'll get him back!"

Dan Visits the Pawnees

DAN nearly dropped his saddle when he heard someone calling him from the Stephen wagon. But it was only little Jerry Stephen.

"Hey, Dan," said Jerry, "what are you doing?"

"Shhh!" Dan said. He glanced anxiously around at the darkened camp. "You want to spoil my Injun hunt, Jerry?"

"What do you mean—Injun hunt?"

Jerry's older sister, Bobo, showed her head over the edge of the wagon box. "Dan, what are you doing with that saddle and rifle? Why aren't you asleep?"

"Got better things to do than sleep," Dan said. "Tell you what I'll do. You keep my secret and I'll bring you a Pawnee scalp. That's fair, isn't it?"

Jim, the oldest of the Stephen children, squeezed up between Bobo and Jerry.

"I'll go with you, Dan," he said.

"Not this time, Jim," Dan whispered. "I've got to go alone. I'll be right back. Promise you won't tell?"

Bobo looked worried. "Dan, I'll bet you're not going after Pawnee scalps at all. You're going after Chieftain. Don't do it, Dan! I'll ask father if you can't use one of our horses."

Dan shook his head. No other horse could ever take Chieftain's place. Carrying his saddle and his rifle, he moved silently away. He left the circle of wagons and hurried to the place where all of the horses had been left to rest and graze.

Dan spotted a bay that belonged to Mr. Armitage. He slipped the saddle on the bay's back and tightened the cinch. Mr. Armitage shouldn't mind his borrowing the horse for a little while. After all, Mr. Armitage was the richest man in the wagon company and had more horses than anyone else.

The stolen horses had left a bold trail, and Dan had little trouble following it in the light of the half moon. He rode cautiously for almost an hour.

119

Then the bay flicked its ears and whinnied softly.

Dan jumped to the ground and looped the reins over a clump of sagebrush. Holding his rifle carefully, he dropped to his knees and crawled forward. He went at least a hundred yards before he came to a low ridge overlooking the Pawnee camp. In the dim moonlight he could see some horses picketed in the sagebrush. Five of them were Indian ponies. The other five had been stolen from the wagon company—and Chieftain was among them. And on the ground nearby lay five Pawnee warriors, asleep in their buffalo robes.

For a while Dan looked down on the quiet camp, wondering what to do next. Then there was a faint rustling sound behind him. Bracing himself against the blow of a tomahawk, he rolled to one side and swung his rifle around.

"Easy, son," a voice whispered. "It's me Doc."

"Doc!"

Dan was relieved that it wasn't a Pawnee, but he wished it had been someone else besides Doc. He didn't want Doc getting any ideas that the Thompsons needed his help.

"How—how did you know—" he said.

"That isn't the point, son. Point is you ought to have your breeches paddled for pulling a trick like this!"

"I . . . I've been doing all right up to now. I found our horses." He pointed to the Indian camp below. "Leave me alone and I'll—"

"Shh!" Doc said. He looked down at the horses and the five Pawnee warriors. "You want me to get out of your way while you surround 'em, Dan? Is that it?"

Dan realized he had been talking foolishly. "Doc, will you—will you help me?"

"What're you planning to do?"

"Those Pawnees are asleep," Dan said. "Can't we rush 'em?"

"Too risky. But if Chieftain means that much to you, we might try that Kiowa trick I was telling you about the other day. You remember it, don't you?"

"Sure. I remember." Dan hoped he sounded a little more brave than he felt.

"All right. I'll cover you from here with the rifles," Doc said.

Dan passed his rifle to Doc. Slipping his knife from its sheath, Doc cut a clump of sagebrush. Then he handed the knife to Dan.

"When you reach 'em," Doc said, "cut all the horses loose so they'll scatter. Grab Chieftain and head back as fast as you can. Savvy?"

"Why not take the whole bunch back?" Dan asked.

"Don't stretch our luck. And once you've got Chieftain, don't stop for anything. Just ride for your life."

Dan took the clump of sagebrush. Pushing it ahead of him, he crawled cautiously toward the Indian camp. A stone clattered under his knee. One of the Pawnees stirred in his sleep, and Dan held his breath until the Indian settled down.

Inching forward behind his sagebrush screen, Dan drew close to the horses—and to the sleeping Indians. His heart began to beat wildly. Suppose one of the horses suddenly whinnied or snorted! He glanced back over his shoulder, uncertain. Doc's hand was raised in a signal for him to make his break.

Dan threw the sagebrush aside, leaped up, and sprinted to the horses. With one slash of the knife he cut the picket string. The startled horses reared and scattered. As Dan reached for Chieftain's mane, a shrill cry came from the Pawnees. It made Chieftain shy back, jerking his mane from Dan's hands.

An Indian charged at Dan, his tomahawk raised to strike. Before he could bring it down, there was the crack of a rifle shot. With a shriek, the warrior fell.

Again Dan took hold of Chieftain's mane, and swung up to his back. By this time another Indian had caught one of the loose horses. He galloped toward Dan, fitting an arrow to his bowstring. A second rifle shot rang out, and the Indian toppled to the ground.

Still on foot, the remaining Indians loosed a barrage of arrows. Little spurts of dust kicked up around Chieftain's hoofs as the arrows struck the ground. But the high-stepping horse quickly carried Dan out of range.

Dan had hardly reached the other two ground-tied horses, when Doc came running up. He tossed one of the two emptied rifles to Dan. Seizing the reins of the extra horse, Doc leaped into the saddle of his own mount.

"Let's get out of here, Dan," he said. "Pronto—before they catch up to us!"

Prisoner of the Pawnees

MORE than a week had passed since Dan had rescued Chieftain from the Pawnees. The wagon train had moved steadily westward. It had forded the muddy South Platte River, swollen with rain. One wagon and several head of cattle had been lost in the quicksand.

Each day the weather grew warmer, as the wagons skirted the sandhills and cut deep ruts across the treeless prairie. And each day the emigrants grew more cheerful. Hank Breckenridge tried to warn them that the Pawnees could not be far off. But the emigrants refused to worry. If the Pawnees hadn't attacked by now, most likely there wouldn't be any attack. That made sense, didn't it?

And then one afternoon the shout went up. "Chimney Rock! Chimney Rock!"

The famous landmark of the Oregon Trail lay ahead. An enormous formation of stone, it rose for hundreds of feet above the flat plain. Chimney Rock marked the end of the prairie, and the end of a good third of the journey. Fort Laramie was not too far away. West of Fort Laramie the emigrants would reach the Rocky Mountains, and South Pass—and then on to Oregon!

"Why isn't the chimbley smoking?" little Jerry Stephen asked. He could not understand why everyone laughed. After all, where there was a chimbley, there should be smoke. Everybody knew that!

Choosing a site near the river, the emigrants circled their wagons and made camp. They would stay here a few days, to give the cattle and horses a chance to rest and feed on the good grass.

That night the wagon camp was a happy place. Someone brought out a concertina. He was joined by a fiddler and a banjo player. Soon there was dancing in the flickering light of the campfires.

"Them fires is big enough to burn a barn," Hank Breckenridge said.

"Big enough to be seen a long ways, too," Doc said. "If the Pawnees catch us in the open like this, the whole tribe will be down on us like a swarm of bees. We've been lucky so far, but—"

As Doc reached the end of John Colter's story, the children were rushed off to bed. Dan was the last to walk away, moving as if he were in a dream. As he fell asleep, he sang part of John Colter's song to himself:

For, it was a race he had to win,
Or, by losing, had to die . . .

When Dan awoke the next morning, the first thing he thought about was the brave mountain man and his strange race against death.

"Dan Thompson," Laura said to him, "what's got into you, mooning around like that? You know there's work to be done."

"Well," said Hank, "Cap Stephen's the boss. An' seein' as how he thinks it's all right, reckon we might as well enjoy ourselves."

Doc nodded and started to walk toward the dancers. But before he could reach them, some children came running up.

"Please tell us a story, Doc!" they said.

Doc smiled, and someone passed him a guitar. "All right. I'll sing you a song that tells the story of a brave mountain man. And that man's name was John Colter."

As Doc strummed the guitar and sang, people gathered around him, youngsters and grown-ups alike. Among them was Dan. He still did not like the way Doc kept hanging around the Thompson's wagon, talking to Laura every chance he got. To make it worse, Laura seemed to like it.

But Dan had to admit that Doc knew how to sing. He soon forgot about his own troubles, listening to the story of John Colter.

On a trapping trip up the old Missouri, Colter was captured by the Blackfeet. The Indians admired his bravery so much that they gave him a chance for his life. Stripping Colter of his clothes and weapons, they turned him loose. Colter ran, and after him ran the bravest of the Blackfoot braves with their sharp lances.

But Colter escaped and walked three hundred miles, barefoot, to the nearest settlement.

124

"I'm sorry, Laura," Dan said.

Together with Myra, the three Stephen children and Tom Foster, he went out to gather firewood.

Before they realized it, they had wandered dangerously far from the wagon camp as they searched for wood.

Dan was a little ahead of the others. As he topped a ridge, he spied a Pawnee scouting party. The five Pawnees saw him at the same time. Digging their heels into the flanks of their ponies, they came rushing up the slope.

"Injuns!" Dan shouted over his shoulder. "Hide —quick!"

The children obeyed, diving into a thicket.

"Come on, Dan!" Jim Stephen called. "Hide!"

"Too late," Dan said. "They saw me. But they didn't see you. You stay hid. Don't move till they're gone. Then run back to camp."

"But Dan—!"

"Keep still! Do as I say!"

Trying to be as fearless as John Colter, Dan strode forward to meet the Indians. The Pawnees stared at him, puzzled. Then, at a word of command from one of the scouts, they pounced on him. Throwing him to the ground, they bound him with strong rawhide thongs.

The Pawnees looked around to see if Dan was alone. But they gave up their search when they saw the wagon camp in the distance. They put Dan on a horse and rode off with him, talking excitedly. Dan could not understand their language. But he could see that they were pleased with taking him prisoner. And perhaps they were pleased, too, with locating the wagon train.

"They must be part of a war party," Dan thought.

It was growing dark when they reached the Pawnee camp. The Indians rolled Dan off the pony and into the dirt. All about him were Pawnee warriors. They were dipping war paint out of clay bowls, smearing it on themselves in jagged lines of yellow, red and blue. Drums sounded,

125

making the air throb with their steady beat. The warriors began to dance, looking like painted ghosts in the firelight.

Yes, this was a war party, all right. Dan trembled a little as he wondered what the Pawnees would do to him. They were paying no attention to him now. But as soon as their dance was over, they would turn back to him. And he had heard tales of what the Pawnees did to their white prisoners—terrifying tales. . . .

Dan strained at the thongs that bound his wrists and ankles. It was no use. He would never be able to work himself free of the tough rawhide.

Desperately he looked around for some way to escape. And then he noticed a clay paint bowl that had been thrown to the ground nearby. Its rim had a jagged edge, a sharp edge—perhaps sharp enough to cut through rawhide.

Keeping his eyes on the dancing braves, Dan stretched out his feet until they touched the bowl. Slowly he drew the bowl toward him, and slowly, cautiously, inched it around behind him. Once it was in place, he leaned back until he could touch

it with his wrists. Moving as carefully as he could, he began sawing the rawhide bindings back and forth against the jagged edge of the bowl.

Once he stopped as a Pawnee glanced at him. But the Indian went on dancing, and Dan started his sawing again. Suddenly, his wrists came free. Watching the dancers, Dan cupped the bowl in his hands and sawed through the bindings around his ankles.

Dan knew there was no sense waiting. Dropping the bowl, he leaped to his feet and ran off into the darkness.

Dan stumbled and fell as a shrill cry of alarm rose behind him. Scrambling back to his feet, he turned and ran, ran with all his strength. For like the race of brave John Colter, *this was a race he had to win, or, by losing, die.*

Dan bounded over a ridge, and raced down the slope into a brushy ravine. After him came five Pawnee braves, shouting with delight at this new game. They were not far behind Dan, and they were gaining.

Dan dodged through the thickening underbrush. He changed direction every few yards,

127

hoping to throw the Pawnees off his trail. He did have one advantage. He was smaller than they were, and could easily slip through openings in the brush. The Pawnees could not get through so quickly, and Dan gained back a little of his lead.

But he soon came to the end of the ravine, and two Pawnees closed in on him. Frantically, Dan scrambled up the side of the ravine to more level ground. Sharp rocks and thorny cactus tore at his feet and cut into his skin. Now most of the Pawnees dropped out of the race, and only one was

left to pursue Dan—but that one was coming closer and closer.

Suddenly the wall of a steep cliff loomed ahead of Dan in the darkness. Panting and exhausted, he was ready to give up. All he could do was brace himself for the Indian's attack.

"But brave John Colter wouldn't have given up," Dan thought—and he began to haul himself up the rocky side of the cliff. A tomahawk flew through the air, just missing his shoulder. And then he heard the Pawnee climbing after him, breathing heavily.

Somehow, Dan kept going, moving up the cliff. As he neared the top, his foot struck a large boulder. The boulder rolled downward, starting an avalanche. With a noise like thunder, more and more rocks went sliding and tumbling down the side. Through the crash and roar of falling rock rose a shriek of despair, and then there was silence.

Dan stopped and clung to the side, gasping for breath. He listened for a sound from below, but heard nothing. The avalanche must have swept the Pawnee to his death, and none of the other Indians had taken up the chase.

Slowly and painfully, Dan pulled himself up to the top of the cliff. Off across the prairie, he could see the small dots of light that marked the campfires of the wagon camp. He rested for a few minutes, got to his feet, and, stumbling and staggering, walked toward the flickering fires that shone out through the darkness.

Battle at the Notch

As soon as Dan reached camp, he had Laura call Captain Stephen and Hank Breckenridge. Quickly he told them what had happened.

"No two ways about it," Hank said. "Them Pawnees will be attackin' us at dawn."

Captain Stephen nodded. The next moment his voice roared through the camp:

"Turn out! Everybody out!"

The men came running up, and one of them asked, "What's up, Captain?"

"We've got to make a run for the Notch," Captain Stephen said. "Young Dan Thompson says there's a big war party on the way. The Pawnees will massacre us if they catch us out here in the open. Our one chance is to reach the Notch. Once we're in the narrow canyon, they won't be able to get at us."

"But it's already turnin' dawn," Spencer Armitage said. "It'll be full daylight before we can reach the Notch."

"We can't stay here like sittin' ducks," Doc Grayson said. "The captain's right."

Hank Breckenridge shouted, "Span your wagons and lighten your loads! Every extra pound you carry makes your scalp that much looser! Throw away everything you can spare, an' half of what you can't get by without!"

The men scattered to their wagons. Everywhere cradles, stoves, chests of drawers were hauled out and placed on the ground. Tears came to the eyes of some of the women as they saw their dearest possessions left to rot on the prairie. But there was no help for it.

Dawn was brightening the sky by the time the wagons were ready to move. Several of the men drove the herd of livestock out ahead of the train.

Doc told Hank, "Send any of the men that can be spared back to the end of the string with all the extra guns they've got. I'm going to rig a couple of the wagons as a rear guard."

"Start 'em rollin', Captain!" Hank shouted.

"Fall in and close up!" Captain Stephen called, and the wagons began to move toward the Notch.

Dan saw the company's best marksmen hurrying toward the rear of the train. Doc told them to climb into the last two wagons and hide under the canvas covers.

"The best shots take the guns," he said. "The others load for 'em."

His rifle in his hand, Dan leaped on Chieftain and started to follow the men.

"Better stick with your wagon, Dan," Doc said. "Your sisters may need a crack shot with them."

Dan wasn't sure whether Doc was paying him a compliment or trying to keep him out of the way. But this was no time to argue. He turned back and rode beside his wagon. Laura sat on the seat, handling the reins, while Myra was out of sight under the canvas cover.

They had gone less than half a mile when Dan saw a long line of Pawnees strung out along the rim of a hill to the right. The chief, in full battle array, sat boldly astride his painted pony. There was another line of Indians to the left. Altogether, there were about three hundred braves in the war party.

As the wagon drivers whipped their teams into a run, the Pawnee chief rode out before his men. He waved his lance, and, yelling their war cries, the Pawnees charged the wagon train from both sides.

Dan heard the crack of rifles, fired by the men in the rear guard wagons, and he fired, too. Soon there was firing from everywhere along the wagon train. There was the whine of bullets and the hiss of flying arrows as the Pawnees returned the fire. The shouts of men, the thud of hoofs, the creak of wagon wheels mingled with the wild war cries of the Indians.

The Pawnees swooped down recklessly from the hills, but many of them fell to the ground as the emigrants' rifles found their marks. And all the while the wagons kept racing on, toward the sheltering walls of the Notch.

Then, at a signal from the chief, the Pawnees drew back to regroup for another charge.

"Looks like they got more than they figgered on," Hank Breckenridge said. "They'll be back—but this is our chance to get into the Notch!"

Captain Stephen nodded. "Keep those wagons right on movin'!" he shouted.

By this time the herd of livestock was entering the Notch, followed by the first of the wagons. As the Pawnees spread out, the wagons kept rumbling up the steep slope that led to the mouth of the canyon. Soon all the wagons were in the Notch except the one belonging to the Benjamin family. Its wheels were jammed tight in a deep rut.

Clutching her baby, Mrs. Benjamin dropped from the wagon and hurried ahead on foot. Two horsemen rode in and looped a rope to the wagon, helping to pull it free. But the added strain sheared off the tongue-pin. The wagon rolled backwards down the slope, and Ed Benjamin leaped to the ground just as it smashed into pieces on the rocks.

Dan was still on Chieftain, keeping close to his own wagon. He saw the men running to the entrance of the Notch, where they took cover behind rocks for their last stand. Before Laura could stop him, he jumped from Chieftain and rushed over to join the group of watchful men.

At first Dan was afraid that Doc was going to send him back. But Doc smiled and said, "Guess

we need all the help we can get, at that. Just don't waste your shots, Dan."

Twice the Pawnees attacked, and twice they were driven back. They left many dead on the field, but they had wounded several of the small party of emigrants.

Dan heard Hank Breckenridge say, "They're gettin' ready to charge again. All they have to do is keep comin' at us, and they're bound to break through."

"Once they do, they'll get to the wagons," Captain Stephen said. "It'll be a massacre. And I don't see any way we can stop 'em."

"Maybe there is a way," Doc said thoughtfully. "A Pawnee would rather take a horse than a scalp, any day. We might try turning the horses against 'em."

Spencer Armitage, who owned the finest horses in the herd, spoke up angrily. "Who do you think you are, Doc, giving away other men's horses!"

"Just a minute, Armitage," Obie Foster said. He was usually the quietest man of them all, but now his voice was loud. "We all got stock in that herd. Anyway, looks like we got no choice. Come on, let's turn the herd loose!"

"Oh, no, you don't!" said Armitage, making a grab for Obie.

Obie's fist shot out, catching Armitage on the side of the jaw. Armitage reeled back and dropped heavily to the ground.

"Somebody give me a hand!" Obie said, and several men followed him as he ran off toward the horses.

Dan stared at Obie, then turned as arrows and bullets thudded all around him. The Indians were charging again. He threw himself behind a rock, raised his rifle, and carefully took aim at a Pawnee brave. He squeezed the trigger, and the brave slumped over on his pony.

"Good shootin', youngster," Hank Breckenridge said. "Keep it up."

For ten minutes the battle went on. Dan lost all track of time. He loaded and fired, loaded and fired, trying to make every shot count.

Suddenly Doc shouted, "Look out!"

Dan and the other men jumped to one side as the herd came thundering down the slope. The stampeding horses galloped on, right into the ranks of the Pawnees. The Indians, amazed, stopped firing and reined in their ponies. Then, yelling wildly, they gave up the battle altogether to run down and capture the horses.

Obie Foster and the men who had been driving the horses joined the other men at the rocks.

"Sorry you had to lose your horses, Obie," Doc said.

Obie smiled. "Don't worry about the horses. We still got our hides, ain't we—thanks to you."

Dan looked at Doc. For a fiddle-footed drifter, Doc wasn't a bad sort. A fellow might even get to like him—if only he didn't hang around Laura so much.

Little Yellow Hair

As the wagon train pushed steadily on, someone shouted:

"There she is! Fort Laramie!"

Ahead, standing on the grassy plain, was a high-walled adobe fort. The emigrants cheered, and soon they were singing:

> There's lots of trails behind us,
> And ahead there's plenty more,
> But now we've hit Fort Laramie
> And we've got a rest in store.

Yes, Fort Laramie meant rest. And it also meant the chance to get supplies, to catch up on many things that needed doing, to repair wagons and care for the lame horses and cattle.

Now the emigrants could see some Indian tepees near the fort, and a man on horseback riding toward them.

"Why, it's Bisonette!" said Hank Breckenridge. "Hey, Bisonette, you ol' hoss! You're lookin' mighty chipper!"

"Hank!" said Bisonette. "So you are still alive, my friend!"

Hank introduced Bisonette to Doc and Captain Stephen. He was a French-Canadian, and ran the trading post at the fort.

"What about those tepees?" Captain Stephen asked.

"They belong to Chief Wolf's Brother and his band," Bisonette said. "They are Sioux, and they don't usually make trouble for wagon trains. But the last train to come through killed a couple of their braves. You better circle your wagons in close to the fort."

"They won't start anything right here at the fort, will they?" Captain Stephen said.

"Probably not, m'sieu," Bisonette said. "But it's Sioux country for a long way west of here."

"Think they might close the trail ahead?" said Hank.

Bisonette shrugged. "Who knows? Better follow me. I'll show you where to camp."

Word about the Sioux spread among the emigrants, but they were too happy at reaching the fort to worry about it.

"If we could handle the Pawnees, I guess we can handle the Sioux," Dan said.

behind the counter. "He is a great Sioux Medicine Man—a very important man among the Indians. He makes dreams for Chief Wolf's Brother."

"Dreams?" said Dan.

"What you call visions," Bisonette said. "He makes a dream and tells the chief what the gods want him to do."

After finishing his work, Dan took Myra to the trading post. They wanted to see what they could get for some untanned buffalo hides the hunters had brought in along the trail.

For once Myra did not ask questions. Dressed in a fresh frock and pinafore, she tugged eagerly at Dan's hand.

Inside the trading post, Dan was amazed. There were stacks of goods heaped up on shelves and counters, and even things hanging from the ceiling. There were bear traps and beads, rifles and ribbons—almost anything a person could want.

Looking around, Dan saw a dignified old Indian standing in a corner. The Indian was watching Myra, staring at her strangely with his sharp eyes.

"That is Many Stars," said Bisonette, who was

Many Stars hurried out, and Dan and Myra did their trading. On their way back to the wagon camp, they saw Many Stars near the gate of the fort. He was talking to Chief Wolf's Brother and Little Thunder, the chief's son. Little Thunder was a boy about the same age as Dan.

Many Stars whispered something to the chief, and Wolf's Brother walked over to Myra.

"Little Yellow Hair," he said, touching Myra's bright blonde hair. "Daughter of the Rising Sun —good medicine!"

"What does he mean—good medicine?" Myra asked Dan.

"Something like good luck, I guess," Dan answered.

Neither of them said anything to Laura about what had happened. But that night, while the emigrants were singing and dancing, Wolf's

134

Brother rode into the wagon camp. With him were Many Stars and three Sioux warriors, leading three fine Indian ponies. Many Stars carried a white buffalo robe rolled up in his arms.

"Be friendly, but be careful," Bisonette said to Captain Stephen. "Hear what they have to say."

Wolf's Brother spread some buffalo robes on the ground near the fire, then sat down to have a pow-wow with Captain Stephen. Dan stood nearby, with Doc, Laura, and some other people of the wagon camp.

After smoking a pipe of peace with the chief, Captain Stephen welcomed him to the camp.

Wolf's Brother spoke, and Bisonette translated.

"Wolf's Brother says those ponies are trained hunters," Bisonette said. "With them you will be able to keep your cooking pots full of game all the way to Oregon. The white buffalo is sacred. That robe Many Stars holds will protect you from bad spirits. Wolf's Brother warns that there are many Sioux to the west. You see that magic whistle Many Stars holds? It is made from the wing-bone of a great war eagle. It will be a sign to the Sioux braves that you are friends. These gifts are the greatest that Wolf's Brother can give."

"In other words," Captain Stephen said, "he's offering us safety for the rest of the journey. But he must want something from us in return. What is it?"

Wolf's Brother spoke again, and Hank Breckenridge broke in. "He wants to trade for Little Yellow Hair—little Myra Thompson!"

"The chief promises to raise Little Yellow Hair as a Sioux Princess," Bisonette explained. "He promises to care for her like his own."

"What!" said Captain Stephen.

Dan gasped, and Laura cried out, "No! No! How could anyone ask for such a thing!"

"You must understand," Bisonette said to Captain Stephen, "if you try to take your wagons on through to Oregon without giving up the little one, Wolf's Brother will set the whole Sioux nation against you. He says that the Great Spirit has

spoken through Many Stars, their medicine man, who claims that the little girl is big medicine. She will bring good luck to the tribe. The chief will do anything to—"

Doc stepped forward, interrupting Bisonette. "Tell the chief that Little Yellow Hair has no magic for his people—no medicine. Tell him she is a child and would sicken and die among strangers. We know the honor he pays us, and the value of the gifts he offers. But we will not part with the child!"

Bisonette translated Doc's words, and for a few moments no one moved. Then Wolf's Brother rose, anger in his face. Turning quickly, he walked off toward the Sioux camp. His men gathered up the war-eagle whistle and the white buffalo robe. Leading the ponies away, they silently followed their chief.

"You were right, of course," Bisonette said to the people of the wagon train. "But Wolf's Brother will have every warrior in the Sioux nation after your scalps."

There was no more dancing or singing in the wagon camp that night.

White Man's Medicine

THE NEXT morning, the people of the wagon camp were quiet and uneasy. Dan could understand why. More than half the summer was gone. Soon the snow would come beating down in the Rocky Mountains. The emigrants would have to hurry to get through South Pass before it was clogged by snow. But if they left now, they might be massacred by the Sioux.

Dan sighed, and started to repair Chieftain's bridle. Doc walked over to help him. They were just finishing the job when they were joined by Hank Breckenridge and Captain Stephen.

"I don't mind sayin' I'm worried," Captain Stephen said. "It's hard to know what to do."

Dan listened to the talk of the men. Then he turned away to watch some Indian boys who

136

were riding up to the open ground nearby. One of the boys flung a short, feather-tufted dart so that it stuck upright in the sod.

Another Indian boy came galloping toward the dart. Clinging to the woven surcingle around his pony, he leaned low, and snatched up the dart. Shouting, he waved it over his head and threw it so that once more it stuck in the ground.

Next it was the turn of Little Thunder, the chief's son. As his pony raced toward the dart, the boy gripped the surcingle with one hand and leaned far down. Suddenly the surcingle broke, and Little Thunder fell to the ground. He rolled over and over, then lay still.

Dan ran toward the fallen boy, but Doc pushed him aside. Doc was kneeling over Little Thunder when Wolf's Brother and Many Stars came rushing up. The chief thrust his lance in the ground near Doc, driving him back. Gently lifting his son, Wolf's Brother carried him toward the Indian camp.

Many Stars angrily pulled out the lance and struck Doc on the shoulder with it. Then he hurried off after Wolf's Brother.

"That boy's badly hurt," Doc said.

"Better not try to help him, Doc," Hank said. "Many Stars hit you with the spear. That means your scalp belongs to him, anytime he wants to take it. He's got it in for you anyway, for sayin' that his medicine was no good. Now he'll blame you for Little Thunder's gettin' hurt. Seems like we're fallin' deeper and deeper into trouble."

All day Dan kept wondering what was happening to Little Thunder. When evening came, he heard a long, piercing wail from the Indian camp.

"What's that?" he asked Hank.

Hank shook his head slowly. "Sounds like Many Stars has tried everything he knows—and it's not doin' any good. You know what comes next. We'd better fort up tight and keep our guns ready."

Before Hank could give the word to Captain Stephen, Doc came walking by. He was going toward the Indian camp, and his medical kit was in his hand.

"Doc!" Hank said. "Keep away from that boy, or they'll kill you! It's too late to help him!"

"Maybe," Doc said. "But I've got to give it a try. The boy's hurt, and I'm a doctor."

"Wait. You'll need help," said Laura, going to Doc's side.

"I'm coming, too," Dan said.

He had to look after Laura. Besides, Doc was risking his life for the sake of everyone in the wagon train. Dan wanted to give him as much help as he could.

"Better stay here. No telling what might happen," Doc said.

But Laura and Dan refused to turn back.

"Seein' as how you're goin' through with it, I'd better come, too," Hank said. "You'll need somebody that can understand Injun talk."

The four walked on in silence. They pushed their way through the Indians crowding around the lodge where Little Thunder was lying. Chief Wolf's Brother rushed out, shaking with anger.

"Go!" he said. "Go—or die!"

Behind him stood Many Stars, a troubled look in his eyes.

"Two medicines are better than one," Hank said in the Indian language. "Many Stars, your prayers are good. The Great Spirit hears. You have great magic. Your medicine has brought the white doctor. Now let him help you."

Many Stars was thoughtful for a moment. Then he spoke to Wolf's Brother, and the two men stepped aside to allow the others to enter.

"Be careful, Doc," Hank said. "Many Stars can put the blame on you if the boy dies. That's why he told the Chief to let us in."

But already Doc was bending over Little Thunder, who lay there unconscious. After a few minutes, Doc reached for his kit.

"He's been stunned by a blow on the head," he said. "But the real trouble is a broken collarbone. Looks like a bone splinter has cut a vein in the neck. Internal bleeding and pressure. That's why he hasn't come around."

Doc took a scalpel from his kit, and Wolf's Brother stepped forward, fear and anger in his face. Doc glanced up. Drawing the hunting knife from the scabbard he wore on his belt, he handed it to Wolf's Brother. The chief nodded. He held the knife in his hand, ready to take Doc's life in payment for his son's.

Again Doc bent over Little Thunder. There was silence in the lodge as Doc's skillful hands did their work. Laura stood close to him, giving him instruments as he needed them.

Several times during the operation Dan had to turn away. It seemed a long time until the operation was finished and Little Thunder was carefully bandaged.

Doc took Many Stars' war-eagle wingbone whistle and placed it on Little Thunder's chest. The medicine man seemed pleased to see that Doc respected the power of his magic.

Doc watched Little Thunder carefully, waiting for the boy to recover consciousness. No one spoke. Wolf's Brother kept his eyes on his son, but his hand still held Doc's knife firmly.

Several minutes went by, then Little Thunder shook as though shivering from cold. He began to breathe more deeply, and his eyes fluttered open. Slowly a smile spread over the face of Wolf's Brother. Still smiling, he looked at Doc and handed back the hunting knife. Many Stars spoke to Doc in the Sioux language, respect and thankfulness in his voice.

Picking up his medical kit, Doc walked out of

the lodge. Laura, Dan, and Hank followed him. The Indians drew back to let them pass.

"Whew!" said Hank. "Well, Doc, how does it feel to be a mighty important man instead of a mighty dead one?"

"Feels fine," Doc said. "Just fine."

As they walked on toward the wagon camp, Dan saw that Doc and Laura were holding hands. Somehow, Dan did not seem to mind. He felt that Doc belonged with the Thompsons—with him and Laura and Myra. And he was glad, for life on the trail had taught him that no one can fight through life alone.

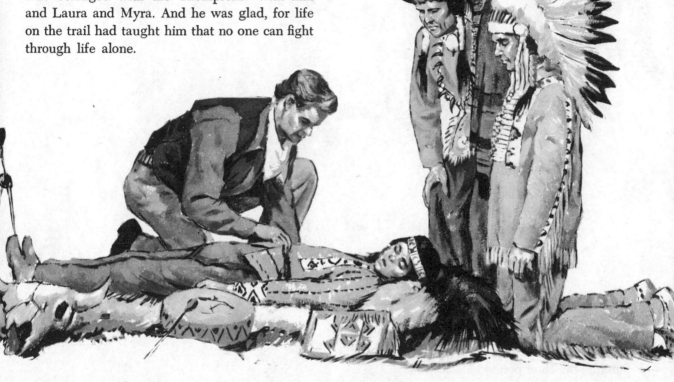

On to Oregon!

THE wagons were strung out in front of Fort Laramie.

Lining each side of the trail were the Indians of the Sioux camp, in their brightest and fanciest dress. Now Chief Wolf's Brother and some of his braves rode to the Stephen wagon and tied three fine ponies to the tailgate. The ponies were the chief's gifts to the white men.

Little Thunder smiled as he sat on a travois drawn by the ceremonial buffalo. He was still wrapped in bandages, but his wounds were healing, and he would soon be completely well.

"Good-by, Little Thunder!" said Myra.

"Good-by, Little Thunder," called children from the other wagons.

Little Thunder waved to them with his unbandaged hand. He watched Many Stars ride up to Myra and hand her a neatly rolled white buffalo robe. Eagerly, Myra unrolled it, and discovered the magic wing-bone whistle inside.

Meanwhile, Chief Wolf's Brother went to the head of the wagon train. He drew up his horse before Captain Stephen, and stretched out his

hand in the sign of friendship. Then he turned to face Doc and Hank as they came riding up. Smiling, the chief pointed ahead.

At his signal, two dozen Sioux warriors swung out on their ponies in flanking positions on either side of the wagon train.

"You are friends," Wolf's Brother said to the white men. "Spirit Wind will bring no storm. Mountains will not be steep. Wolf's Brother will take you safe to the Big Water!"

"The Big Water," Doc repeated softly. "The Pacific Ocean—and Oregon." He smiled and thanked Wolf's Brother.

"Let 'em roll!" Hank said to Captain Stephen.

Rising up in his stirrups, Captain Stephen shouted, "Roll the wagons!"

Doc rode back to the Thompson wagon, where Dan was sitting next to Laura and Myra.

"Say, Dan," Doc said, "Chieftain could use a little exercise, couldn't he? How would you like to go up ahead and ride with Hank? He needs a good man up there."

"Why, Doc?" Dan said, grinning. "So you can ride with Laura? Is that it?"

Doc stared at Dan; then he had to grin himself.

"Well," he said, "a medical man's got to do some studying if he wants to settle down and start a good practice in Oregon. And a man can't study, riding ahead of a wagon train all day."

Dan jumped to the ground, and Doc climbed up on the wagon. Sitting down beside Laura, he picked up the reins.

140

"Don't forget to study," Dan said.

With a whoop of delight, he leaped astride Chieftain.

As he galloped to the head of the wagon train, he could hear the crack of whips and the shouts of the drivers calling to their horses:

"Hiyah-hup!"

"Heeyah-ho!"

The wagons were moving now, rumbling and creaking as they rolled along. Dan rode up beside Hank, who pretended to be surprised.

The old scout smiled and said, "I reckon you've growed up some since we first hit the trail."

"Reckon I have," said Dan. Sitting straight in the saddle, he joined in the song that rose from the long line of wagons:

> There's a magic in the wind,
> And a brightness in the sky,
> There's a Promised Land a-waitin'
> And we'll get there bye an' bye!
>
> Westward ho the wagons!
> Always westward roll!
> Westward ho the wagons!
> For Oregon's our goal!

> All America's in motion
> And her hopes are turnin' west.
> Come on, let's get a-goin',
> For a new land's always best!
>
> Westward ho the wagons!
> Westward roll them far!
> Westward roll the wagons
> Toward the western star!

The Love Bug

Jɪᴍ Douɢʟᴀs was young, handsome, healthy, and usually had a big smile on his tanned face. But on this particular day, his smile had been replaced by a frown. The reason for the frown was that Jim had a problem—he didn't have a car or the money to buy one. For Jim this was an especially important problem, for he was a race-car driver. And how can a racing-car driver drive when he doesn't have a car, let alone win any money or prizes?

Jim wasn't made to feel any better when he got home to his old converted fire station high on

a San Francisco hill. His roommate, Tennessee Steinmetz, a far-out sculptor, tried to talk him out of being a racing-car driver and into a job as a mechanic on a used car lot.

When Jim exploded, Tennessee tried to explain that he had discovered his real self by going to Tibet and meditating with monks and swamis. Jim said he already knew what his real self was. He was a racing-car driver, and that was that.

To make some money, Jim decided to enter some dirt track races in Bakersfield, about a hundred miles away. But when he asked Tennessee for the loan of the "beast," Tennessee's ancient Edsel sedan, he was surprised at the answer he got. Tennessee told him he had done the only thing that could make the old car happy. He had cut it up and used the parts in a sculpture.

Jim then set out to buy a cheap car in a used car lot—and the result was the wildest, weirdest experience of his life.

It began when he spotted a pair of beautiful legs below a sign in a display window. Peering around the sign to see what came with the legs, he found himself face to face with Carole Bennett, a beautiful girl indeed. She was so startled by the sudden confrontation that she dropped the sign. Forgetting that there was a window between them, Jim bent over to pick up the sign and gave his head a nasty whack against the glass.

Carole motioned for him to come inside and get first aid for the bump on his forehead. Once inside, Jim noticed for the first time what kind of establishment he had literally bumped into. It was an agency for expensive foreign sports cars, and he forgot the bump on his head when he saw the bright yellow Thorndyke Special revolving on a turntable in the center of the showroom. As he stared at it, the owner of the agency, Peter Thorndyke, approached, sure that he had a customer for his costly racing machine.

"May I offer you sherry and a biscuit?" he asked.

Jim nodded and went on admiring the splendid car, hardly aware of Thorndyke's presence.

"What price range did you have in mind?" said Thorndyke as he offered the sherry.

"Oh, about seventy-five dollars," Jim said.

"Seventy-five dollars!" screamed Thorndyke, quickly withdrawing the sherry.

"I might be able to go eighty."

"I bid you good day, sir!" said Thorndyke indignantly, turning on his heel and walking away.

Jim was about to leave, when a little white Volkswagen nudged his leg.

"Hey! Watch it!" Jim said, and turned to bawl out the careless driver. Then he noticed that there was no one behind the wheel.

Thorndyke returned and, spotting the little car, let out a bellow:

"Havershaw!"

A little man with large round glasses came running in answer.

"Yes, sir, Mr. Thorndyke, sir."

"What is *that* doing in my showroom?" demanded Thorndyke, pointing at the little car. He ordered it taken out, and, to emphasize his feelings, gave it a hard kick.

"Hey! What did you do that for?" Jim said. "It's a good little piece of machinery." Then, apologizing to Carole for speaking out of turn, he left.

The next morning he was awakened by the ringing of his doorbell. Leaning out of the second-story window, he saw a strange man looking up at him.

"Police," said the stranger, waving his identification card.

"What!"

Pointing to a car parked in front of the old firehouse, the policeman asked Jim if he had ever seen it before. It was the same little car which had nudged him in the showroom. But when Jim tried to tell the story, the policeman said he was under arrest on suspicion of theft.

Jim went to the showroom with the policeman. He accused the haughty Thorndyke of planting the Volkswagen in front of his house so that it would look as if he had stolen it, and would be forced to buy it to keep from being jailed. And that's exactly what Jim had to do.

He took the car out for a trial spin and immediately noticed something different about it. It seemed to have a mind of its own. It would go only where it wanted to go and do what it wanted to do. Jim decided to return it and demand that Thorndyke refund his small down payment. He

reached the showroom just as Carole and Thorndyke were leaving in a Rolls Royce to have dinner together. Thorndyke refused to listen, but Carole slid in behind the wheel of the Volkswagen to take it for a drive and prove to Jim that the car was perfectly normal.

Strangely enough, the car did run properly while Carole was at the wheel. As they chatted, Jim learned that she was quite a racing fan and knew all about the many cars he had wrecked during his career. She was also a good mechanic, and she assured him that the little car was in fine shape.

Stopping at a traffic light, she told Jim to take the wheel. A pair of teenagers in a souped-up jalopy pulled alongside and challenged him to a drag race.

"Get lost," said Jim. Who ever heard of drag racing a Volkswagen?

The jalopy roared off with tires squealing as the light changed, sending exhaust fumes back at the little car. Suddenly the Volkswagen reared back on its rear wheels and started down the street after the teenager's car. With a roar like a jet plane, it passed the speeding jalopy as if it were standing still, and came to an abrupt halt at the next traffic light.

"Wow! Did you see this thing take off?" Jim said.

"Another one of your cute little tricks, Mr. Douglas?" asked Carole coldly.

"I had nothing to do with it, so help me!"

"As long as the customer is pleased, I'll step out and take a taxi," Carole said, and opened the door to get out.

Wham! The door slammed shut, the little car reared up on its wheels again, and barreled down the street like a runaway rocket.

"Stop the car!" yelled Carole.

"I'm trying to!" said Jim, desperately working the brakes.

The car refused to stop. Then, without warn-

ing, it shot into a rundown drive-in, tooted its horn for service, and shut off its engine.

Carole again reached for the door.

"Good-*bye*, Mr. Douglas, and I hope I never—" She stopped in mid-sentence, discovering that the door wouldn't open. And nothing she or Jim could do seemed to help. They were prisoners of the little car.

Jim made the best of it by ordering hamburgers and coffee. After they finished eating, he drove off, apologizing to Carole for all the strange happenings and for making her miss her dinner with Thorndyke. Still in a bad mood, she told Jim none of the strange things would have happened if *she* had been driving the car.

Screech! The Volkswagen suddenly stopped in the middle of the street. Jim knew he hadn't

stepped on the brake, and he invited Carole to take the wheel. She started to drive back to the showroom, but the car, as Jim figured it would, went just where it wanted to go. That turned out to be Seabreeze Point, a lovers' lane overlooking the ocean. After a while, it allowed Carole to drive herself home, with Jim sitting happily beside her.

Later that evening, when he told Tennessee about the strange behavior of the car, Tennessee made a most unusual statement.

"Well, it's finally starting to happen," he said. He had a theory, which had come to him while he was meditating with the monks in Tibet. Machines were becoming more and more human. They actually had souls and feelings and wanted to be loved just like everybody else.

146

Jim said the whole idea was nonsense. Every once in a while, for some unexplainable reason, a car came off the assembly line and turned out to be faster than all the other cars supposedly exactly like it.

"And luckily," added Jim, "I happen to have got one of these super cars."

Tennessee didn't believe it. He even went so far as to give the little car a name. He called it Herbie. Jim insisted that Herbie was only a piece of machinery, with an engine, not a heart.

At the same time, Jim realized he had a super-speedy car, and he entered it in a desert road race. Sure enough, even though the competition looked awesome and sounded worse, Herbie put on a burst of speed and took the checkered flag.

It happened that Thorndyke and Carole were at the race. Thorndyke offered to buy the Volkswagen back, but Jim turned down his generous offer. He did agree to a bet. If he beat Thorndyke's powerful Special in the next race, Herbie would be all his. Thorndyke would pay the twenty-three installments still due. But if Jim lost, Herbie would go back to Thorndyke. Aided by

Tennessee, who seemed to understand the little car's feelings, Jim won the race, and Herbie was his.

Jim then ran up a streak of wins that were the talk of the racing world. With each victory, Thorndyke became angrier. The fact that the little car kept beating his expensive machines irked him no end. No doubt about it—the bug bugged him, and he was determined to do something about it, even if it meant skullduggery.

One night, when Jim was out on a date with Carole—driving a big, expensive car Thorndyke had lent her—Thorndyke turned up at the old firehouse.

"I just wanted to pay my respects to that brave little car," he said to Tennessee.

Plying Tennessee with Irish coffee, he tried to wheedle the secret of Herbie's speed out of the befuddled sculptor. But all Tennessee could say was that Herbie had heart and, frustrated, Thorndyke poured Irish coffee, with plenty of whipped cream, into Herbie's oil intake.

The scheme worked. In the race the next day, Herbie was in the lead when he suddenly felt the

effect of the Irish coffee. Coughing and wheezing, he sputtered to a grinding halt, and Thorndyke breezed by to victory. Herbie managed to squirt whipped cream all over Thorndyke's fancy racing costume, but that was small consolation for losing the race.

When Carole learned what Thorndyke had done, she quit her job and headed for Jim's house to join his team. She found Jim gone and Tennessee with his head buried under Herbie's rear hood, trying to figure out what was wrong with the little fellow. Donning coveralls, Carole pitched in, and soon she had Herbie running as smoothly as ever. As she took Herbie outside to wash him, Jim came driving up in an expensive, brand-new Lamborgini, an Italian racer.

"What's that for?" asked Tennessee. "You already have Herbie."

"Not after today I don't," Jim said.

To help pay for the Lamborgini, he had agreed to sell Herbie to Thorndyke.

"Oh, no!" groaned Tennessee, pulling Jim inside the house so that Herbie wouldn't overhear any more of their conversation. He and Carole were arguing with Jim when they heard the sound of crashing metal from outside. Dashing out, they found Herbie demolishing the Lamborgini. Jim

grabbed a shovel and brought it crashing down on Herbie, but it was too late. The Lamborgini was in ruins.

Jim went back into the house, thinking hard. Suddenly he realized that Tennessee and Carole were right. Herbie *did* have a heart. And it was Herbie who was responsible for winning all those races, and not his own driving skill. Thorndyke soon turned up to claim the little car, and Jim told him the deal was off. He wouldn't sell at *any* price. Furthermore, he praised Herbie to the skies.

Unfortunately, Herbie didn't hear a word of this, and Tennessee came in to say that he was gone. His heart broken because Jim had whacked him, the little car had run off. Jim rushed out into the foggy night to search for Herbie—and so did Thorndyke. But Jim was on foot, while Thorndyke sent out a squad of radio-controlled trucks, and it was Thorndyke's men who were successful. They dragged the little fellow back to Thorndyke's showroom, where he ordered them to cut the car apart with torches.

Frightened at such a fate, Herbie blasted through a plate-glass window and escaped. His heart still heavy, he headed for the Golden Gate Bridge. He would end it all by diving into the

bay. It was on the bridge that Jim found him and persuaded him not to jump—but only after nearly falling into the bay himself. Herbie managed to save him, and after that they were firm friends.

With Carole and Tennessee as his crew, Jim entered Herbie in the El Dorado, a rugged cross-country race. Their chief rival was Thorndyke, driving his Special, with Havershaw as crew. True to expectations, the two cars left all the other competitors far behind and went roaring over the winding mountain road. Again Thorndyke did not hesitate to use skullduggery. He and Havershaw poured oil over the road, and, wheels spinning, Herbie crashed down the mountainside. Herbie survived—but that wasn't the last of Thorndyke's tricks.

When it was time to add gas from the spare can, Jim found it filled with water. Next, one of Herbie's wheels came off and bounced away down the mountain. Thorndyke had loosened the bolts. Because of this, Herbie fell far behind and finished last for the first day's run.

With the help of his crew, Jim patched up Herbie as best he could and went all-out in the final leg of the race the following day. Right at the start, he took a short-cut down the mountainside, passing all their competitors except Thorndyke. Fighting every inch of the way, Herbie strained with all his might—and the effort tore him apart. Just as they were about to catch up with Thorndyke, the little car broke into two halves.

But the rear half, the half with the motor, relieved of the weight of the front end, zoomed ahead. Sitting proudly in the back seat, Tennessee urged him on, cheering, yelling, shouting endearments. Putting on a final burst of speed, Herbie ripped across the finish line a fraction of a second before Thorndyke. Herbie came in third as well, his front end rolling across the line behind Thorndyke, carrying Carole and Jim.

It was the happiest day of Herbie's life. But an even happier day came not too long after, when, all repaired and as good as new, Herbie drove Jim and Carole away on their honeymoon. Tennessee saw them off, and tossing a last handful of rice, he said to no one in particular:

"Didn't I tell you that little car has a heart?"

149

The Great Locomotive Chase

Down a narrow muddy road that led eastward from the town of Shelbyville, Tennessee, moved a group of twenty-three men. They walked quickly, yet with caution, as if fearful of being seen.

It was the night of Monday, April 7, 1862. Almost a year had passed since the bombardment of Fort Sumter and the start of the American Civil War.

This group of men, stealing through the night, were soldiers of the North. But instead of the blue uniforms of the Union Army they wore rough civilian clothes. For each man had, that night, taken his life in his hands and volunteered to go on a still unknown mission—as a spy.

Twilight had long since faded from the sky and black clouds covered the moon. The thunderstorm that had been threatening all evening was growling closer, and a chill drizzle of rain was falling.

For over a mile the men slogged ahead, rarely talking and then only in whispers. When they reached a section of woods, they halted.

"This is the place," one of them said.

The group turned off the road and pushed inward through tangled underbrush to a small clearing. In the center of the clearing they saw a lone figure. It was James Andrews, the man who was to command them.

"Good evening, gentlemen," he said.

Then he gestured to the men to gather around him.

"We're here so we can talk without being overheard," he said. "But before I tell you the details of our mission, I want to issue a warning. You soldiers are to be sent in disguise over two hundred miles behind Confederate lines to do a job. The risks are great. If you're caught, it might mean death by hanging."

The rain had now increased to a downpour. Lightning slashed across the clearing followed by crashes of thunder. Some of the men shifted uneasily, their faces tense.

Andrews waited until there was an interval of quiet and then went on. "Since you have volunteered blindly without knowing exactly what is in store for you, it will not be considered dishonorable for you to back out. . . . Those who wish to withdraw, will you please leave us now."

Again he paused.

When no one in the group moved or spoke, he said, "Good. You're the men for me. Now listen carefully, all of you."

The men pressed in closer as Andrews, his voice lowered, outlined the scheme.

The spies were to break up into small units of three or four and travel southeast through the Cumberland Mountains, cross the Tennessee River, and reach Chattanooga. From Chattanooga, they were to go to Marietta, Georgia—their destination.

And there, in the heart of the enemy country, with Confederate troops encamped around them, they were to execute the amazing feat of capturing a train. They were to race it north, stopping in isolated sections along the way to rip up tracks, cut the telegraph lines, and burn bridges behind them. Thus all rail communications between Chattanooga and the large Confederate supply base at Atlanta would be severed.

"On the very day we cripple the railroad," Andrews said, "Union soldiers under General Mitchel will be advancing on Chattanooga from the north. The town is lightly garrisoned. With no reinforcements of troops or ammunition from Atlanta possible, General Mitchel will easily be able to take and hold Chattanooga.

152

"But more than that. The whole of East Tennessee will be at his mercy and the Confederate Army in Virginia will be threatened with disaster. Gentlemen, if our plan succeeds, it might will result in a major defeat for the Confederates and an early end to the war."

The boldness of Andrews' scheme sent a wave of excitement through the rainsoaked men. Few of them knew much about this tall, well-dressed man who was to lead them. With his soft voice and polished manners, he seemed more like a poet than a man of action. Yet they had heard stories told of his daring adventures as a secret agent for the North and how he had hoodwinked the South into believing that he was a spy for their side.

"I will meet you at Marietta, Georgia, in the hotel adjoining the railroad depot," Andrews said. "Additional instructions will be given you then. If anyone fails to show up before sunrise Friday morning, the attempt will be made without him. . . . Are there any questions?"

There were.

What would the raiders tell the Confederate pickets if they were stopped on the way south?

"Say you're Kentuckians escaping from Yankee rule to join a Southern regiment," Andrews answered. "If they press you closely, tell them you hail from Fleming County, Kentucky. I'm from Flemingsburg myself. No man from that county has ever joined the Southern Army. So you should be safe from discovery."

What if the Johnny Rebs insisted that they enlist in the Confederate ranks then and there?

"Don't hesitate to join their army on the spot," Andrews said. "I'd be sorry to lose any of you, but it would be better to serve with the enemy for awhile than risk discovery of our plan. You can always escape back to our lines some dark night while on picket duty."

How was Andrews himself going to reach Marietta?

"I'll ride along the same road, sometimes before you, sometimes behind. But treat me like any stranger. Don't recognize me unless you're sure we're not observed. Do you have your pistols?"

The assembled spies unbuttoned their coats and showed their revolvers, some thrust in holsters, others tucked into belts.

"Good. Keep them hidden. In this business you never fight unless you have failed. And we are not going to fail. Nothing can stop us. Nothing!"

The softness was gone from his voice and the words came out harsh and clear.

"All right. Choose you own companions and form into squads. Three or four to a group—no more. Quickly now!"

As the raiders broke into small units, Andrews went from man to man, distributing Confederate money and shaking hands.

Finally he stepped back.

"We'll meet again in Marietta," he said. "Good-by and good luck."

And thus began the strange adventure that was to become one of the most celebrated incidents in the Civil War.

The Inn

For three days, through almost continuous rain, the separate groups of spies headed south. Some slept at night in haystacks, others in barns and farmhouses.

Many were able to slip by the Southern pickets unchallenged. A few were stopped. Two were obliged to join the Rebel ranks and were lost to the expedition. But the others found that the story of being Kentuckians on their way to enlist in the Confederate Army got them by.

Andrews was like a will-o'-the-wisp. His reputation in the South as a daring Confederate agent gave him complete freedom of movement. On horseback he moved slowly southeastward with his agents, cautiously checking on one group, then another, ever alert for trouble.

At the bank of the rain-swollen Tennessee River, he turned up at a small inn where four of his men—Pittenger, Campbell, Knight, and Brown—had found lodging. Andrews knew the inn's landlady and he knew the type of guests she had—hot-headed Confederates, all of them. The slightest slip on the part of the inexperienced spies might have disastrous results.

When Andrews arrived, supper was being served in the inn's firelit dining room. A dozen guests were seated around a long table, among them the four Northerners. Several women were present—and a Southern army officer in uniform.

The landlady gave Andrews a warm welcome.

"Well, look who's here!" she said. "If it isn't Mr. Andrews. You're just in time to eat with us."

"Sounds mighty good and smells better," Andrews said.

The landlady introduced him around to her guests.

The secret agent shook hands with his men without a sign of recognition. Then, picking up a glass from the table, he said:

"Ladies and gentlemen, I bring great news. On the strength of it I would ask you to drink a toast with me—if I knew the color of your politics."

He glanced suspiciously at his four men.

"Don't worry about these boys," the landlady said. "They've been livin' among the Yankees but they've come to join our army."

"Good," Andrews said. "I'm proud to tell you that we've won a great victory at Shiloh!"

"Did Beauregard lick that buzzard Grant?" the Confederate officer asked in an excited tone.

"Cut him to ribbons," Andrews said. "The whole Yankee force has gone up the spout!"

"Yippee!"

All the Southerners jumped to their feet, shouting with joy. The Northerners were slower to get up. One of them, the powerfully built Campbell, didn't move. A look of annoyance passed over Andrews' face. He raised his glass in a signal for Campbell to rise.

Scowling, Campbell finally obeyed.

"I give you a toast—our beloved Confederacy!" Andrews said.

Everyone drank, but again Campbell was slow. Only when his companion, Corporal William Pittenger, nudged him did he drain his glass.

The Southern Army officer eyed him.

"You don't seem very happy over our victory."

Before Campbell could reply, quick-witted William Pittenger spoke up:

"He's not. He wants to kill all the Yankees himself!"

Some of the men guffawed. Campbell looked glum.

"Sounds like a Kentuckian," Andrews said.

"We're all from Kentucky," Pittenger replied.

"Well, you'll find plenty of action later on, sir," Andrews said to Campbell. "But before you go any farther south, there's one thing we should teach you."

"What's that?" Campbell growled.

"*Dixie!*"

There were cries of delight from the Southerners. "Good. That's it! *Dixie!*—we'll teach him!"

Andrews moved toward the piano at the side of the room. "May I?" he courteously asked the landlady.

"Go right ahead," the landlady said. "Come on, boys. Gather round."

Andrews seated himself at the piano and began playing the popular Confederate song. Soon the whole company of guests, even the reluctant Campbell, were loudly singing, *"Oh, I wish I was in Dixie . . . away, away. . . ."*

And the crisis had passed.

Late that night, when the inn was quiet, Andrews stole into his men's bedroom.

"Mr. Campbell," he said quietly, "I'd like a word with you."

Campbell was surly. "And I'd like a word with you. Do we have to be better Southerners than the Johnny Rebs are themselves?"

"Let me tell you this," Andrews said severely. "If you can't sing their songs and love Jeff Davis and hate Abe Lincoln until next Friday, you'll never reach Marietta."

"All right . . . all right," Campbell muttered.

"Were we as badly licked at Shiloh as you made out, Mr. Andrews?" William Knight asked.

"No. When I bring them good news, I'm doubly welcome. But the truth is bad enough."

"Bad enough to stop General Mitchel's advance?" Pittenger said.

"Shiloh can't stop him," Andrews said. "But these rains can. Trouble is, our movements and his have to dovetail. And with the roads a sea of mud, he'll be slowed down. We'll have to take a chance and postpone our plans to seize the train and burn the bridges. We'll change it from Friday to Saturday.

"Tomorrow you men go on to Chattanooga. I'll make contact with the others and meet you there in time to take the train to Marietta Friday night. Be careful. Bite off your tongue rather than let anyone suspect who you are. I'm depending on you."

Andrews sent a look in Campbell's direction. Then he left the room.

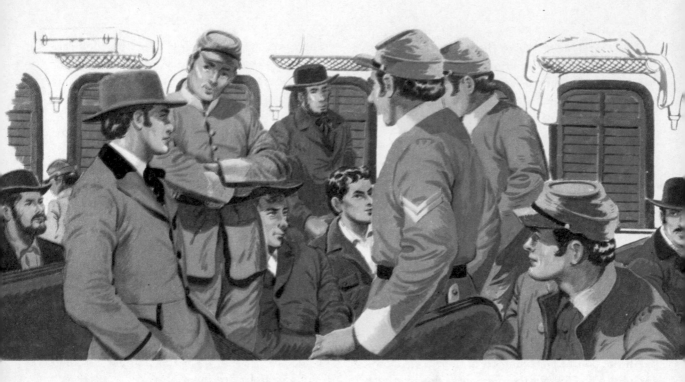

Dangerous Journey

By FRIDAY evening, all the raiders but four had reached Chattanooga. There, together with Andrews, they boarded a passenger train south for Marietta, Georgia.

So far everything had worked out well, and Andrews was breathing a little easier. Yet there were lines of strain on his face as he settled down in his seat.

This was to be his last mission as a Union Army secret agent. Once it was accomplished, he was to quit his dangerous profession and return to his home in Kentucky. There he planned to get married and live a quiet life.

But for now, he was determined that his bold scheme must succeed. Not so he could go out in a blaze of glory, but because he passionately believed that the cutting of the railroad line would shorten the bloody war that was tearing his country apart.

As the train rattled southward, Andrews reviewed his plans. If the expedition could only reach Marietta without trouble, perhaps it would be a good omen for the next day!

But there, on the train, danger once again threatened. And again it involved the burly William Campbell.

The passenger cars were crowded with Southern soldiers, happy to be going home on furlough. Gibes against the North were shouted up and down the car where the spies were seated.

"How many Yanks can one Southerner whip?" a lanky Confederate soldier yelled.

"Five!"

"How many?"

"Ten!"

"That's more like it," shouted the lanky one. "Why, one company of Southerners armed with popguns could run a regiment of Yankees clean out of the country. . . . Anybody like to deny it?"

Andrews had sat close to Campbell in the hope of restraining his quick temper. Ever since the shouting had started, Andrews had seen that the big man was finding it more and more difficult to hold himself in check. The last gibe had reddened his face with anger. Already he was starting up from his seat, fists clenched.

At that moment the train swung around a curve and Andrews managed to bump heavily against Campbell, knocking him back.

"Sit down!" he whispered fiercely.

The ruse would have worked except that, as Campbell fell back in his seat, his coat opened, showing his service revolver.

The Confederate soldier who had been leading the shouting saw the gun.

"Look at that cannon!" he roared.

Campbell closed his coat over the revolver but the soldier lunged toward him.

"Let's see it!"

Andrews acted quickly. "Don't be ornery, Bill," he said. "Go on, show it to him."

Campbell hesitated, then handed over the gun.

"Huh!" the soldier exclaimed as he examined the weapon. "Yankee army issue. Where did you get a Yankee gun?"

Campbell didn't answer. His red face got redder.

"He took it off a dead Yank," Andrews said lightly. "Didn't you, Bill?"

"Which battle?" the Southern soldier demanded.

Campbell looked up at him, his jaw squared. "Battle for our hen-coop!" he said.

Andrews slapped his thigh and chuckled. "That's all those Yankees are—chicken stealers!"

The Confederate soldier joined in the laughter and handed back the gun.

"Hear that, y'all?" he yelled. "Chicken stealers. That's sure 'nuff right. Chicken stealers. Hah . . . hah . . . !"

And so ended another crisis. But for the rest of the trip Andrews watched Campbell closely.

Peril Ahead

It was close to midnight when the raiders arrived in Marietta. They obtained rooms in the hotel near the railroad station, and Andrews immediately called a conference.

With window shades carefully lowered and a single candle burning, the secret agent whispered out the final details of the reckless plan that was to be launched at dawn.

"At five-thirty," Andrews said, "we will board the northbound mail train from Atlanta. You will buy tickets for different stops to avoid giving the appearance of traveling together.

"Eight miles from Marietta, the train will make a breakfast stop at Big Shanty—a place where there's no station or telegraph. Just a hotel and a freight shed on one side and a Confederate Army camp on the other.

"The engineer, the conductor, and most of the passengers will get off to eat in the hotel dining room.

"And there . . ." Andrews' voice grew tense . . . "there we will seize the train!"

None of the men in the shadowy room stirred.

"Now listen carefully to every word I say," Andrews went on. His voice was low, yet distinct. "Not only does success depend on your following instructions to the letter—but your very lives!"

He faced Brown and Knight, the two experienced locomotive engineers in the party.

"You men will uncouple the passenger cars, leaving just the engine, tender, and boxcars for us. Then, get in the engine cab and start the train—fast!

"Alf Wilson, you'll go with them as fireman. I'll be riding in the engine cab, too.

"The rest of you will run for a boxcar, get in, and hide. Your time will come later, when we start ripping up the tracks and setting the bridges afire. . . . Is everything clear to everyone?"

Again there was a tense silence. Andrews looked from face to face. He knew how his men felt. The trip down through enemy country had been nerve-wracking. But it was nothing to what lay ahead.

Sergeant-Major Ross spoke up.

"That army camp at Big Shanty. There must be four thousand Rebs there. Do we have to steal the train in full view of the Southern army? Why don't we pick a deserted part of the tracks any place north of here?"

"At Big Shanty we'll have an empty train to deal with," Andrews replied. "If we made the attempt anywhere else, we'd have to overpower the crew and passengers. It would mean a fight."

William Campbell broke in. "And what's the matter with a fight?"

"For one thing," Andrews said, "you never know how it's coming out."

Campbell grunted. "Well, I know one thing. I've had my fill of bowin' and scrapin' and sweet-talkin'. I'm all for capturin' this train in a fair fight."

Andrews stared at the big man.

"Mr. Campbell," he said. "I was told you'd be worth ten in a scrap. That's why I brought you along. Just in case of trouble. But we didn't come here to fight. We came to burn the railroad bridges. . . . If you don't like it, drop out now! But if you come along, you'll do it my way!"

"There's just one last thing," Andrews said to the knot of raiders. There was powerful feeling in his voice.

"We must succeed! We must! I tell you that I am going to accomplish my purpose—or I will leave my bones to bleach in Dixie!

"Now go to your rooms. Get as much sleep as you can. I'll call you in plenty of time. . . . Good-night, gentlemen."

A few of the spies managed to sleep. But for the majority, the prospect of seizing the train right in the middle of a guarded enemy camp kept their eyes open all night.

Nor did Andrews get much rest. For the moment the door had closed behind his men, he sat down at a table and began carefully writing a letter—a letter he hoped would prove useful the next day. He wrote it on stationery of the Army of the Confederate States of America. And he signed it with the name of the dashing Southern general, P.G.T. Beauregard.

Before five o'clock in the morning, Andrews had the raiders assembled in his room. Even Campbell had sullenly shown up.

In spite of little or no sleep, Andrews appeared surprisingly fresh. He had changed from the dark suit he had been wearing and put on a frock coat, white shirt, and gray striped trousers. On his head rested a tall silk hat.

"What are the fine clothes for?" Sergeant Scott gasped.

"There may be an occasion when I'll have to pull a bluff and be an official of the Western and Atlantic Railroad," Andrews said.

He glanced at his watch. "Thirty minutes till train time. Now, about your tickets. . . ."

He went down the list of the nineteen men quickly. Ross, Pittenger, and Campbell were to get tickets to Allatoona. Shadrack, Slavens, Brown, Knight, and J. A. Wilson—Kingston. Wollam, Robinson, Parrott, and Buffam—Calhoun. Bensinger, Reddick, and Scott—Resaca. Alf Wilson, Wood, Dorsey, and Mason—Dalton.

"We'll all ride in the same car, but in separate groups. When the train stops at Big Shanty, keep your seats until I give the signal."

Andrews gave a tap to his silk hat and walked toward the door.

"Now let us proceed to the station," he said. "Follow me in groups, at intervals. Good luck, gentlemen."

Big Shanty

THE SPIES and a few other passengers were strung out along the platform when the balloon-stacked engine, named the *General,* huffed to a stop at the Marietta station. Behind the engine were a tender filled with wood, three boxcars, and two passenger coaches.

Andrews waited until all his men had entered the rear coach before he climbed the steps. He had scarcely taken his seat at the back of the coach when the train lurched forward.

"Mornin', Mr. Fuller. You goin' to get us to Kingston on time?"

"Yes, ma'am, right on time today, Mrs. Preston."

Andrews opened a newspaper he had bought and held it up in front of him. But he kept sneaking quick glances as Fuller came nearer. When the conductor was beside his seat, Andrews lowered his paper and handed him his ticket.

"Good morning, Conductor," he said.

"Mornin', sir." Fuller took the ticket and held it in his hand. But his eyes swept thoughtfully over Andrews from his silk hat to his polished shoes. He seemed to be debating something.

Finally Fuller said, "Didn't you get on at Marietta?"

"Why, yes," Andrews said.

"Do you know anythin' about those men up front there?"

Andrews' heart skipped a beat. "Should I?" he parried. "Is there anything remarkable about them?"

"Well, it's the first time so many folks ever got on at the same time at Marietta. And I've a hunch they're really all together but just actin' like they don't know each other."

"Why would they do that?" Andrews spoke with a good deal more calmness than he felt.

The conductor leaned down. "I think they're deserters. If they are, I'm goin' to turn 'em over to the military authorities at Big Shanty."

"But why tell me this?"

"Well, sir," Fuller said, "from your appearance it's plain you're a man of position. And seein' you got on at Marietta too, I thought you might know somethin' about 'em."

"Sorry not to be of any help," Andrews said. "But I wouldn't worry. They look all right to me."

"Maybe they are and maybe not," Fuller said, with a backward look. "That's not for me to judge. When we get to Big Shanty, I'm going to turn the whole caboodle over to the military."

Andrews drew in a deep breath. Here was trouble—real trouble.

The conductor was about to go on down the aisle when Andrews touched his arm.

They were on their way at last. In less than half an hour, the big moment would be at hand.

Andrews looked up the length of the coach. He saw his men sitting in separate groups. So far, everything was going well.

The front door of the coach banged open and the conductor appeared. He was a bearded man in his middle twenties, broad-shouldered and vigorous.

Andrews watched him as he made his way down the aisle, taking tickets. The conductor was looking each passenger over carefully, particularly the spies.

It was almost as if he were suspicious. But that was absurd. Why should he be?

An old lady who had got on at Marietta smiled brightly at the conductor.

"You are an official of this line and therefore I can trust you. I *do* know those men. They're on government business bound for Yankeedom and so am I."

The conductor's eyes widened. "Well, I'll be. . . . Blockade runnin'?"

"Maybe that. Maybe something else." Andrews reached into his coat pocket and took out the letter he had written the night before. He handed it to Fuller.

"This may explain things better."

The conductor read the letter slowly.

"*To whom it may concern. . . . The bearer of this document, James J. Andrews, and the party with him are on official business. All courtesy and cooperation extended to them will be appreciated. . . . P.G.T. Beauregard, Brigadier General.*

"General Beauregard!" Fuller exclaimed. "You don't get a letter like this from Beauregard for nothing."

"No," Andrews said dryly.

"I'd give my right arm to serve under that man."

"You are, sir," Andrews said. "Without men like you to run this railroad, Beauregard and Robert E. Lee would perish."

Fuller raised his head proudly. "I never thought of it that way."

The whistle from the engine sounded. Fuller glanced out the window. He called loudly, "Big Shanty! Twenty minutes for breakfast!"

The train was coming to a stop in front of a frame building which bore a sign: BIG SHANTY, and under it, Lacy Hotel.

"Our inspector, Mr. Murphy, is on board today, Mr. Andrews," Fuller said. "I know he'd be proud to have you take breakfast with us."

"Thank you," Andrews said. "I've already eaten. But you have a good meal. My men and I will watch your train for you."

Fuller shook hands, then followed the other passengers out the door, leaving the coach to Andrews and the spies.

Andrews, nerves on edge, stared through the window. Outside he saw Fuller walk to meet the train's engineer and a well-dressed man, undoubtedly Mr. Murphy, the inspector. The three of them, along with a number of train hands and passengers, headed for the door to the hotel dining room.

Andrews sent a quick look out the window on the other side. There the land was crowded with row upon row of tents. The Confederate Army camp extended to within a few yards of the railroad.

A half dozen soldier bystanders were looking over the train. And nearby a sentinel slouched back and forth, his musket on his shoulder.

A drop of sweat ran down Andrews' face. The train would have to be taken in full view of those soldiers.

But now that the time had come, he had a wild desire to hurry.

"Come on, gentlemen!"

Getaway

Casually, Andrews opened the door at the rear of the coach and went down the steps on the side next to the army camp. Under the eyes of the Confederate sentry, he walked leisurely in the direction of the engine, with the air of a man killing time.

Over his shoulder he saw Knight and Brown, his two engineers, close behind. So was Alf Wilson, who was to be the fireman. And back of them came the others.

Many times in the past weeks, Andrews had gone over in his mind each move they would make, even to using the train itself to screen them from view of the people in the hotel. But the nearness of the armed sentry now presented a problem.

Andrews' fingers tightened around the handle of the pistol in his pocket. If the sentry should try to stop them, there would be only one thing to do—shoot him. Yet the sound of a shot would bring everybody on the run, and the chances of stealing the train would be slim.

The sentry *was* watching them. At the moment he appeared just curious. But there was no telling when curiosity might turn to suspicion.

Andrews walked a little faster. When he reached the gap between the first coach and the third boxcar, he spoke quietly to Knight.

"Uncouple here."

Partly shielded by Andrews, Knight reached in and quickly removed the coupling pin, disconnecting the front end of the train from the back.

"You three go on," Andrews said.

Knight, Brown, and Wilson moved toward the engine cab while Andrews turned to the rest of

164

the spies. He jerked his head toward the empty rear boxcar, the door of which stood open.

"Get in!" he said in an undertone.

As the men scrambled to obey, Andrews stole a look at the sentry. The soldier had brought his musket from his shoulder and was holding it in his hands ready for action. He seemed about to issue a challenge.

"Come on, boys," Andrews said loudly for the sentry's benefit. "When it's orders from General Beauregard, we can't waste time."

The use of the magic name worked. The sentry relaxed and shouldered his musket again, though he continued to watch.

It was all Andrews needed. The instant the last of the spies disappeared into the boxcar, Andrews ran for the engine, where Knight, Brown, and Wilson were nervously waiting. He swung up on the step, holding fast to the rail.

"Let her roll!" he called.

Knight was in the driver's seat. He released the brakes and opened the throttle.

The big driving wheels spun on the slippery rails. They took hold, and with a jerk that almost threw Andrews off his feet, the *General* surged ahead, pulling the front section of the train after it. They were away!

Looking backward out of the window of the cab, Andrews had a glimpse of the sentry staring, of Confederate soldiers in front of their tents waving. He thought he saw the hotel door open and three men come plunging out. But the train, picking up speed, was swinging around a bend, and he wasn't sure.

Nor did he care. For there was no telegraph at Big Shanty. It would be impossible for Fuller or anyone to send an alarm ahead. The Rebs would have to go back to Marietta to despatch a message, and by that time the raiders would have cut the telegraph lines.

The most difficult and dangerous part of the plan had now been accomplished. The train was in their possession. The next thing to do was to tear up a section of track to avoid any possible pursuit by rail.

Two strong crowbars were needed. But a look into the engine's tool box was disappointing. The only tools there were a hammer and a rusty fine-tooth saw.

Then fortune smiled. They hadn't gone two miles from Big Shanty when Andrews spotted a section gang repairing a switch.

"Stop by those men!" Andrews said.

As Knight halted the engine, Andrews swung down. Passing himself off to the gang boss as an official of the railroad in the service of General Beauregard, he obtained two stout iron bars. And once again the train streaked north.

A short distance from Allatoona, Andrews called another halt. And there in a desolate section of country, the entire band of raiders went to work.

While nimble John Scott climbed a telegraph pole and cut off a length of wire, Campbell and a group went to work prying loose a rail. They threw it into a boxcar so it couldn't be found and reset.

Another group under Andrews' direction descended on a pile of crossties at the side of the roadbed. They heaved the ties into the boxcars for possible future use in blocking the track.

Then, with Alf Wilson hastily stoking the *General's* fire with wood from the tender, they were underway again.

"Do you think we're being followed?" Brown asked anxiously.

"That torn track will block everything below us," Andrews said. "Anyway, I happen to know that there are no trains south of us short of At-lanta. The only train we have to worry about is a

southbound express-freight we're due to pass in Kingston. After that—"

A rare smile twisted Andrews' lips. "After that we'll put on full speed, burn the bridges I have marked out, and race on to meet Mitchel as he advances on Chattanooga. We've got the upper hand on the rebels now. No one can stop us!"

Pursuit

But Andrews failed to take into account one rebel—the husky young conductor, Robert Fuller.

As the stolen train began to move out of Big Shanty, Fuller was sitting down to breakfast in the hotel, with Murphy, the inspector, and Jeff Cain, the engineer. Startled by the sudden loud puffing of the engine, he rushed to a window.

"My train!" he gasped. "Somebody's making off with it."

Fuller charged for the door, followed by Murphy and Cain. By the time they got outside, the *General* with the three boxcars in tow was disappearing around the curve to the north.

Believing that deserters from the camp were responsible and that they would soon abandon the train, Fuller started running up the tracks in pursuit. Murphy and Cain followed along the tracks behind him.

Bystanders hooted at the sight of men chasing a train on foot.

"You're going to have to go some to catch that en-jine," one of them shouted.

But Robert Fuller was a proud man and a determined one. He was the conductor of that train. It had been put in his care. And nobody was going to take it from him.

In good physical shape, with strong leg muscles, Fuller set such a fast pace that Murphy and the frail Cain found it difficult to keep up.

167

For well over a mile the chase continued. Cain was at the point of exhaustion and Murphy was gasping for breath but Fuller waved them on.

Then, just as the conductor himself was about ready to admit it was hopeless, he saw the repair gang ahead.

"Did you get a look at the men who stole my train?" Fuller shouted at the gang.

"Stolen was it!" the gang boss said in astonishment. "Why, they stopped here and the official asked for some tools."

"What official?" Fuller demanded.

"The gent in the stovepipe hat!"

It was Fuller's turn to be astonished. "Andrews!" he said. "It must have been Andrews!"

"Faith, I didn't ask his name. But he said he was on business for Beauregard."

"That's the fellow!" Fuller said angrily.

"Then they weren't deserters?" Murphy asked.

"No!" Fuller said. "This man Andrews told me he and his party were secret agents for Beauregard. But they sound more like Yankee spies to me now."

The conductor smacked his right fist hard against the palm of his left.

"We've got to catch 'em!"

His eyes lighted on the gang's push car at the side of the roadbed.

"We'll use that!" he said. "Put it on the tracks. Quick!"

The workmen lifted the push car onto the rails, and Murphy and Cain seated themselves at the end facing south. Fuller climbed aboard and stood in the middle. He took the long pole the gang boss handed him.

Then, with Murphy and Cain kicking with their heels at the crossties and with Fuller pushing hard with his long pole, the car was put into motion.

The track at this point ran downhill and the car picked up speed rapidly. Fuller poled with savage vigor, his mind fixed on only one thing—overtaking the train thieves.

He knew the road well—every curve, every grade. But such was their speed that Fuller didn't see the gap where the Northerners had lifted a rail until it was too late to stop. There was only one thing he could do. "Jump!" he yelled. "Jump!"

The three leaped free just as the push car left the track. They landed in a ditch half filled with water.

No one was hurt. Fuller and his companions quickly lifted the car back onto the tracks beyond the break.

Fuller was furious. He pointed up to where the telegraph line had been cut.

"This proves it!" he said. "Those scoundrels aren't from Beauregard. No one would rip up the track and slash the telegraph wires—unless they were Yankees!"

With a jerk, the push car shot ahead.

"We'll never catch them on this thing," Murphy pouted. "Maybe we could if we had a locomotive. But that's hopeless."

Fuller's face suddenly brightened.

"No, it isn't! At Etowah there's an old freight engine, the *Yonah*. Used by the iron works on their private line. If we can get hold of it. . . ."

He dug his pole in harder. "Faster! Faster!" he shouted. "I'll catch those Yankees if it's the last thing I ever do!"

Delay

Unaware of Fuller's desperate pursuit, Andrews cautioned Knight and Brown against pushing the *General* at too high a speed.

"We must hit Kingston on schedule and not before," he said. "If we roll in there ahead of time, we might be forced to wait on the siding a long time for that express-freight to come through. And I don't want to give anybody a chance to snoop around this train and ask a lot of questions. That could be fatal."

Allatoona had long since been passed when Brown leaned out the window of the cab. Ahead was a bridge over a river and beyond a station with a spur track that led away from the main line toward the hills in the distance.

"Must be Etowah," Brown said. "There's a locomotive on the spur, steam up."

"Likely the yard engine of the ironworks east of here," Andrews said.

"Hadn't we better destroy it?" Knight asked.

"She's not worth the risk. Look at the number of passengers on the station platform. Must be a dozen Confederate soldiers among them. . . . Ease through the station but don't stop. Let 'em hear your bell."

Back in the rear boxcar, where sixteen of the raiders were riding, Campbell and Pittenger had found peepholes in the wooden sides.

"How do you like that!" Campbell said. "Andrews runs right past that locomotive. Why didn't he stop and wreck it—and burn that bridge? I thought our job was to cripple this railroad."

"There wouldn't have been a chance with all those soldiers around," Pittenger said.

Campbell snorted. "He's afraid to fight. That's all. Plain afraid."

"He knows what he's doing."

"He won't if some Johnny comes along and grabs that engine and chases us."

A few miles before they reached Kingston, a stop was made at Cass to take on a supply of wood and water. The tank-tender accepted Andrews' story that he was a Confederate officer bringing a cargo of gunpowder to Beauregard at Corinth.

But at Kingston, the raiders ran into trouble. The express-freight they were to meet was late. Moreover, a train from Rome was on a siding waiting to pick up the Atlanta mail that was usually carried on Fuller's train.

Andrews had his engineers back his shortened train in ahead of the Rome local on the siding.

"This is going to be touch and go," Andrews said in a low voice to Knight, Brown, and Wilson. "You boys oil up the engine. Be too busy to bother with anybody. I'll do the talking."

And he had plenty of talking to do. He had no sooner stepped down from the cab than he was met with a barrage of questions. Who was he? Where were Fuller and the regular crew? What was the reason for half a train?

Forcing himself to keep calm, Andrews told the story of Beauregard and the powder supply. He said that Fuller was outfitting another train and would be along shortly, bringing passengers and the Atlanta mail.

Andrews, a master of bluff and evasion, had never before been put to such a test. Yet such was his striking appearance and assured manner that he smothered all doubts.

How long could he keep up the deception? He himself wondered.

Andrews strolled up and down the crowded platform, chatting with the waiting passengers. Always he kept one hand on the cocked pistol in his coat pocket, and his ear alert for the rattle of the telegraph key. With the wires cut to the south, there was no danger of an alarm from that direction. But if the telegraph operator tried to send a message north, checking on the story of Beauregard and the ammunition, Andrews was determined to act.

Thirty agonizing minutes passed before the southbound train arrived. To Andrews' dismay, he learned that it wasn't the expected express-freight, but a local. And to make matters worse,

the train was carrying a red flag, which meant that another local was behind.

"I must get this powder to Beauregard without delay!" Andrews stormed. "What's the reason for this blocking of the road?"

The answer was upsetting. A Union force under General Mitchel was advancing on Chattanooga, he was told. Supplies were being rushed south before they could fall into Yankee hands.

Andrews winced inwardly. Mitchel hadn't been held up by the rains. And now the clogged main line might defeat the whole plan.

Yet there was nothing to do but wait.

At length the next train chugged in. It too carried a red flag!

Clenching his hands, Andrews heard the explanation. The load on the second train had been too great for one engine. The train had therefore been split into two sections.

Meanwhile, the sixteen men shut up in the rear boxcar were in fearful suspense. Frantic over the delay, not knowing what went on outside, they could only crouch there in utter silence, guns ready.

Another long interval followed before the sec-
ond section of the southbound train showed up. And with it came the information that the express-freight that the *General* was to meet at Kingston still was miles to the north.

Andrews could now feel suspicion mounting through the crowd. Questions were being asked about the train Fuller was supposed to be bringing up from Atlanta. Why hadn't it arrived? And the discovery that no telegraph messages could be sent south was adding fuel to the feeling that something was wrong.

Andrews took a bold stand. "I can't wait any longer," he said to the station master. "If Chattanooga is being attacked, they'll need my ammunition there more than Beauregard will."

Signaling for Knight to put the *General* into motion, Andrews himself strode to the switch and threw it open. As the train rumbled off the siding and on to the main track, Andrews swung up to the cab.

"Give her everything she's got!" he said.

And before anyone in authority knew quite what was happening, the *General* with its three boxcars was steaming off.

Four miles outside Kingston, Andrews ordered

the train stopped. The cooped-up men poured thankfully out of the boxcar. The telegraph line was cut and another section of rail pried loose.

A few minutes later the raiders were speeding north again.

"Keep that throttle open!" Andrews ordered. "I heard the station master's last report. That express-freight hasn't reached Adairsville yet. We must meet it there on the siding."

With Wilson desperately throwing wood on the fire, the *General* was streaking along.

"What if the freight clears Adairsville before we get there?" Brown asked. "We're liable to run slam-bang into it!"

Andrews' face was grim. "That's a chance we must take," he said. "Keep her going, Knight.

On the Trail

THE GENERAL had been gone from Kingston a scant four minutes when a locomotive came streaking up the tracks from the south.

The station master squinted his eyes. "What in thunder!" he said. "Looks like that old ironworks yard engine from Etowah, the *Yonah!*"

It was the *Yonah*. And riding its cab with its engineer was the determined young conductor, Robert Fuller, together with Murphy and Cain.

Fuller's plan to use the ancient locomotive in the pursuit of the Northern spies had succeeded. And now with a dozen armed Confederate soldiers from Etowah perched on the *Yonah's* tender, Fuller was hot on the scent.

The conductor's arrival and his story of the theft of the *General* caused a sensation in Kingston. But Fuller wasted no time in talk when he heard that the raiders had left just a few minutes before them.

The Kingston tracks were jammed with trains. It would take considerable shunting to clear the main line for the *Yonah* to get past. And Fuller was in too much of a hurry. Leaving the *Yonah*, he sprinted to the Rome local, the only train in the clear.

"Uncouple your cars and get ready to pull out!" he yelled to the engineer.

Then Fuller seized the station master by the arm. "Try to get a message through to every station up the line—quick! They're probably cutting the wires right now. . . . Has Pete Bracken brought his express-freight in yet?"

"No, but he's cleared Calhoun and is making up time," the station master said.

"Then the *General* may run into him," Fuller said.

"Unless Andrews gets to the siding at Adairsville first."

The cars were now uncoupled, and Fuller and Murphy climbed into the engine cab. Cain, utterly spent, was left behind.

"Get in the tender, boys," Fuller shouted to the Confederate soldiers. "We're going to need your guns!"

The soldiers bustled aboard, and with a hiss of steam the engine was away.

Fuller kept a sharp lookout for a break in the tracks. A short distance from town he spotted the place where the raiders had lifted a rail.

"Throw her in reverse!" he shouted.

Wheels locked, the Rome engine came to a shuddering stop. Fuller was out of the cab like a shot.

"Come on!" he yelled. "Let's run for it. We're sure to meet Bracken's express soon."

Once again the footrace was on, with the sturdy conductor in the lead. But soon a whistle sounded, and around a bend came Pete Bracken's southbound express-freight.

Fuller waved it to a stop.

"So that's who was on the *General!*" Bracken said when he heard Fuller's quick story. "It came high-balling up to Adairsville just as I was pulling out. A gent in a silk hat yelled that he was carrying powder to Chattanooga. He talked me into taking to the siding and letting him pass!"

"Andrews has talked his way past his last train," Fuller snapped. "Back up your freight to Adairsville. We're going to need your engine."

At Adairsville, Fuller himself handled the switch as the freight cars were sent rolling onto the siding. Then, with the engine, the *Texas,* still in reverse and with the determined Fuller on the forward end of the tender, the chase was on again—in earnest.

173

Flight

With no way of knowing what had happened behind him, Andrews rode the cab of the *General* in a glow of satisfaction. Now that Bracken's express-freight had been passed, the tracks ahead would be clear of traffic straight through to Chattanooga. Success of the mission seemed sure.

The *General* covered the ten miles to Calhoun at a fast clip. On the far side, Andrews stopped the train.

"We'll cut the telegraph wire and take up another rail," he told his men. "But it will be the last time. After that, all we have to do is fire the bridges over the Chickamauga, then race on to meet Mitchel."

The raiders' spirits were high and they joked among themselves. Scott went about his job of clipping the wires while the rest began prying at a section of rail.

But the rail resisted all efforts to raise it.

"If we only had a claw on this crowbar, it'd be easy," Campbell grumbled.

Two spikes were finally knocked free and an end of the rail was loosened. Still the other end refused to budge.

Feeling reasonably safe, yet fearing to delay too long, Andrews started forward to help with the job. He had taken just one step when, from down the tracks to the south, came the unmistakable scream of a locomotive whistle.

Every man in the party seemed to freeze.

"A train!" Pittenger gasped.

For a few seconds, Andrews could do nothing but stare at the black plume of smoke that had suddenly appeared back of a stand of pine trees far to the south.

"Must be Bracken's express!" he said. "They're after us! Let's get that rail up!"

In a flash the comforting sense of security was gone. In its place was urgency, almost panic.

Savagely the men attacked the rail, trying to knock it loose with rapid blows.

"Hurry!" Andrews said.

Fuller's locomotive had now come into view around a curve. It was traveling fast. Again its whistle screeched.

The spies worked in a frenzy. In their haste they got in each other's way.

The light drizzle of rain that had been falling was now a downpour, soaking the ground. One of the raiders slipped and fell.

The rail was now definitely loosened and pushed inches out of line.

"That should do it!" Andrews said. It had to do it. There was no more time to spare. "Get aboard!"

Knight, Brown, and Wilson were already in the *General's* cab. As the rest of the spies scrambled into the rear boxcar, the train surged ahead.

Andrews had followed his men into the third car. Seizing one of the crossties that had been put aboard earlier, he crashed it against the back wall of the wooden car until he had made a large opening.

If worse came to worst and the *Texas* was able to get past the bent rail, he had a plan to stop her or at least slow her down.

Somehow the pursuers had to be held up long enough for the Northerners to get to the first Chickamauga bridge and burn it.

Staring through the jagged hole he had punched out, Andrews could see the *Texas* clearly as she thundered after them in reverse. Confederate soldiers were riding atop her tender. There was no mistaking the color of their uniforms. And all of them had rifles.

That was bad. For a showdown battle might happen, and the raiders had only pistols.

Then the hope that the *Texas* would be derailed by the loosened track was dashed. The engine shot across the bent rail as if nothing were wrong!

"Grab some of those ties!" Andrews ordered. "Toss them out this hole on to the track. Maybe that will stop them!"

The raiders instantly obeyed. Most of the thrown crossties bounced and went end over end down the embankment. But some stayed, and the gap between the *General* and the *Texas* widened as the pursuers were forced to stop to throw aside the obstacles.

Time and again Andrews thought they had outdistanced the enemy. But always, careening around a curve, came the *Texas*, whistle screeching like a banshee.

The raiders looked at Andrews, and at each

other. None of them spoke, but the same thought was in all their minds. Was there no way to stop the *Texas*? Was there no way to stop the men in Confederate gray?

Andrews' jaw was set. There was one other thing he could do that might block them.

"Knock a hole in the forward wall!" he shouted to the raiders. "Clean through to the next car. Then everybody clear out of this one!"

With a splintering of wood, a section of the wall was broken open. The spies scrambled through it to the second boxcar, with Andrews following.

Waiting until the *General* was on an upgrade, Andrews then pulled out the coupling pin. The freed third boxcar shot down the slope toward the approaching *Texas*.

But the shattering collision Andrews hoped for didn't happen. Seeing the car coming for them, the crew of the *Texas* stopped and reversed. Then, with nothing more than a slight jolt, contact was made with the loosened boxcar. And in an instant, the *Texas* was steaming north again, pushing the car in front of it. At Resaca, the boxcar was shunted out of the way onto a siding and then the chase was on again.

Into deep valleys, up hills, through tunnels, the wild race continued as mile after mile flashed away. Knight and Brown and Wilson were giving the *General* everything they had. And the *General* was responding well.

Swaying dizzily and with sparks spitting from her wheels, she tore around sharp curves at breakneck speed. Still it wasn't quite enough. The *Texas* hung on doggedly.

Andrews cut loose his second boxcar. And again the crew behind picked it up on the run and slammed it out of the way onto a siding.

But the maneuver had widened the gap between the two engines and Andrews meant to make use of it.

They were now coming closer and closer to the first Chickamauga bridge. If it could be fired, they would be safe. If they failed, it would be the end.

The *General* was dangerously short of wood.

Yet to make a stop now and refuel would destroy all their advantage.

Andrews turned to his men. "All right," he said. "This is our chance. First, knock a hole in that front wall, so we can get to the tender." He pointed rapidly to four of the raiders. "You . . . you. . . you . . . and you. The rest sweep this straw on the floor into piles against the sides. Quick, we must hurry!"

Eagerly, the spies went to work. The instant the opening was made in the front wall, Andrews yelled to Pittenger.

"Get the can of coal oil from Wilson. Bring it back here."

Pittenger scrambled through the opening and across the tender to the cab. When he returned, Andrews took the can from him and poured the coal oil over the heaps of straw.

The Chickamauga bridge was just ahead—a covered structure that spanned a deep chasm.

When they were halfway across, Andrews ordered the train stopped. Hurrying to the engine cab, he came back carrying a shovelful of glowing coals.

With a sweep he scattered the live coals over the soaked straw. Flames instantly swooshed up and began eating into the wooden walls.

"Get to the tender!" Andrews snapped.

He was the last to step through the jagged opening. As he did so, he jerked out the coupling pin.

"Pull ahead!" he shouted to Knight.

The *General* rumbled on, leaving the burning boxcar in the center of the bridge.

Holding to the tender, Andrews tensely watched the rear. The boxcar was flaming like a torch inside the long covered structure. Given a little time, even the rain-soaked timbers of the span would be set ablaze. The vital link in the railroad would be destroyed and victory would go to the Union.

But Andrews wasn't given that little time. Horrified, he saw that the flaming boxcar, instead of staying where it had been left, was moving through the bridge. Behind it, pushing it—was the *Texas*.

176

The gamble had failed. All they could do now was run for it again.

But even that chance was denied them.

"We're out of wood!" Knight yelled. "We're down to nothing."

Everything the raiders could lay their hands on was thrown into the *General's* fire.

"There's a wood-station this side of Ringgold," Andrews said. "Can you get another mile out of her?"

The *General* itself gave the answer. Its speed dropped to twenty-five miles an hour . . . to twenty . . . to fifteen. The engine was wheezing and groaning.

His face drawn, Andrews turned to see his pursuer shunt the flaming car onto a siding. Shrill rebel yells cut through the air as the *Texas* closed in on them.

Andrews knew it was the end.

"Scatter and make for the back country," he said. "Get to our lines as best you can. May luck be with all of you!"

Honor

AND so our story is all but done. For luck wasn't with the raiders. Though they escaped from their train, news of the daring exploit that had come so close to success swept through the countryside. Confederate troops combed the area, and the Northerners hadn't a chance. Within a week the raiders were all captured. They were taken in chains to Atlanta, and there put in prison.

Expecting their execution as spies, the raiders made one last effort together. Secretly, William Knight carved a key from a bone to fit the locks on their manacles. And one day at sundown, when they were being returned to their cell after an exercising period, they overpowered their guard, and Knight unlocked their chains.

The raiders headed on the run down a narrow passageway between two buildings that stood close to the outer wall.

One by one the men were hoisted up by the powerful Campbell. But even as the first raider

disappeared over the top, the alarm sounded.

Campbell could hear shouts from the prison yard and the thudding of running feet. Soldiers would come pouring into the passageway.

Campbell worked faster, practically throwing each man bodily upward until he was alone.

It was only when he himself had scrambled to the top of the wall that he realized how they had been given those last few precious moments.

One of the raiders had turned back and planted himself at the entrance to the passage. Standing there alone, battling to hold off a squad of soldiers, was Andrews.

For a moment, Campbell hesitated. Possible

freedom lay ahead for him. All he had to do was leap to the other side and run.

But the big man didn't. Instead he jumped down inside the wall and sped to join his leader.

Together the two fought until they were overwhelmed and returned to their cell.

"Mr. Andrews," Campbell managed to gasp. "I once said you were afraid to fight. But I was wrong! Really wrong."

Some of the spies got away. Some were caught. Some gave up their lives—Campbell and Andrews among them.

A year later, eight of the raiders stood in the office of the Secretary of War in Washington, D.C. They had just come from a visit to the White House, where they had been received by President Abraham Lincoln.

The Secretary looked at the men before him.

"Your leader was a brave, resourceful man," Edwin Stanton said. "No less may be said of your comrades who perished with him. . . .

"Congress has by a recent law prepared a medal to be awarded for conspicuous bravery. You gentlemen are the first ever to receive it."

Opening a box, Stanton moved forward to present each man with the military decoration that was to become the highest in the land—the Congressional Medal of Honor.

The Happiest Millionaire

John Lawless arrived on Walnut Street in Philadelphia on a summer afternoon in 1916. John walked briskly, in spite of the heat, until he came to the most imposing house on the street.

"Elegant!" said John Lawless to himself. He looked at the address on the slip of paper that he carried, and then at the house—and a handsome house it was, with bay windows both upstairs and down, and an ornate iron fence. John smiled. His luck was holding. Just one day off the boat, and a job with a millionaire was practically his.

John took off his hat and brushed back his fair hair with his hand. Then he went up the steps and rang the bell.

It was the cook who answered the door. John knew she was the cook by the dusting of flour

on one cheek. John smiled again. The woman was nearly as broad as she was tall. Worse things could befall an immigrant fresh from Ireland than to go into service in a house where the cook enjoyed her work.

"Good day to you, ma'am," said John. "Would this be the home of Mr. Anthony J. Drexel Biddle?"

The woman's eyes traveled from the crown of John's head down over his tweed suit (which was, to tell the truth, a bit on the tight side) to his well-polished black boots. She did not seem impressed by what she saw, and for a moment John was afraid that she might close the door on him.

"I've come to be interviewed for the position

of butler," said John quickly. He offered her the slip of paper from the employment agency, but she ignored it.

"Mrs. Biddle does the interviewing," she said. "She's not at home just now."

John bowed. "Well then, I'll be pleased to call again."

The tiniest trace of a smile crinkled the corners of her eyes. "What part of Ireland?" she asked.

"County Tyrone."

It seemed the right place to be from, for she stepped back and swung the door wide. "Perhaps you'd like to wait in the kitchen," she said. "Mrs. Biddle will be coming home soon."

John Lawless followed as she led the way across a hall where small rugs gleamed with rich colors against the hardwood floor. There were great double doors to right and the left. A broad, carpeted stairway led up to the second floor, and beside the stairway was the most stylish telephone booth he had ever seen. It had three walls made of leaded panes of glass.

"My name's Mrs. Worth," said the woman. She stepped quickly past the telephone booth and through a narrow passageway into the big, white-tiled kitchen. "Have a seat and I'll pour you some coffee."

John sat down at the wooden table in the center of the room. "Might you be from Ireland yourself, Mrs. Worth?" he asked. It was a safe question; he already knew the answer.

"I came over as a young girl." Mrs. Worth was busy pouring coffee from the pot which simmered on the back of the gas stove.

"Not so long ago, then?" said John.

Mrs. Worth knew blarney when she heard it, but she laughed in spite of herself. She handed the coffee to John and he sipped with care. It was good. He would like it here. Or would he?

"Tell me, Mrs. Worth, what became of the last butler?"

"I couldn't say." She sat down across the table from John. "He left in the dead of the night, after being here less than a month." She leaned closer. "We've got a servant problem in this house. No use saying we don't."

John looked around. The kitchen was neat— very neat indeed.

"It must be hard to work for the very rich," said John. "I mean, they're used to having things just so."

Mrs. Worth shook her head. "That's not exactly the trouble."

"Are the wages very low?"

"No. The Biddles are quite generous."

"Long hours, then?"

"I wouldn't say so."

John frowned. If the Biddles were not too fussy, and the wages weren't too low and the hours weren't too long, why on earth would a butler run away in the middle of the night?

"Cordelia!"

John jumped, and almost spilled his coffee.

"Cordelia!" the shout rattled the window-panes.

"That would be Mr. Biddle," said Mrs. Worth calmly.

A tall, trim, dark-haired man burst into the kitchen. John started to get to his feet, but Mr. Biddle paid no more attention to him than if he had been a pan hanging on the wall.

"Where's Mrs. Biddle?" he demanded.

John noticed that Mr. Biddle was clutching at one hand with the other. There was just the tiniest trace of red showing between his fingers. John also noted the blue turtleneck sweater Mr. Biddle wore. Big, black letters across the front spelled out "Biddle Bible Class." Now, wondered John to himself, how could a man cut his hand at a Bible class?

"Is there something I can do, Mr. Biddle?" asked Mrs. Worth.

"Yes! You can call Dr. Dunlavy and tell him I've been bitten by an alligator!"

"Oh, dear!" Mrs. Worth got up and ambled toward the door.

"Alligator?" said John aloud. Strange. He had heard that there were alligators in America, but it had definitely been his impression that they lived somewhere in the southern part of the country. Certainly he had never heard of anyone in Philadelphia being attacked by one.

"Might as well live alone," said Mr. Biddle miserably. He looked around to John. "Are you a married man?"

"Me, sir? No, sir."

"Then you wouldn't understand." Mr. Biddle offered his hand so that John could examine it more closely. There was a tiny wound on the index finger. "I've been bit," said Mr. Biddle with some heat. "Suppose it hadn't been my finger. Suppose it had been my leg! Or my head! I might have died! And where is my wife when I need her? And where are my three fine, intelligent children?"

"I couldn't say, I'm sure, sir," said John.

"Cordy!" bellowed Mr. Biddle. "Tony! Livingston!"

"What is it, Papa."

John spun around. The girl who had appeared suddenly in the kitchen was sixteen. Or perhaps she was seventeen. No matter. She was bright and pretty. Like Mr. Biddle, she wore a Bible class sweater. She had completed her costume with black gym bloomers. "Is something wrong?" she asked.

"Yes, something's wrong." Mr. Biddle held out his hand.

The girl didn't seem alarmed. "What were you doing shaving at this time of the day?" she wanted to know.

"Blast! I haven't been shaving! And since when do I shave my finger?"

"Well, you don't shave your ear, either, but last week you cut it."

John Lawless put down his coffee cup and edged toward the doorway. He was beginning to understand why the previous butler might have left suddenly.

"It's a bite, blast it!" cried Mr. Biddle. "George turned on me, after all these years!"

The girl smiled. "It's not really such a bad bite."

Mrs. Worth returned to report that Dr. Dunlavy was somewhere between his office and the hospital and couldn't be reached.

"Keep trying," commanded Mr. Biddle. He turned toward John again. "Blasted alligator!" he

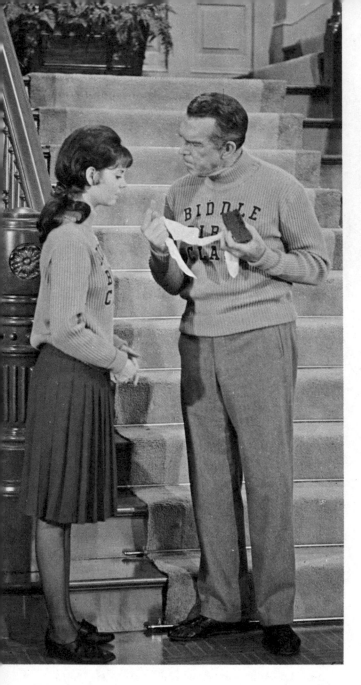

to pry, but I can't help wondering. Is it forever like this?"

"Like what?" asked Mrs. Worth.

"Like . . . like this!" repeated John. "It isn't as if this was the only job in Philadelphia. Not for a likable lad like myself."

The telephone rang, and Mrs. Worth went to answer it. She seemed quite unconcerned about John.

"Perhaps I can call another day," said John to her retreating back.

She gave John an absent-minded wave of the hand as she shut herself in the telephone booth.

Just then the doorbell rang. There seemed no help for it, so John went to answer the door.

The woman who stood on the doorstep was hardly a large person. She scarcely came to John's chin. She was thin, and had the tissue-dry skin of the very old. Yet her back was ramrod straight and her head was held high. John knew instantly that this woman might break, but she would never, never bend.

She fixed John with a cold stare. "Who are you?" she demanded.

"John Lawless, ma'am," said he. He fumbled in his pocket for the paper from the employment agency. "I came about the butler's position."

Like Mrs. Worth, the newcomer cared nothing about that paper. "If you are the new butler, you may announce me," she told John. "I'll wait in the music room." She swept past John and through the double doors to the right of the stairway.

Announce her? Of course, announce her. But to whom? Mrs. Worth was still shut up in the telephone booth, bobbing and nodding as she talked to someone. John went in search of Mr. Biddle. He found the master of the house in the stable, which was on the far side of the garden and was fitted out not as a stable, but as a gymnasium. There was even a boxing ring in the center of the place.

Mr. Biddle seemed somewhat calmer now, and Cordy was putting the finishing touches to a bandage on his injured finger.

exclaimed. "And after I've treated him like a son." He stormed out, and the girl, Cordy, followed him.

Mrs. Worth settled herself at the table again. "The doctor's nurse will call me when she reaches him," she said comfortably. "Shall I be heating up your coffee for you, Mr. Lawless?"

"What? Oh! Oh, no. It's fine!" John, who had been standing, staring after Mr. Biddle, sat down and picked up his cup. "Mrs. Worth, I'm not one

"There's a lady in the music room, sir," John reported.

"A lady?" Mr. Biddle turned a puzzled eye on John.

"She didn't give a name, sir—like there was no need for it."

"Aunt Mary!" exclaimed Mr. Biddle. "Drat!"

Cordy very quietly went away, and Mr. Biddle turned his back on John and proceeded to ignore him.

Back went poor John to the music room. He had not the faintest idea of what to do. But he was saved by the appearance of a very lovely woman with auburn hair. She came in carrying several parcels, and seemed genuinely glad to see the formidable old lady who had taken possession of the big chair by the fireplace. "Aunt Mary!" she exclaimed. "What a lovely surprise!"

"Is it?" The old lady glared at her.

She glanced at John, a question in her eyes.

"I'm John Lawless, ma'am." Again he offered the paper from the employment agency and again it was ignored. "I came about the butler's position."

The auburn-haired lady seemed very pleased to hear this. She gave her parcels to John to take away, and she ordered him to summon Mr. Biddle to the parlor and to bring in the tea tray.

So John tucked the paper from the employment agency back into his pocket. And he carried Mrs. Biddle's parcels to the kitchen (for the lady was, indeed, Mrs. Biddle), and he carried word to Mr. Biddle that he was to appear in the parlor, and then he carried the tea into the parlor, as he had been told.

For John had suddenly decided that the Biddle household might be a somewhat odd one. The ordinary, run-of-the-mill butler might not really suit the Biddles. But for John, the position might be just the combination of luck and accident that John, in his own mind, called "fortuosity." And, lucky or not, it wouldn't be dull.

"Heaven help me," said John, and he settled down, more or less, in the house of Anthony J. Drexel Biddle.

Soon John became acquainted with the family. There was Mr. Biddle, who stirred things up. There was Mrs. Biddle, who calmed things down. There was Cordelia, the pretty seventeen-year-old who was always called Cordy. The boys, Tony and Livingston, were younger than Cordy.

George, the alligator, remained in residence in his tank in the conservatory beyond the parlor. Although he had treacherously bitten Mr. Biddle on the finger, Mr. Biddle was extremely proud of George. He had captured George himself, down in Florida. "I went into the swamp with a party of Seminoles," he told John. And he continued to make much of George and the other, smaller alligators which had practically taken over the conservatory.

Mrs. Worth was always there, presiding over the kitchen. She had been with the Biddles for many years. By now she believed that the Biddle way of doing things was the only way possible.

The maids who came and went in the house didn't agree with her. Some stayed a day. Some stayed a week. A few stayed for a whole month. One stayed only as long as it took her to open the conservatory door and catch one glimpse of George and his friends. Alligators were not her idea of proper house pets.

Aunt Mary came and went regularly all summer. She did not quite live *at* the Biddle house, but to hear Mr. Biddle tell it, she lived much too close to it. And to hear Aunt Mary tell it, the Biddle house was not a proper place to educate a young girl like Cordy.

It wasn't the alligators in the conservatory that Aunt Mary objected to. Any strong-minded young lady could overlook a few alligators—or even pretend they weren't there. It was the Biddle Bible Classes that Aunt Mary didn't like.

The classes, which were held in the gymnasium, combined prayer meetings, hymn singing and calisthenics. Some boxing practice was usually thrown in for good measure, and a number of the young men who attended the classes were what Aunt Mary called "pugilists." Everyone else in the house called them what they were—boxers. Professional prizefighters.

Aunt Mary did not approve of these young men. She did not approve of gym bloomers and black stockings and turtleneck sweaters for Cordy. She did not approve of the fact that Cordy could hit a punching bag better than most young ladies could pour tea.

Cordy must go away to school, Aunt Mary announced. School was the only answer. After all, did Anthony Biddle think that any man in his right mind would want to marry a lady prizefighter?

Mr. Biddle did not like the idea at all, and Mr. Biddle usually got his own way. But in this case, Aunt Mary won out. Fall came, and Tony and Livingston left for classes at St. Paul's, while Cordy was exiled to the Loretta Wingfield School in Lakewood, New Jersey. Peace descended upon the Biddle house on Walnut Street in Philadelphia.

Or comparative peace. For it was never terribly peaceful when Mr. Biddle was anywhere about. John Lawless was kept busy. There was the serving to do, and the silver to be polished. Sometimes John helped when Mr. Biddle fed the alligators. And of course the Biddle Bible Classes continued, Aunt Mary or no Aunt Mary. John enjoyed the classes immensely. Back home, in County Tyrone, John had been somewhat noted for his skill with his fists. Here in Philadelphia he became unofficial sparring partner for Mr. Biddle. And, since Mr. Biddle thoroughly approved of those skilled in the art of self-defense (all other things being equal), he thoroughly approved of John.

Autumn wore away into winter, and John became accustomed to the routine—or lack of it—at the Biddle mansion. Then there was a change. It began on a very cold night when Mr. and Mrs. Biddle came home rather late. There was an icy draft of air swirling through the front hall. Mr. Biddle felt it the moment the front door was shut behind him.

Mrs. Biddle announced that she believed the draft was coming from the conservatory.

Instant terror set in.

"My alligators!" shouted Mr. Biddle.

He rushed into the conservatory. It was true. It was horribly, terribly true. Every window in the place was wide open, and the water in the alligator tanks was frozen solid.

"John!" shouted Mr. Biddle. "My alligators! Look at my alligators! JOHN!"

John Lawless had been enjoying a late cup of tea in the kitchen. He appeared in the conservatory with the cup still in his hand. "You yelled, sir?" he said.

"What happened here?" demanded Mr. Biddle. "Why are these windows open?"

John quickly busied himself closing the windows. "It must have been the new maid, sir," he explained. He did not dare even to glance at the alligator tanks.

"What new maid?" asked Mr. Biddle.

As usual, Mrs. Biddle managed to keep her

voice calm. "Her name is Florence, dear," she explained. "She started this afternoon."

"She was complaining about the smell," put in John Lawless.

Mr. Biddle was insulted. "What smell?"

"We're accustomed to it, dear," said Mrs. Biddle, "but the alligators do have a certain . . . a certain . . ."

"She probably decided to give the room an airing, and forgot to close up again," John concluded.

Mr. Biddle decided, and very promptly, too, that the maid was a stupid thing. He demanded an axe. Mrs. Biddle was very startled until Mr. Biddle assured her that the axe was not to be used on Florence, the maid, but on the alligators. Mr. Biddle intended to chop the ice away from them and thaw them out—provided they were still capable of being thawed.

An hour or so later, it began to appear that the alligators were a lost cause. They had been chipped out of the ice and were heaped in front of the blazing fire in the parlor, but they remained stubbornly frozen stiff.

"Dead!" mourned Mr. Biddle. "Dead, dead, dead!"

Mrs. Biddle offered silent sympathy and mopped at the puddles on the parlor floor with a towel. "Anthony," she reminded Mr. Biddle, "it's after midnight."

"I hate to give up."

"I know, dear, but there comes a time when . . ."

Mrs. Biddle stopped and listened. The front door had just opened. Mr. Biddle got to his feet and crossed to the hall.

Cordy was standing just inside the front door. Her cheeks were very red and her eyes were very bright. She looked as if she was happy, but she looked as if she might have been crying, too—just a little.

"Cordy!" exclaimed Mr. Biddle.

"Cordy, what are you doing here?" asked Mrs. Biddle. "Why aren't you at school?"

"Did they call?" asked Cordy quickly.

"Did who call?"

"The school? When they missed me, I mean. I'm glad if they didn't. I was hoping we'd get here first!"

John paused in the doorway. His hands were filled with damp towels.

"We?" questioned Mr. Biddle. "Cordy, is someone with you?"

"Yes," said Cordy. Her color became even higher. "My fiancé is outside. His name is Angier Buchanan Duke and he's in the car."

John could see the back of Mr. Biddle's neck growing quite red. Mr. Biddle breathed quickly

once or twice. Then he spoke in a strangled voice. "Do you mean to tell me that some boy is sitting out there in front of this house thinking that he's going to marry you?"

Cordy smiled and it was clear that this was exactly what she meant. "He wanted to be sure I got in all right," she told her father. "I'll tell him he can go now." She opened the door and threw a kiss to someone John couldn't see. "Good night!" she called.

"Aren't you going to ask him in?" said Mrs. Biddle in her gentle way.

"No, Mother, I don't think so." She went to her father and kissed him. "I'm not going to let you get at him until you get used to the idea," she said. "I think you'll like him very much—if you just give him a chance."

Then Cordy kissed her mother, and she shook hands with John (who had to juggle the damp towels) and went up to bed.

Then Mr. Biddle announced several things in a loud, clear voice. Cordelia was still a child, said he. He would never permit the marriage. She was not ready for it.

"You mean *you're* not ready," said Mrs. Biddle. "Anthony, you'll be making the greatest mistake

of your life if you try to stop this engagement. Cordy has a mind of her own. Faced with an obstacle, she'll proceed with still greater determination."

Mrs. Biddle smiled then. "You know," she said, "I'm anxious to see what he looks like."

"Cordelia, you amaze me!" said the flabbergasted Mr. Biddle.

Then he and Mrs. Biddle went upstairs.

"It never rains but it pours," mused John Lawless. "To lose your only daughter and your pet alligators all on the same black night." And he carried the damp towels out into the kitchen.

In the morning it became clear that John had taken too dim a view of the situation. Mrs. Worth was first into the kitchen and had the coffee singing merrily on the gas stove by the time John came down. Last to appear was Florence, the new maid. She was humming to herself as she went to hold out her hands to the warmth of the stove.

John looked at her severely. "You left the windows open in the conservatory last night," he accused.

Florence's head, which was very blonde, swiveled so that she could look at John. Her wide, blank blue eyes became even wider—and more blank. "Oh?" she said.

"A fine to-do there was when Mr. Biddle came home," said John.

The girl shrugged. It seemed to her a great deal of fuss about nothing. She twitched her skirt straight and sauntered out toward the front of the house.

"That's a careless piece," exclaimed Mrs. Worth, slicing bread for toast.

From the front of the house came a soft, rumbling grunt.

"Mrs. Worth!" cried John. "Mrs. Worth, that sounded very much like . . ."

John was interrupted by a piercing shriek.

"Aha!" John raced into the hall just in time to see Florence gather up her skirts and rocket upstairs. Behind her, in the hall, George rolled his eyes and grunted the happy grunt of an alligator who has just warmed up after a frozen night.

Mr. Biddle rushed out of his room in his bathrobe. His slippers were still in his hand when he collided with Florence on the upstairs landing.

"What's all the blasted screaming?" he wanted to know.

Florence simply knocked him down and ran on. The nearest haven which beckoned to the girl was the bathroom. In a twinkling she had locked herself in there. But not for long. With another jarring scream she unbolted the door and rushed out. Behind Florence, a small alligator crawled out from under the bathtub and yawned a gaping alligator yawn.

"The girl's crazy," Mr. Biddle concluded. "That stuff she uses to color her hair must have gone to her brain."

Then he noticed the little alligator. "Well, I'll be . . . !" he exclaimed.

"Anthony, what is it?" called Mrs. Biddle.

"Everything's all right now," replied Mr. Biddle happily. He picked up the alligator. "Did that nitwit girl frighten you?" he wanted to know.

Mr. Biddle started down the stairs calling to John that the alligators were not dead after all.

"I know, sir," said John.. He had George by the tail and was trying to drag him toward the conservatory.

"George!" exclaimed Mr. Biddle. There was real delight in his voice. "Good old George! Cordelia! Cordy! It's George! He's all right!"

Mr. Biddle had reached the foot of the stairs with the smaller alligator still in his arms. Poor, silly Florence darted into the telephone booth. Then she discovered that one of the very tiny alligators was happily curled up in a corner of the booth. Florence came out of the telephone booth more quickly than she had gone in. Screaming with new energy, she bumped into John, who lost his grip on George's tail. George scrambled for the kitchen.

"George!" called Mr. Biddle. "George, come back here!" Without pausing to think about it, Mr. Biddle handed the small alligator to Florence and started after George.

The terror-stricken Florence hesitated not a moment. She knew exactly what to do with small alligators. She threw the little one up in the air, screamed again and streaked out through the front door.

Cordy came down the stairs in time to catch the little alligator and carry it to the conservatory. Mrs. Biddle came down and extracted the second small alligator from the telephone booth. And in the kitchen Mrs. Worth, who had breakfast to get, had no intentions of putting up with nonsense from any alligator—not even George. "I'll teach you to make yourself at home in my kitchen!" she shouted. George had gotten himself wedged in under the cupboard. He thrashed to and fro as Mrs. Worth belabored him with a broom. Pots and pans flew in every direction.

"Come out of there!" cried Mrs. Worth. "Come out, I say!"

George just took a huge bite out of the broom.

"My new broom!" Mrs. Worth paused for a second to assess the damage, and the alligator made a run for the door. He had a slab of bacon in his mouth.

"You drop that! Drop it, I say, you big, ugly beast! You'd be a handbag if I had my way!" She chased after him, beating at him with her amputated broom, until he had scuttled to safety in the conservatory.

"You should have let out a call, Mrs. Worth," said John Lawless, very politely. "I would have been happy to give you a hand with the animal."

"Thank you, Mr. Lawless," said the cook. Her tone indicated that she did not thank him at all. "I managed very well on my own," she said, and she turned and headed back toward her kitchen. She was breathing only a trifle more quickly than usual. "Breakfast will be in half an hour," she announced. "I have to slice some more bacon."

John Lawless went to the door. Florence had left it open behind her when she fled. "I suppose we'll have to send her things after her," said John. He shut the door. "These maids do come and go."

Mr. Biddle felt better that day. Much, much better, in fact. How can a man help but feel better when his alligators have thawed out?

Still, there was the question of Cordy and the young man named Duke. Cordy was determined. There were no two ways about it. She was going to marry young Angier Duke and no one was going to stop her.

For once Mr. Biddle held his tongue and kept his own counsel. He did not forbid the match. Not again. Instead, he asked Mrs. Biddle to invite Mr. Duke to dinner.

The dinner itself was not a rousing success. Mr. Biddle asked about New York, which was Angier Duke's home. Mr. Biddle then announced that he could not stand New York.

"Tell me, Mr. Duke," said Mr. Biddle, with the air of a man who is trying very hard to be pleasant, "what do you like to do? Do you hike? Do you ski?"

"I broke my ankle once, skiing," admitted Angie miserably.

"Did you get right back up on those skis and try again?" demanded Mr. Biddle.

"No, sir," admitted Angie.

"Well, you should have," said Mr. Biddle.

"The bone was sticking out," explained Angie.

Mr. Biddle opened his mouth, then shut it again quickly. John smiled to himself as he passed the dessert plates.

"Do you box?" asked Mr. Biddle at last. There was a crafty look on his face. The whole conversation had been leading up to this, John knew.

"Box?" echoed Angie. "No, sir. I just don't seem to have the time."

"You should take time," insisted Mr. Biddle. "Life is a precious and wonderful thing. You can't just sit there and let it lap around you. You have to dive into it. You have to feel it and taste it and use it. The more you use, the more you have. That's the wonder of it!"

Angie did not seem to be paying very close attention to this sound advice which Mr. Biddle was offering him. Angie's eyes were fixed on a spot behind Mr. Biddle. Both John and Mr. Bid-

dle turned to look. A very small alligator—the one called Lucy—was crawling out from underneath the radiator.

"Well, look at that," exclaimed Mr. Biddle. "I'll bet she's been hiding there all day, where it's warm."

194

Mrs. Biddle hastily suggested that they all go into the parlor and have coffee.

When they were safely out of the dining room Cordy whispered, "I told you he keeps alligators."

"It's not that," said Angie. "Cordy, he scares me half to death!"

"You've got to stand up to him," urged Cordy.

"He'd punch me in the nose."

"Then punch him back!"

Angie turned pale at the very idea.

"Better still," insisted Cordy, "punch him first! Angie, you've got to talk up to him. Contradict him. Even when he's right, tell him he's wrong."

"But I couldn't do that!"

"Angie," explained Cordy, "I'm telling you how to go about getting him to like you. I *want* him to like you."

It didn't make any sense at all to Angie. On the other hand, he had to agree that Cordy knew Mr. Biddle better than he did. So, by the time John carried in the coffee tray, he was boldly disagreeing with everything Mr. Biddle had to say.

If Mr. Biddle liked cold weather, Angie liked it hot. If Mr. Biddle was sure it would rain, Angie was equally sure it would be dry. Mr. Biddle approved of hiking, but Angie preferred yachting.

Then, quite deliberately, Angie spoke up about boxing. There wasn't much to it, decided Angie. "Two men just standing there hitting each other doesn't offer a lot of challenge," he said.

There was a sudden cold glint in Mr. Biddle's eye. "John," said he, "go out to the stable and get the gloves."

"The boxing gloves, sir?" asked John. He knew quite well which gloves Mr. Biddle wanted.

"Anthony, what are you thinking of?" asked Mrs. Biddle.

"I want to show Mr. Duke a little of the art of boxing," said Mr. Biddle. "I want to correct his false impression. John and I can go a couple of quick rounds."

"In my parlor?" Mrs. Biddle was shocked.

"It will be just a demonstration," Mr. Biddle assured her.

"Anthony, I really don't think this is the time or the place."

"We don't have to stand on ceremony with Mr. Duke," countered Mr. Biddle. "After all, he's practically a member of the family. Right, Mr. Duke?"

Angie smiled for almost the first time that evening. "Right, Mr. Biddle," he agreed. "As a matter of fact, I was just wondering, why can't *I* try it?"

"What's that?"

"Why can't I fight you?" persisted Angie.

"Without knowing what you're doing? I don't think so."

Angie took a deep breath. "I thought this was one house where a man could get a fair fight," he said softly.

Mr. Biddle straightened up, and the red flush which John now knew so well appeared on the back of his neck. "John, get Mr. Duke the gloves," he ordered evenly.

John did as he was told. Then he stood by to hold the stopwatch for the bout between Angie and Mr. Biddle.

The first round did not last long. It took Mr. Biddle only seconds to flatten Mr. Duke.

"You ran right into my fist," complained Mr. Biddle.

Angie got to his feet.

"I hope you're not upset with me," said Mr. Biddle. John thought his anxiety was rather put on.

"If I were upset, I'd take care of you," said Angie calmly.

"Oh?" Mr. Biddle was surprised. "I wonder about that."

"You do? Well, sir, if you'll just take your boxing stance . . ."

Mr. Biddle tried to hide an amused smile. He put up his fists and again prepared to flatten this outrageous young man.

Instead, Mr. Biddle suddenly found himself stretched out flat on the floor of his own parlor, staring at the ceiling.

"Merciful heavens!" exclaimed John.

Mr. Biddle sat up carefully, feeling his back to make sure nothing was broken.

"Anthony, are you all right?" Mrs. Biddle looked very pale.

"Of course I'm all right. He caught me unawares, that's all."

"Care to try it awares?" asked Angie.

"Couldn't all this wait for another time?" asked Mrs. Biddle quickly. "The coffee is getting quite cold."

"Don't worry, Mrs. Biddle," Angie told her.

"No one's going to get hurt. At least, I'm not."

This made Mr. Biddle really angry. "What do you want to do, wrestle?" he asked.

"It's a little like wrestling, sir," admitted Angie. "It's called ju-jitsu."

Mr. Biddle immediately assumed a wrestling crouch, and Angie threw him to the floor a second time.

"I hope I didn't hurt you, sir," said Angie, and this time he helped Mr. Biddle get up.

"Nothing that won't wear off." Mr. Biddle laughed at himself.

More than a little relieved, John laughed, too. "That's a grand style of fighting, sir," he told Angie. "I'd like to learn it myself. I've got a feeling it might come in handy some day."

"We've *all* got to learn it!" cried Mr. Biddle. "That's a remarkable thing. Why, it could mean the difference between life and death in hand-to-hand combat. You *will* teach it to me, won't you?"

"Of course, sir," promised Angie.

"How lucky that young Mr. Duke should know ju-jitsu," said John to himself. "A real piece of fortuosity, that is."

Now the winds of real change began to swirl through the big house on Walnut Street. Cordy's engagement was announced, and she and Angie were off to New York for a round of parties given by Angie's mother and her friends. Then the wedding date was announced, and it was back to Philadelphia for another round of parties given by the Biddles and the Drexels.

Cordy began to look tired. John noticed it. On too many days there were dark shadows under her eyes. Once John overheard her in the parlor, talking with Angie. There was some argument about the future. Angie's mother had some ideas, it seemed—some very definite ideas. And Cordy didn't agree.

Then, all at once, the wedding was almost upon them. The house swarmed with dressmakers and milliners and caterers and florists. Mrs. Biddle spent hours checking and re-checking lists. There were lists of guests and lists of things to do. There were lists of things to buy. There were lists of wedding gifts.

Then Angie's mother arrived in Philadelphia, and the newspapermen hurried down to meet

her. For Mrs. Duke traveled in her own private railroad car—and that sort of thing didn't happen every day in Philadelphia.

It was plain from the very start that Mrs. Duke was not impressed with Philadelphia. Nor was she impressed with the Biddles. To Mrs. Duke, it was unthinkable to keep alligators in the house —even if you caught the alligators yourself. It was ridiculous to have your own Bible class. And some of the people who attended the Bible class were completely impossible.

Then there was Mr. Biddle himself. Mrs. Duke was struck with real horror at a garden party one day when Mr. Biddle took his place near the musicians and began to sing. It didn't matter that Mr. Biddle enjoyed singing. It didn't matter that he sang rather well. In Mrs. Duke's circle, one did not sing in public.

"At least he *feels* like singing," said Cordy, defiantly.

"So do I, sometimes," replied Mrs. Duke, "but I keep it to myself."

John, passing with a tray of small sandwiches, frowned to himself. He did not like the way things were going. He didn't like it at all.

John went into the kitchen to get more sandwiches from the boxes the caterer's men had brought. "I'm thinking there'd better be a wedding soon, or there'll be no wedding at all," he told Mrs. Worth.

She was wiping punch cups and putting them on a tray on the drainboard. "They haven't a moment to themselves, those two," she said. "Miss Cordy was crying last night. I heard her when I went up. She's tired, poor lamb."

"And that mother of his is no help," put in John. "He and Miss Cordy want to go and live in Detroit. He wants to make cars, he says. His mother wants them to live in New York, under her thumb."

"And make money, I suppose," said Mrs. Worth. "As if the Dukes hadn't enough of that."

John picked up his tray and went out. He caught sight of Mrs. Duke and Aunt Mary in the parlor. These two awe-inspiring ladies had met

200

once and taken an instant dislike to one another. Aunt Mary regarded Mrs. Duke as an upstart. Mrs. Duke thought Aunt Mary was a stuffy old biddy. Now John invaded the parlor with his tray, attempting to ease the chill with Irish charm and offerings of watercress sandwiches.

John failed. The ladies were speaking very little, either to each other or to John. And Mr. Biddle, when he appeared, was greeted with real coldness.

Mrs. Duke was annoyed. It seemed there had been some mix-up, and not all of the members of the Duke family had received their invitations to the wedding. "How would you feel if the Biddles had not been invited?" said Mrs. Duke.

"They'd come anyway," snapped Aunt Mary. "They're relatives."

Cordy, who had wandered in with Angie, suddenly hit at the Chinese gong that stood in one corner of the parlor.

"Stop it!" she cried. "Stop it! I'm sick to death of it! Duke pride! Drexel pride! Biddle pride! Philadelphia versus New York! You're turning our wedding into the biggest fight in history. I'm not going to have it! Angie and I will elope!"

"Elope?" Mrs. Duke was horrified. "Elope and make us all look like fools?"

"At this moment, Mrs. Duke, I don't care *what* you look like."

"Cordy!" cried her mother, who had just come in.

"Angie, you had better speak to your bride," commanded Mrs. Duke. "This wedding is going to take place on schedule and it's going to be done right. Once you are safe in our railroad car and on your way to Hot Springs, you can . . ."

"Hot Springs?" cried Cordy. "I thought we were going to Detroit?"

Angie sank miserably into a chair. "Cordy, I'm sorry," he groaned.

"What, please tell me, is the matter with Hot Springs?" demanded Mrs. Duke.

"I'm sure there's nothing wrong with it, Mrs. Duke. But I'm not going to spend my honeymoon there—just as I'm not going to live in New York!"

203

"Of course you're going to live in New York," flared Mrs. Duke.

"I am *not* getting married!" announced Cordy angrily.

"What? You certainly are getting married!"

Mr. Biddle quickly stepped in. "She doesn't have to if she doesn't want to."

"Well, if you're not getting married, then neither am I," shouted Angie. And, having stated this very obvious truth, he marched out of the house.

Cordy rushed upstairs in tears.

"John!" Mr. Biddle looked rather worried. "I think perhaps you had better follow Mr. Duke."

"Yes, sir," agreed John. And, without even stopping to get his hat, John went out onto Walnut Street after Angie.

It was very, very late when John returned. There were no lights on in the Biddle house. John used his key to open the back door, then crept up to bed without making a sound.

He was up and dressed early in the morning, and down in the kitchen before Mrs. Worth was stirring. He was standing near the window, measuring coffee into the pot, when Cordy came out of the stable and crossed the terrace. Mr. Biddle was with her.

"I don't want to talk about it, Papa," John heard Cordy say. "There's nothing to talk about. You never really approved of Angie, and you were right. He's a mama's boy! He doesn't know what life is all about."

"He'll learn," said Mr. Biddle. "Maybe you'll learn together. I've got nothing against that boy, Cordy. I never did, except that I wanted you to stay at home. Now, whatever you decide to do, Cordy, I'll back you a hundred per cent. It's your life."

Cordy began to cry then, and her father gave her a handkerchief. And the doorbell rang. John put the coffee pot on the stove and went to the door, where he found Mrs. Duke in a state bordering on frenzy. She swept past John without a glance. "Where is he?" she demanded.

Mr. Biddle and Cordy came in from the terrace.

"Where is Angier?" cried Mrs. Duke. "He wasn't in his hotel room all night! His bed hasn't been slept in!"

"JOHN!" shouted Mr. Biddle.

"Yes, sir," said John softly.

Mr. Biddle frowned at John. "I thought I asked you to watch out for Mr. Duke."

"I did, sir."

"John, you have a black eye!" said Mr. Biddle.

"Yes, sir," explained John. "Mr. Duke hit me, sir."

"What?" exclaimed Mr. Biddle.

"He was going to go to China, sir, or some such place, to make his own fortune. But he's safe in the jailhouse this morning," said John proudly. "Somehow he had the idea that I told the police sergeant—a fine lad from County Cork—that he told me that all Irishmen were pigs and Ireland was a proper sty for them. They'll release him as soon as I withdraw the charges, sir."

"John!" exclaimed Cordy.

"Well, Miss Cordy," John defended himself, "I thought it might make you unhappy if he went off to China."

Mr. Biddle stirred himself. "Mrs. Duke, why don't you wait out on the terrace," he suggested.

"John, bring the car around front and we'll have this situation cleared up in no time."

And clear it up they did—so far as the police were concerned. To straighten things out with Angie was another matter. Angie had spent the night in jail, and he was tired and very angry. He stated that he wasn't going to leave for China, but he wasn't going to leave for anyplace else, either. It was then that Mr. Biddle had a stroke of inspiration.

"Young man, it's time you woke up to your responsibilities," he said. He was standing in the doorway of Angie's jail cell and his manner was that of one explaining things to a backward child. "I want you to get this wedding over with," he told Angie. "Then you can take that honeymoon at Hot Springs and then get back to your desk in New York. You may think you want other

things for yourself. You may think you have dreams of your own. But you'll get over all that —just the way other people do."

Angie started up in anger. "*You* didn't get over it!" he shouted.

"Darn few like me!" declared Mr. Biddle.

"Is that so?"

"Yes—that's so."

"Now you listen here, Mr. Know-it-all Biddle, no one is going to run my life for me. I've decided that much. And what's more, I'm going to ask Cordy to elope with me—today!"

"If you ask Cordy to elope, she won't," warned Mr. Biddle.

"Then I'll tell her," said Angie.

Which is exactly what he did.

Cordy said no at first. But then she didn't say no. At least, she didn't say it loudly.

So Cordy and Angie were off together, headed for Detroit, just as they had planned.

And there wasn't any need for the Dukes to worry about being invited to the wedding, because there wasn't any great big wedding.

Mrs. Duke was very, very upset. And Mrs. Biddle cried a bit. She was, after all, the mother of the bride, and she was supposed to cry. Mr. Biddle felt a little sad. But Mr. Biddle couldn't stay sad for long. He was, after all, a very happy millionaire. Which, as John was fond of saying, was fortuosity at its finest.

The Ugly

Dachshund

ONCE there were three little Dachshund pups named Chloe, Heidi and Wilhelmina. All day long they squeaked and yelped and waddled about as fast as their short crooked legs could carry them. They were the favorites of Mrs. Garrison, who was very fond of Dachshunds.

With them lived a fourth pup. His name was Brutus, and he was a Great Dane—and he was the favorite of *Mr.* Garrison.

At first Mrs. Garrison didn't like Brutus very much.

"He'll grow on you," said her husband hopefully. "You'll see—you'll grow to like him."

But it was Brutus who did most of the growing. And as he grew he continued to act more and more like a Dachshund. Now, there are some things that Dachsies do very well—they scamper about, they wag their tails, and they curl up to sleep on somebody's lap. Brutus tried to do all these things, too. When he ran, he stayed low and close to the ground, the way Dachshunds do. But his hindquarters wouldn't cooperate. They always stuck up high in the air. When he wagged his tail, he swept lamps crashing off their tables to the floor. And when he attempted to jump on Mrs. Garrison's lap, she couldn't breathe.

As he grew older, Brutus grew bigger, and he grew heavier, and he grew stronger. But he didn't grow on Mrs. Garrison. She still didn't like Brutus at all.

One day she put the Dachsies in a toy wheelbarrow to take their picture. With a joyous bark, Brutus jumped in to join them. *Crash!* The wheelbarrow splintered and fell apart, and the Dachshunds went flying in all directions.

Chloe, Heidi and Wilhelmina pattered into the house one day. And Brutus, his tail wagging happily, hunkered down and scrambled after them. Leaping and tumbling, the three little pups raced around. They found a ball of wool on a chair, but they didn't see the half-knitted sweater at the other end of the wool.

Chloe grabbed the ball of wool in her mouth and ran. Yipping and squealing, Heidi and Wilhelmina chased after her. And big Brutus lumbered after them, trying to join in the fun.

The ball unwound and the sweater unravelled. Soon nothing was left but a tangled trail of wool which looked like a big red web spun by a giant spider.

The three little dogs scurried under the sofa and hid, and when Mrs. Garrison came into the room, Brutus was the only one she saw.

Then, another day, the three little Dachshunds raced into Mr. Garrison's workroom. Brutus loped along after them.

Mr. Garrison was an artist, so his workroom was full of pencils and paints and brushes and paper. Grunting and squealing, the Dachshunds zig-zagged in and out among drawing tables, cabinets and easels.

Suddenly Brutus' tail knocked down a jar of paint brushes. The big pup gave a startled yelp and backed into a cabinet. *Crash!* The cabinet toppled over, and paint tubes, pencils, pads and clouds of powdered color scattered all over the floor. Brutus yelped again and, lurching forward, crashed into an enormous easel. The three puppies slithered out the door, but big Brutus wasn't so lucky. When Mr. and Mrs. Garrison ran into the room, poor Brutus flumped down on the floor and whimpered sadly. Mrs. Garrison looked about at all the wreckage and said, "Well, he's done it again."

"Yes," said Mr. Garrison. "But after all, he's only a puppy."

"I know," sighed Mrs. Garrison. "That's what frightens me. What will he do when he gets bigger?"

Finally Mr. Garrison was forced to put Brutus outdoors in a pen. "Why can't you be good for something?" said Mr. Garrison in dismay. He left Brutus and went back into the house.

After several mournful whimpers, the Great Dane pup settled down and closed his eyes. One hour went by. Two hours. Three. There were no stars out that night. It was very dark.

Slowly, slowly, the stranger backed along the ground. Suddenly he jumped to his feet and headed for a tree, with Brutus lunging after him. Leaping for a low-hanging branch, the man swung upward, barely in time. And there he clung as Brutus circled below, barking loudly.

Inside the house, Mr. and Mrs. Garrison thought that Brutus was barking because he was lonely. Burrowing their heads deep in their pillows, they went back to sleep—and slept until morning.

All at once Brutus' eyes snapped open, and he growled deep in his throat. Rising, he began to paw the sides of the pen. In the darkness, a strange man—stealthily, on tip-toe—was coming closer and closer to the house. Brutus backed to one side of the pen. And then he charged. In one big jump he was out of the pen. He raced across the lawn. With a flying leap, he knocked down the stranger—and a gun flew through the air.

Days and weeks and months passed. By now Brutus was no longer an oversized pup. He was a full-grown Great Dane. But he continued to think of himself as a Dachshund.

Things came to a crashing climax the night of Mrs. Garrison's big party. It was one she had planned for a long time. She had invited the editors for whom her husband worked, and all the other people who had purchased his paintings,

Poor Brutus. In the morning, the strange man he had chased up the tree was found to be a policeman who had been looking for prowlers. Mr. Garrison was sorry that the policeman had spent all night up in the tree. But he was delighted that at last Brutus seemed to be good for something.

"Don't you see how valuable he is?" Mr. Garrison asked his wife. "Why, if we keep him, no burglar will ever come within miles of this house."

So Brutus stayed on with the Garrisons and the three Dachshunds.

as well as the neighbors and many old friends. And—most important to her—she had invited an expert on dogs who would advise her on entering Chloe in the forthcoming Fairview Dog Show.

Preparing for such a party was too much for her alone, so Mrs. Garrison hired a caterer, a Japanese named Mr. Toyama. Mr. Toyama spent two days at the Garrison home. First he strung paper lanterns all over the back yard. Then he prepared trays and trays of little sandwiches and other things to eat. Finally, he spent one entire morning on a three-tiered cake with fancy decorations in the frosting.

Mr. Toyama first saw Brutus when he was hanging the Japanese lanterns. He rounded a corner, and there was the Great Dane. Mr. Toyama looked at Brutus, and the dog looked at Mr. Toyama, and the caterer fled. He ran out of the house crying, "Lion! Help! Lion!"

It took Mrs. Garrison two hours to comfort Mr. Toyama and convince him that Brutus was a friendly (if large) member of the household. After he had calmed down, Mr. Toyama continued to prepare for the party, but he kept well away from Brutus.

The night of the party, Mrs. Garrison was the perfect hostess. She told all of Mr. Garrison's business associates how brilliant they were. She told the women how charming they were. And she told her friends how happy she was to see them. Then she found the dog expert and proudly showed off little Chloe. "Isn't she a darling?" Mrs. Garrison said. "She never gets into trouble the way Brutus does."

The dog expert replied, "She's a fine Dachshund, Mrs. Garrison. Ah, who—or what—is Brutus?"

At that moment his question was answered. Mr. Garrison had carefully tied Brutus in his pen to keep him out of the way. But the excitement of the party was too much for the Great Dane. He wanted to join in the fun. With a lurch he broke away from his rope and ran to join the party.

He brushed by two women, sending them sprawling on the grass. He put his paws on a publisher's shoulders and slurped him affectionately on the face. He put a foot on a tray of food and squashed all the little sandwiches into one big mess.

In the confusion chairs splintered, tables toppled and guests scattered in all directions as Brutus galloped through the yard.

Mr. Toyama was carrying the cake from the kitchen to the patio when he saw Brutus again. "Lion! Help! Lion!" he called, and he ran for dear life. Brutus happily jumped on his back, and Mr. Toyama sailed into his carefully decorated cake.

The last anybody ever saw of Mr. Toyama, he was running down the street with green and blue frosting all over his white jacket.

And abruptly the party ended.

Brutus was in disgrace. Even Mr. Garrison agreed with his wife that something would have to be done about Brutus.

But the next day everything changed. At mid-morning the trash men arrived to collect the paper cartons, broken glasses and china, squashed sandwiches and remnants of the big cake which were left over from the party. As they were throwing litter into their truck, little Chloe was sniffing around in a carton of leftovers. The trash men didn't see her as they hefted the carton and threw it into the truck.

But Brutus saw. He raced around and tried to attract the attention of the trash men. They paid no attention to him and started to drive off.

"Wurf! Wurf!" Brutus barked and blocked the way. The men sounded their horn to scare Brutus, but he held his ground. He wouldn't budge from in front of the truck.

Mr. and Mrs. Garrison heard the honking and barking, and they came running outside. At first they scolded Brutus severely. But Brutus loped to the back of the truck and clawed at the side panel. Mr. Garrison didn't know what to think—until he heard Chloe yipping faintly inside the truck.

Quickly the trash men rescued the little Dachshund. "Gosh," said the driver, "I bet that's why Brutus wouldn't let me leave. He knew the little pooch was in the truck."

"It does look that way, doesn't it?" said Mrs. Garrison. And she patted Brutus fondly.

Mrs. Garrison no longer complained about Brutus, but to her he was still nothing more than a sweet, clumsy ox of a dog. This troubled Mr. Garrison. It troubled him so much that he tried to teach Brutus to heel and stay and walk obediently on a leash. When Mrs. Garrison saw this, she said, "You're wasting your time."

"Oh, am I?" said Mr. Garrison grimly. "We'll see about that." And then and there he decided to enter Brutus in the Fairview Dog Show. But the show was only a few weeks away, and Mr. Garrison wondered if he could train Brutus to be a show dog in so short a time.

"Well, I can try," he told himself.

With the help of Doc Pruitt, a friendly kennel owner, he tried and tried. Brutus learned to heel and stay, but after many hours of hard work Doc Pruitt could only scratch his head in puzzlement.

"Why does he droop that way in the middle?" he asked.

"I'll tell you why," Mr. Garrison said gloomily. "He still thinks he's a Dachshund."

"Then you better do something about it," Doc Pruitt advised. "I don't know what to suggest, but it better be good."

All this time Mrs. Garrison was grooming little Chloe for the Fairview show. Whenever Mr. Garrison was home, he saw his wife brushing Chloe or instructing her in the fine points of behavior in the show ring. Mr. Garrison never admitted to

his wife that he was also training Brutus. But every afternoon he and Brutus went quietly into the hills to meet with Doc Pruitt. Together Mr. Garrison and the vet sought to convince the Great Dane that he wasn't a Dachshund.

The day of the Fairview Dog Show arrived. Mr. Garrison and Doc Pruitt led Brutus to a large tent. The big dog kept looking about nervously. Mr. Garrison said, "He's not used to all these dogs. Come to think of it, he's never seen any dogs other than our Dachshunds."

Just then, his eyes wide and staring, Brutus saw for the first time—a cocker spaniel, a bulldog, a poodle, a bassett hound, and—

"Great Danes to the ring, please," called a judge.

Swallowing hard, Mr. Garrison led Brutus to the show ring. And there Brutus—for the first time—saw other Great Danes.

How tall and strong they were! How handsome. What a proud, Great Dane look they had about them. Brutus eyed the other Danes. Then he

looked down at himself. Suddenly he seemed to walk taller. He lifted his head proudly. At last he knew he was a Great Dane.

Suddenly, in the middle of the judging, Mrs. Garrison and Chloe approached the ring. Mrs. Garrison was surprised to see her husband, but Brutus was more shocked to see Chloe. All of his old instincts came flooding back, and he began to sag in the middle, scooch down and waddle like a Dachshund. However, a tug on the leash from Mr. Garrison reminded him of his Great Dane breeding. Again he stood proud and true.

Can you guess which Great Dane won First Prize that day?

Brutus won!

As for Mrs. Garrison, she was both surprised and delighted.

There are still three little Dachshunds living with the Garrisons. And with them lives a fourth dog of whom they're very proud. He is a huge and handsome Great Dane, and Brutus is his name.

Kidnapped

The Trap

THUNDER rumbled in the distance and an angry sunset outlined the figure of a young traveler stopped at the crossroads. As he puzzled over the signpost's dim lettering, ruddy twilight touched David Balfour's face, making it seem even more youthful than his seventeen years.

The old sign, David decided, was unreadable in any light, blurred by too many seasons of Scottish weather.

"I'll wait," he said aloud. "Perhaps somebody will come by and I can ask the way."

Wearily he lowered his plaid bundle and sat down on one of the large stones which propped up the signpost. Then, for the twentieth time in two days, he took from his pocket the sealed letter that Mr. Campbell, the minister, had given him.

"It's in my father's handwriting," he pondered, "addressed to Ebenezer Balfour, Esquire, the Laird of Shaws. A relative! That's a strange thing! Father was a worthy Christian man, but poor. He never told me we were related to the gentry. I suppose the Laird of Shaws will have a great house, full of servants. I hope my high relations will not take me for a beggar in these plain, dusty clothes."

The slow tapping of a cane interrupted David's thoughts. Into the crossroads hobbled an aged crone bent nearly double under a load of firewood faggots. As she was about to pass him, David stood up.

"Mother," he asked, "which is the way to the house of Shaws?"

The old woman lifted a bitter, toothless face. Turning, she pointed to a tower which showed black against the far skyline.

"*That* is the house of Shaws," she croaked. "Blood built it, blood stopped the building of it, and blood will bring it down. Black be its fall! And if ye see the laird, tell him that Jennet Clouston once again has called down her curse upon him—him that sold her out of house and home!"

She hobbled on. There was something so hateful in the tapping of her cane that it made David shiver. He took a deep breath, slung his bundle onto his shoulder and walked rapidly down the road toward the tower which stood sharp and bleak against the red sky.

When he reached the place David's heart sank. There was still light enough to show him a huge, unfinished building already falling into disrepair. Empty windows stared out like black eye sockets. The raw ends of rafters jutting out of one side suggested broken ribs . . .

After some moments the boy's first shock of disappointment gave place to rising anger. In some mysterious way, David felt, he had been betrayed; but he could not turn back at this point. He pushed the gate open and strode across the courtyard.

A rat, disturbed by his entrance, scuttled up the steps. It ran up the masonry to the carved stone coat-of-arms above the door, paused to look down with beady eyes, and dropped into the shadows.

"The place looks deserted," David thought; "but the old woman, Jennet Clouston, said, 'If ye see the laird—'"

The big, rusty iron knocker waked hollow echoes. A pair of crows flew out of an empty window and flapped away, cawing.

"The house of Shaws!" David exclaimed with a bitter laugh. "Either the laird has abandoned it or he is dead, like this musty ruin. Whichever it is, I'll have to make sure because of the letter."

He turned back toward the gate. Halfway there he heard a sound behind him—the double click of a gun being cocked. He swung about. In an upper window a dim figure held a bell-mouthed blunderbuss aimed at him.

"It's loaded," the figure cackled. "Who are ye, and what's your business here?"

Anger edged David's response, as he looked up into the mouth of the gun.

"My name is David Balfour," he answered. "I have a letter from my father to Ebenezer Balfour. If he's alive tell me where I can find him, and I'll be gone. And you can put down your cannon."

The blunderbuss wavered and was drawn back.

"Wait," said the cracked voice. "I'll come down. The letter is for me. Your father must be dead, and that is what brings ye to my door."

* * * * * * *

Seated in the cold, empty, flagstoned kitchen, the boy gazed with dismay at the person who claimed to be his Uncle Ebenezer. It was true! This creature in the long flannel nightgown and soiled nightcap must be his relative, for in the old man's features David could see a wizened caricature of his father. The old hands were shaking as they folded up the letter he had just read—hands which looked as dirty as the pinched, gray-stubbled face. But Ebenezer's eyes were as sharp as flints. They probed David's features.

"Do ye know what's in this letter?" he asked. "Did your father ever talk with you about me?"

"No," the boy replied, "he never mentioned that he had a brother. I did not know till after his death that there was a house of Shaws. But now there are things I mean to find out. What does his letter say, Uncle?"

"Ay, his letter," Ebenezer wheezed. "He was a secret, silent man, my brother Alexander. A strange man! You're seventeen years old, and he never told you . . ."

The stony eyes left David's face.

"Eh, Davie," he said at last, "do ye see yon little stairway across the room? It leads up the tower. At the top of the tower there's a room with a small chest in it. Bring the chest down to me, lad. There are papers in it which will tell you everything."

David arose and reached for the candle. As he did so a crash of thunder shook the room. A heavy gust drove rain against the cobwebbed window panes.

"Davie," the old man quavered, "don't take the light. I'm not well. A storm makes me nervous. Gang along, lad. You can feel your way till ye come to the top."

David had no trouble climbing the circular stone stairway even in the dark. There were landings at each floor, but he did not pause for breath until he neared the seventh. Then, as he felt for the next step, the lightning flashed.

Where the step should have been was—nothing!

He swayed backward with a choked cry. As his weight shifted, the stone flag beneath him gave way. His hands shot out to a beam which the lightning had showed projecting from the unfinished wall. Hanging there, David heard the stone slab land with a thud in the courtyard.

Captain Hoseason

DAVID'S knees were still shaking as he sat down on the stair and thought of the awful height from which he had nearly plunged. Light was what he needed now, he told himself. Flint and steel were in his pocket, but he must find something that would burn—something that would dispel the horror of darkness.

He moved down to the next landing. There should be a room here, he thought, judging by the size of the tower . . .

There was a room—a sort of garret used for storing odds and ends, or so it seemed to David's exploring fingers. Here was some old paper . . . Tinder-dry, it caught fire with the first shower of sparks struck from the flint.

Holding the paper up like a torch, David looked around. A battered metal box caught his eye. He opened it. Inside were some old toys and—by great luck—the stub of a candle.

By candlelight the room's contents looked worse than useless: a child's broken chair, a cradle with one rocker missing, old barrel staves, a rusty weathervane. Going back to the box of toys, David rummaged till he found a child's picture book. On the flyleaf was a line of clear, firm handwriting.

With growing excitement David read the inscription again, then tucked the book under his jacket, picked up the candle stub, and went softly down the stairs.

In the kitchen old Ebenezer was shuddering as if with a chill. The brandy he was trying to pour kept missing the edge of his glass.

"I heard him fall," he muttered, half aloud. "I'll look in the morning. If I didna have to go out in the dark—"

"Why not, Uncle?" David spoke from the stairway. "You sent *me* out—in the dark."

With a strangled wail the old man clutched at the table. His legs gave way and he crumpled to the floor.

"Davie," he moaned, as the boy came toward him, "you're not coming to take me? Dinna touch me. Please, I'm not ready to go."

"I'm alive—no thanks to you, Uncle," David said grimly, lifting the old man to his feet.

He held up the picture book.

"I found this, in my father's handwriting. Let me read it: 'To my brother Ebenezer on his fifth birthday.'" He paused . . .

"My father must have been older than you, Uncle. Therefore he was heir to the house of Shaws. By rights I am now heir and the lawful laird; and by law I could put you out of house and home. That is why you sent me up the tower in the dark, to fall to my death—you murderous old miser!"

Ebenezer's hands groped out in silent pleading. At last he found his voice.

"For pity's sake, Davie," he whimpered, "let me go to my bed. I'll tell you everything in the morning. I promise you."

The boy eyed him coldly.

"Very well, Uncle, but I'll go with you. Lead the way."

The bent, nightgowned figure shuffled to a door opening off the kitchen into a room with iron-barred windows and cracked panes. A chest of drawers and a sagging four-poster bed were the only pieces of furniture.

"Now I'll take these," David said, unhooking the heavy bunch of keys from the nightgown's girdle.

Ebenezer Balfour's eyes were like points of flint in the candlelight.

"Good night to ye, David," he whispered.

"Good night, Uncle," the boy replied cheerfully. "I'll lock you in, and be sure of not having my throat cut tonight."

* * * * * * *

A loud banging at the front of the house waked David early. He rose, dressed quickly and unbarred the door, to find a half-grown boy in sea clothes holding up a letter.

"This is for the laird," the youngster piped with a cocky grin. "From my master, Cap'n Hoseason of the brig *Covenant*. Take it. My errand's done."

228

David scowled at the missive, resisted a temptation to open it, and took it back to his uncle's room. Ebenezer read it, sitting on the edge of his bed. Afterwards he scratched his chin thoughtfully.

"See what it says, Davie," he invited, offering the letter.

David glanced quickly through the message.

"Captain Hoseason wants you to meet him at the inn, and then go to the lawyer, Mr. Rankeillor, to settle some business," the boy observed. "A lawyer's might be the place to settle *our* business, too, Uncle. I think I will go along with you."

"I hoped ye would stay that," Ebenezer responded. "After all that's happened I doubt if ye would take my word for anything; but you'll see for yourself. Mr. Rankeillor is lawyer for half the gentry in these parts—an old man, and he knew your father, David. As for Hoseason, I have a trading venture with him, and we must settle the terms. His ship is at Queensferry, a short walk from here."

Captain Hoseason, David found, was a burly man with a quarterdeck voice. He boomed, "Ahoy!" as Ebenezer introduced his nephew. Then the two men stepped into the inn's side parlor and closed the door. For half an hour the murmur of their voices rose and fell, while David paced the floor impatiently.

When the door opened, Captain Hoseason came striding toward him with hand outstretched and a wide smile.

"Master Davie," he exclaimed, "your uncle tells me great things of you! I wish we had time to get better acquainted," he went on, "but I must sail with the tide. You will meet Mr. Rankeillor aboard my ship in the harbor. The laird and I will finish our legal business, and then I must put you all ashore—but not before we drink a bowl together."

Hoseason's ship was only a small trading brig, but her deck was the largest David Balfour had ever set foot on. He forgot for the moment his uncle in the gig below the ladder, as the captain's hearty voice rambled on at his side.

"Mind ye, she's home to me, Mr. Balfour. Here

is the deck house and the lockers where I keep the more valuable of the ship's stores. Step inside, young sir . . ."

Minutes passed, and all at once the captain's rambling talk seemed out of place.

"You had legal business to finish with my uncle and Mr. Rankeillor, didn't you?" David interrupted him at last. "By the way, where *is* my uncle? He came aboard, didn't he?"

Grimness masked Hoseason's heavy face as he moved to block the doorway.

"Now, did he, young man?" the captain mocked. "Ay, there's the point!"

David lunged. His shoulder knocked the man aside. He sprang to the ship's rail, and a shout of anger burst from him. This time he knew he had been caught. The ship's gig was pulling strongly for shore, with Ebenezer Balfour in the stern-sheets, looking nervously back.

A heavy hand fell on David's shoulder.

"Back from the rail, me bucko," the man said. "You're a deck hand, now."

David shrugged free. His leap took him nearly overboard, but the two men behind him were just as quick. He was hauled back, struggling wildly. A fist crashed into his face. Through a red haze David saw the man who had struck him— a brute with heavy shoulders and bloodshot eyes. The fist struck again, and David's world exploded in a flash of light.

The Cabin Boy

STRUGGLING up through the sea of pain and darkness, David heard the rumble of voices. Captain Hoseason was saying, "Take the lad out of this hole and put him in the forecastle, Mr. Shuan. With the fever he has, he might die here; and I'll have no part in murder."

"Very noble of ye, Captain," the other voice replied. "If he dies, ye'll not be able to sell him in the Carolinas for twenty pounds, to work out his indenture in the tobacco fields."

Opening his eyes, David saw the face of the man whose blow had felled him. It was leering

231

at the captain, who had started up the ladder. Hoseason snorted and tossed back a last word.

"You will obey my orders at once, drunk or sober. Take the lad to the forecastle, and see that he has food and water."

"I told yer," piped a Cockney voice, as soon as the captain had gone, "I told yer that's where 'e should have been in the first place—in the fo'c'sle —*ow!*"

A thud followed the sound of a hard slap.

"Take him there yourself, ye little imp," the mate said harshly. "One day I'll wring your skinny neck and put an end to your back talk."

Mumbling drunkenly to himself, the mate climbed the ladder. David closed his eyes, feeling sick again. When he opened them he saw the wizened cabin boy—the one who had brought the letter to Shaws that morning—gazing up at the hatch with a ferocious look. In his hand was a long-bladed knife.

"One day you'll go too far, Mr. Bully Boy Shuan!" he muttered through his teeth.

In a flash the boy's manner changed. He turned to David with a cheery smile.

"Come on, matey, I'll help you out of 'ere. Get up and lean on me. I'm little but I'm strong. Can yer stand now?"

"I think so," David answered.

Slowly, with the cabin boy's help, he got up the ladder and across the ship's heaving deck to the forecastle. One deep determination steeled his will to recover: he must escape to settle accounts with his uncle and claim the inheritance which was rightly his own.

For the next few days the brig *Covenant* stood well off the rugged Scottish coast, battling with contrary winds. By the time the weather moderated, David was well again.

Without complaint, he took orders, did his work, as best he could, and prudently kept out of the surly mate's way.

The Cockney boy was not so lucky. One bright moonlit night, as David sat practicing sailor's knots, Mr. Shuan's drunken shouting issued from the deck house. It was followed by the boy's frenzied screams. Suddenly there was silence. Captain Hoseason ran to the deck house door, followed by a sailor.

Moments later the sailor came out carrying a limp burden. The cabin boy's face was as pale as wax. While David watched, numb with shock, a little procession of deck hands moved with the dead boy to the rail. There was a low mumbling of voices, then a splash sounded from overside.

"Balfour! Balfour, come here!"

The captain's call startled David out of his horror. Hoseason stood in the deck house doorway, beckoning.

"Move your berth aft, Balfour," he said. "Ye'll serve in the deck house—in his place."

He stepped aside as the mate lurched out into the moonlight.

"As for you, Shuan, ye sot and ye swine," he roared, "ye'll get forward with the lookout and stay there till ye come to your senses. There's a fog coming up, and we're not yet clear of the Hebrides. I hope you're not too drunk to know the sound of breakers on the rocks."

David shuddered as he passed the cabin boy's murderer. Even with the captain at his side, he dreaded to enter the room where the murder had taken place only a few minutes before.

"Balfour," Hoseason said heavily, "this night's work must never be known. The lad went overboard, and that's the story. I'd give five pounds if it were true."

As the night hours wore on, the fog thickened. All hands were on deck, listening anxiously for the sound of the reefs, which might be nearer than the captain had calculated. Toward morning David was sent around with mugs and a pitcher. He was returning to the deck house when the lookout yelled, "Starboard your helm!"

The mate's voice had barely echoed the order when a shock struck through the brig. The captain was thrown against the deck house. There was a grinding, bumping sound under the *Covenant's* keel.

"Fishing boat from the shore," the mate's shout answered Hoseason's query. "We cut her in two. No use lowering a boat—we'd never find them—"

"There's a man here," the lookout's cry interrupted him, "a man on the bobstay!"

Hoseason ran forward. Two sailors climbed out on the bowsprit. They reached down and pulled the man in.

When he finally stood on the deck the rescued man was a striking figure. A greatcoat swung jauntily from his shoulders, and he still wore his hat with a scarlet plume. He was broad shouldered, tall, in his middle twenties, David guessed. His gray eyes singled out Hoseason with a glance as quick as a rapier.

"Good evening to you, Captain," he said. "It seems to me that ye keep a poor lookout on your ship. Thanks to you, my friends are at the bottom of the sea."

Hoseason eyed him coldly.

"Ye've a Scottish tongue in your head and the French King's uniform on your back," he challenged. "As ye say, your *friends* are all at the bottom of the sea. You will be wise to give an account of yourself."

The Swordsman

THE TALL young man shrugged his greatcoat open. He touched the hilt of his sword.

"I'll give an account of myself in any situation where I must, Captain," he said with a touch of mockery. "For your information, my name is Alan Breck. I was on my way to France, and if I get into the hands of King George's redcoats it will go hard with me. If ye will take me where I was going I can reward ye highly for your trouble."

"To France," Hoseason replied with a short laugh. "No, sir, that I cannot do. But if ye'll step into the cabin with me, we may come to some other agreement."

He turned to David and held out a key.

"The pannikins, and the bottle from the locker, boy," he said. "The best brandy, mind ye!"

Beneath his blue uniform jacket with the silver buttons, Alan Breck wore a red waistcoat and a gold sword belt. As the captain watched him greedily he removed a money belt and poured out a handful of gold.

"Thirty guineas, Captain, if ye set me on shore by the Linnhe Loch," he said pleasantly. "Take it or not, as ye please; I'll not arble-bargle with ye. The money belongs to my chieftain, and I'll not use it to buy my carcass too dear."

Hoseason's greedy look turned shrewd.

"Your chieftain," he repeated thoughtfully. "Ay, there's many a Highland gentleman who fought for Prince Charlie in the year forty-five, and then when defeat came followed him to France. I'm for King George, but I can be sorry for a man with his back to the wall. Thirty guineas will set you ashore—and here's my hand on it."

The captain left his guest sipping brandy and went out on deck. After some moments Alan Breck turned to David.

"Why such a long face?" he asked with a smile. "Is this the first time ye have seen a wicked rebel?"

"I'm for King George, my lawful sovereign," David answered him; "but if I'm long faced it's not because of you, sir. I have troubles of my own."

Alan laughed merrily.

"Aboard this ship I don't doubt you have troubles," he agreed. "I like you, lad. And I'd be grateful if ye would bring me a drop more brandy. The bottle's empty."

"The captain has the key, sir," David said. "I'll fetch it."

Hoseason was having a whispered conversation with the mate. He nodded at David's request and tossed him the key. Then he called the boy back.

"Do ye know, David, where the pistols are?"

"Ay, sir, by the other door."

The captain brought out another key.

"Look you, David, yon wild Highlander is a foe of our King and a danger to my ship, besides being a touchy man. Now, it so happens that all our firelocks are in the deck house with him, and if *we* were to take them out under his nose he might run us through with his sword. On the other hand, a lad like you could snap up a powder horn and a pistol or two without rousing his suspicion. Ye follow me?"

"Ay, sir."

"Take the key, then, lad—and good luck!"

Before he re-entered the deck house, David's mind was made up. He closed the door.

"There's something I have to tell you, sir." he said, meeting Alan Breck's eyes. "They're planning to kill you. They've murdered a boy already, for nothing, and now it's you—for your money, I think."

The young Highlander's eyes never left David's face. At last he nodded.

"I was right, when I took a liking to ye, lad. Ye'll stand with me? It will be the two of us against the whole ship."

"I'll stand with you, sir. My name is David Balfour."

"And mine is Alan Breck *Stewart*. Here's my hand . . . And now, let us look to our defenses. I have my sword and dirk, and there is a rack of cutlasses."

David turned away, suddenly unable to trust his voice. He opened the pistol locker.

"The firelocks will be yours, David," said Alan Breck. "Load them all. Then bolt your door. When I open my door on this side I'll have just enough room for proper swordplay."

David's hands grew steadier as he worked.

"What about the window, Mr. Stewart?"

"That will be your post. If they lift a hand against the locked door, ye're to shoot. Dinna fire to this side unless they get me down or break through the skylight . . . Ah! Here comes the noble captain."

Captain Hoseason stopped with Alan Breck's swordpoint mere inches from his chest. He looked grimly past the Stewart at David's white face and the cocked pistol in David's hand.

"I see," he said angrily, "the boy has turned traitor and set ye against me. If it's war ye want, so be it, Highlander."

Besieged

THE FIRST rush came with half a dozen cutlass-armed sailors, led by the mate. In the narrow doorway Alan could not be reached by more than one man at a time, but the mate's aim was clearly to beat him down by sheer strength and weight. His cutlass sang through the air in a terrible downstroke.

Alan parried it expertly. The force of the blow brought him almost to his knees, but he came up like a steel spring. His sword flicked out. Thrust through, the mate gave a howl, flung up his arms and fell.

"Look to your window, Balfour!" cried Alan Breck.

The captain and four sailors were rushing toward the locked door with a heavy pole. Aiming quickly, David fired. Captain Hoseason yelped, clutched at his arm. His men paused. In swift succession David brought up two more pistols and fired them into the haze of powder smoke. The battering ram crashed to the deck. Scurrying feet retreated behind the smoke screen.

At a ringing of blades behind him, David turned. The sailors had forced Alan back from the door so that now three of them had room to slash at him. David reached for his fourth pistol. As he did so, Alan, with a burst of fury, drove his enemies back. Only one cutlass opposed him now, wielded by a huge seaman. Their blades clashed, Alan lunged, and the giant fell back with a groan. The other sailors fled.

While Alan carefully cleaned his sword, David reloaded the pistols.

"I think I winged the captain," he said, breaking the silence.

"Good, that makes three," murmured Alan Breck. "Hark, now, to their voices. They're planning something. Next time they come they'll be in earnest."

With a pistol in his hand and the others laid out ready on the berth, David stood listening.

"They're all around us," he whispered to his friend.

Before Alan could reply the bosun's whistle sounded. Four sailors rushed the open door. The skylight shattered. A man dropping through it landed squarely on David. The impact brought both of them to the deck in a heap. David lost his pistol and the sailor's cutlass skidded from his hand.

The man lunged after it, but David caught him around the legs. They struggled.

Alan, too, was in difficulties. A man had run

238

under his sword and was grappling him around the waist. With his free sword arm Alan kept back the others, for the moment.

The sailor wrestling with David swung a fist, breaking his grip. A kick slammed the boy back against the berth. The sailor stooped to snatch up his cutlass. As he swung it high, David raised a pistol from the berth and fired. The man crumpled, with a horrible groan.

"Balfour! Balfour!" Alan shouted.

The Stewart was on one knee, parrying the blades of three enemies, while the fourth dragged him down. David seized the dead man's cutlass and jumped into the fight. His jabs and slashes took two men's attention, and that was all Alan Breck needed.

With his dirk, the swordsman stabbed the man who clung to him, then leaped up to engage the others. They fell back, outmatched.

The doorway was suddenly clear. Every enemy was in flight, with Alan and his sword in close pursuit. At the break of the quarterdeck the Highlander stopped. He stepped over the two corpses outside the deck house, and entered.

"David Balfour, I love ye like a brother!" he exclaimed. "And, oh, man, am I no a bonny fighter?"

David sat on the berth. He made no answer. Suddenly he threw himself down on the berth, his face in his hands, and sobbed.

Alan touched his shoulder gently.

"I know how ye feel, Davie," he said. "It's because ye killed a man. It was the same with me, at your age. Ye need rest now, so I'll clean up the cabin."

* * * * * * *

They were eating breakfast from the captain's stores when Hoseason called to them that he wanted a talk. He stood below the rail of the quarterdeck with his arm in a sling.

"Ye've made a sore hash of my crew," he complained, "and I haven't enough men to work the ship. Ye've killed my mate, and he was the only one aboard who knew this coast. There's nothing left but to run south to Glasgow for fresh hands—"

"And turn me over to the redcoats?" Alan cried. "Ho! What an innocent ye must take me for, Captain! Put me and the lad ashore now—anywhere within twenty miles of my own country, Appin or Morven or Ardgour—and I'll pay ye thirty guineas as agreed. After that ye may go to Glasgow or Timbuctoo, for all I care. Remember, in weapons we have the advantage of ye."

Hoseason shook his head like an angry and baffled bull.

"Be it as ye will, then," he replied, "but I'll need your help to pilot my ship. There's dirty weather in the making, and I do not know the reefs." He stamped away.

David frowned. "Asking you for help may be a trick, Mr. Stewart," he suggested.

Alan Breck nodded gloomily.

"It might be, but we'll have to take the risk. I think the captain is afraid of us and of the reefs, about equally."

The young Highlander drew his dirk. With its keen edge he sliced off one of the crested silver buttons from his coat.

"A keepsake," he said, handing the button to David. "If we're shipwrecked and ye reach dry ground alone, it will be of help. Wherever ye show this button the friends of Alan Breck will come around you.

"Now lock up all but three of the pistols," he continued before David had time to thank him. "We'll arm ourselves, and join the captain when he calls us."

240

Stranded!

Clouds were blowing across the face of the moon when Hoseason hailed the deck house again. Alan and David came out, alert for treachery; but the captain's face was so genuinely worried as they joined him that they forgot their suspicions.

"Look yonder to starboard where the sea breaks on the reefs," he bellowed above the howl of the wind. "And yonder to port! Do ye recognize them, Highlander? And if ye do, can ye pilot us through?"

For a long moment Alan studied the fountains of white water which spouted in plain view of the brig.

"I'm thinking these are the Torran Rocks," he said finally, "ten miles of them. I've been picked up and set down on this coast often enough. Somehow it runs in my mind that the channel lies close under the land."

"Pray Heaven ye're right!" Hoseason returned, and shouted a change of course to the man at the wheel.

"Port your helm! Port your helm!" the foretop lookout cried desperately a moment later.

Hoseason leaped to aid the helmsman with his one good arm. The brig's bow lifted on a wave, then sheered off in a deluge of spray. The sails slatted as the brig rolled. They caught the wind again, and the roaring of the reef fell astern.

David glanced at Alan's face. It showed drawn and bleak in the moonlight, and this shocked David worse than the bloody attack on their lives that morning.

"You're not afraid, are you?" he asked.

"It's no the kind of death I would choose," Alan Breck replied. "I'm a fighting man, not a sailor, and that rock came too close."

The moon slipped under a black cloud. Minutes later, when it reappeared, the lookout's cry was more cheerful: "Clear water ahead!"

The tension on deck relaxed, but not for long. To windward a dark mass of cloud was sweeping toward them preceded by sharp gusts. Before the crew had time to take in canvas the squall struck.

A studding sail split with a sound like a cannon shot. A yard with its tangle of ropes fell to the deck. The ship spun like a top. Thrown off their feet, David and the captain slid across the quarterdeck. Alan managed to grasp the rail.

There came a great shock and the grinding of broken timbers. The brig's top rigging carried away with a ripping noise, barely heard above the wind. David had lost sight of the captain. As he scrambled for a foothold Alan's shout reached him: "Hold on! Hold on!"

241

A huge wave towered above the deck and broke across it. The deep rush of water carried David overside. Tumbled in the maelstrom beyond the reef, he fought to hold his breath. When he finally surfaced, the wreck was many fathoms away, barely visible in the combing waves, and fast receding.

The powerful current which swept David out of sight of the brig proved to be his salvation. Before long, moonlight showed him white rollers breaking on a beach. He swam for it with all the strength he had left.

He felt hard sand under his feet just before the surf slammed him down against it. An undertow seized him. A wave hurled him flat again. Minutes later he staggered onto dry land and collapsed. He fell into a deep sleep.

It was full daylight when David waked, shivering. The sleep which followed exhaustion had restored most of his strength. Now his first clear thought was for the fate of his friend Alan.

The waves breaking on the beach were less angry, but neither wreck nor reef were in sight. The current, David concluded, had carried him to the other side of the island or point of land on which he stood. He started out, following the curve of the beach.

Half an hour's walk brought the brig's broken masts and listing hulk into view; but the only sign of life was a lean and ragged Highlander gazing toward the wreck—a smaller man than Alan Breck. At sight of David the scarecrow-like figure clapped a hand to his dirk. He shouted angrily in Gaelic. At the same time his bony arm made motions toward the brig.

David caught the meaning of his gestures, though he made no sense of his talk.

"Listen," he said, "if you want to loot that miserable wreck it's no concern of mine. I was swept ashore last night on the other side of that headland. All I want is somebody to guide me to the main. Do you understand English?"

The ragged Highlander sheathed his knife.

"Ay, when it's necessary," he admitted.

"Good! Tell me, then, did you see anyone from the ship? Did they get ashore safe? Was there a gentleman with a red plume on his hat?"

"Ay, there was a great gowk like that," the man replied, grudgingly. "They went away to the mainland."

He peered shrewdly at David, held up five dirty fingers, and began counting them off.

"Two shillings to guide ye to the main; then I'll have to give ye food, and that'll be another shil-

243

ling. And then, while I'm gone away some other may find this wreck of mine and steal from it. So altogether it will cost ye five shillings. Either that or ye find your own way, mannie."

David shrugged and pulled out his purse.

"A greedy guide is better than none, I suppose," he said as he dropped the money into the outstretched hand, "but for the price I'll expect ye to take me to some place where I can find lodging."

The Highlander grunted, tested the coins with his teeth, put them in his pocket, and set off. At a place where the low tide exposed a sandy isthmus they crossed to the mainland. Beyond them, in rugged steps, the hills climbed to a craggy mountain range.

Skirting a great, rocky peak, they came finally to a little lake bordered by purple heather. And there on a thick bed of the feathery stems the guide plumped himself down. After pulling off his brogues, he waved vaguely toward the farther heights.

"There's where ye go, mannie," he said. "Over the hills and far away! I'm stopping here."

The Murder

THE LONGER he looked into the mocking eyes of his guide, the angrier David became.

"I paid you to take me to a lodging. If you don't, you're a thief and a skellum," he accused.

The Highlander flapped his ragged sleeves and poured out a spate of Gaelic words. David smiled grimly. He opened his purse. The torrent of Gaelic words stopped. With his eyes fixed on the purse as if held by a magnet, the man got to his feet.

"Five shillings more," he said, "and I'll lead ye to the ferry."

He took a step forward, his bare toes gripping the sod.

"Gie me the money in my hand, and I'll take ye there now," he promised in a wheedling tone. "Five shillings!"

David laughed.

"You're a cheat and a liar. I'd rather starve to death than give you another penny."

As David snapped the purse shut the ragged man leaped for it. They grappled. David flung him off, tripping him at the same time. The Highlander bounced up, whipping out his dirk. This time it was no mere threat.

Desperately David grabbed the knife wrist. His right fist drove into the man's face. The Highlander went down again, dropping his dirk. David snatched it up. As he glanced over at the dour face of his attacker something else caught his eye —the angry wriggling of bare toes in the heather. The toes gave David an idea.

He stepped quickly to the man's shoes, picked them up and tossed them into the lake. Then he tucked the knife under his belt, and strode away, smiling to himself.

Only a few miles from where he had left his fuming guide, David reached the margin of Loch Linnhe. He had spotted its wide expanse from a bend of the path he had found, leading down from the heights. At the same time he had noticed something else—a small wharf and a boat moored beside it. Now, as he approached them, he saw a small cock-sparrow of a man mending a net. This was probably the ferryman his guide had mentioned.

The face with its keen, quick eyes looked honest, if not very friendly, David observed, and he decided to come straight to the point.

"I am seeking a man named Alan Breck Stewart. Did he come this way?"

The ferryman's gaze became piercing. After studying David for a minute he laid aside his net and stood up.

"Are ye by any chance a shipwrecked man?" he asked. "And have ye, by any other chance, a silver button?"

"A silver button with the Stewart crest," replied David, taking it from his purse. "So Alan Breck did come here?"

The little man turned the button in his fingers and handed it back.

"Ay, and I have the word to see that ye reach Appin land safely. Come away to my boat now."

The skiff moved lightly over the choppy wavelets of the loch, propelled by short, brisk strokes of the oars. The gloomy mountains drew nearer, towering above a misty coast.

"Yonder is Duror of Appin," said the ferryman at last, "and there ye must ask for the house of James of the Glens, who is brother to their chief. Your friend will join you there when he can; but mind ye, there's one name ye must never speak in this country, and that is Alan Breck.

"The rumor is," he continued, "that Colin Roy Campbell, who is called the Red Fox, has his soldiers coming—to turn the Stewarts out of hearth and home. It's a bad day for Appin, and ye must take care to walk softly, lad."

Following the ferryman's directions, David found the bridle path which ran along the steep shore of the loch. Above him a birch forest clung to the craggy mountainside. It was a lonely spot —until David heard the sound of voices, mingled with a ringing of horseshoes on the stony track.

Around a bend of the path rode a tall, stout, red-haired gentleman. In his dress and in his manner he had the plain mark of authority. Behind him rode a smaller man in black—a lawyer, David guessed—and after him a servant. As David stepped off the path to let them by, the big man pulled up his horse.

"Where are you going, boy?" he asked crisply.

"To Duror of Appin. And I'd be obliged, sir, if you would tell me where I will find James of the Glens."

The large man's eyes opened wider. He turned to the lawyer behind him.

"Is this an omen, do ye think, councillor? Today, of all days—"

"Today of all days it is an ill subject for jest, Mr. Campbell," the man in black replied.

"Very well, what *does* it mean?" the red-haired Campbell insisted sharply. "A rising of James's people against us?"

With an inward start David realized that this must be the one called the Red Fox—the man of whom he had been warned. He spoke up quickly.

"If you're thinking of me, sir, I am neither of James's people nor of yours. I am an honest subject of King George, owing no man and fearing none."

The Campbell's look was stern.

"This day, young man," he said, "I must take nothing for granted. I am the King's agent and have twelve files of soldiers at my back. I must tell you—"

"Take care, sir!"

The lawyer's warning was drowned by a firearm's deafening report. The Red Fox lurched, then fell heavily from the saddle. His horse shied away. With a despairing shout the lawyer flung himself down beside the wounded Campbell.

For a moment David stood staring helplessly —until a movement on the hillside above him broke the spell. His eyes picked out a man with a long gun darting away among the birch trees. The murderer!

"There he goes!" David cried, and raced up the slope in pursuit.

He had just reached the spot where the ambusher had disappeared when he heard the lawyer shouting, *"Mr. Campbell is killed!* Stop that boy! He was posted as an accomplice—to delay us!"

"To the Heather— or Hang!"

The PATH below David was filling with redcoated troops. At a sharp command, he saw weapons whip up to point-blank aim. At a second command, smoke and sound burst from the gun muzzles. A bullet tore bark from the tree six inches from David's head. Something plucked at his sleeve, and a cut twig fell spinning before his face.

Only then did the horror of his false position come over him. They were trying to shoot *him* down, as a party to the crime! He turned and ran.

The redcoats, emerging from the cloud of their own powder smoke, charged up the hill. They climbed fast, but David's heels were winged with desperation. He gained—until he reached a crag whose sheer rock face blocked his way. As he

hesitated a low, familiar voice spoke from a thicket: "In here, Davie!"

"*Alan!*"

He dived after the vanishing form. They emerged from the thicket, doubled back, and raced up a steep gully. Alan Breck sped like a mountain goat over the high rocks, through a narrow slot between cliffs and down another gully roofed over with green bushes. Then they climbed—until David was sure his lungs would burst. The soldiers saw them now, and raised a great shout; but the firelocks had not been reloaded. At the top of the cliffs, Alan turned for a taunting wave to the redcoats.

Out of sight, on the high moorland, the fugitives paused for breath.

"Man, I thought they had you with that great volley," Alan panted. "But they seldom sight on a target. Come, now! They're still after us, and we must fool them with the fox's trick."

He dived into a dense mass of bracken, leaving not so much as a broken stem to show where he had disappeared. David followed him.

The breathless soldiers arrived with little noise except the thumping of feet and the whistling of hard-drawn breath. Their eyes were slightly glazed with the stress of climbing. They broke into a shambling trot as they reached level ground, picking the easiest way through the masses of bracken. When they were gone Alan motioned David to get up.

"Are ye still wearied?" he asked.

"Not now, and I can speak," David answered coldly. "I liked you very well, Alan Breck. But now a Campbell man lies dead of a murderer's shot. I'll have no part nor lot with anyone who kills from ambush. We'll say good-by now."

The corner of Alan's mouth drew down in a mocking smile.

"So that's the trouble," he remarked. Then suddenly his eyes were serious. He drew his dirk.

"I swear by the Holy Iron," he said, reverently touching the cross of its hilt, "that I had neither art nor part in that man's death—neither act nor thought of it. If I were going to kill a man I would do it face to face—and not in a way to bring vengeance on my clan, as this killing will surely do. Ye believe me, Mr. Balfour?"

For answer David thrust out his hand, and Alan took it, with a light-hearted laugh.

"Now," said the Stewart, "if ye have finished arguing, we'll go down to speak with James of the Glens. We canna bide in his house, lest the redcoats catch and hang us all; but he'll furnish us with what food we can carry. From now on, and for many a day, our bed must be the moorcock's and our life like the hunted deer's; for we're both wanted men, David. The Red Fox's killing will be blamed on us two by all the Campbells. We'll not be safe from them till we're out of the Highlands."

* * * * * * *

Night was falling as Alan and David paused for the first time since leaving the home of James of the Glens. David carried a bag of provisions over his shoulder; Alan's was slung underneath his greatcoat. Far below them, water glimmered like a piece of broken mirror among the trees, and the path led up through frowning crags.

"Poor James!" Alan sighed. "He is old, and wearied with taking orders from the Campbell conquerors whilst trying to protect his own clansmen. He'll be forced to post a reward for our capture. Many a home in Appin will be harrassed by the redcoats tomorrow as they seek friends of the slayer. You and I must be far away."

"You and I?" David retorted. "Alan, I am tired of running, when this matter is no quarrel of mine. My quarrel is with my uncle. All I want is to get back and settle it. I've done nothing wrong—so let me go my own way as an honest traveler. If I'm taken by the King's men, I'll trust to the justice of my country."

Alan Breck looked at him in withering silence.

"Justice!" he burst out at last. "Man, I wonder at ye. This is a *Campbell* that's been killed; and if ye're taken ye'll be tried with Campbells packing the jury box and a Campbell magistrate on the bench. They'll hang ye higher than Haman. Make your choice once for all, David Balfour. To the heather with me—or hang!"

Outraged by the brutal injustices of his position, David still could use his head.

"You're right, Alan Breck. We'll run together."

The first rays of the morning sun lanced down at the hunted pair through a mountain notch. Alan halted with a groan.

"What a gomeral I am!" he lamented. "The day has caught us where we should never have been—the pass of Glencoe. Like as not, there'll be a company of dragoons searching through it from the other side—planning to catch us between them and the soldiers behind us . . . But it's not worse to go forward now than to go back."

Keeping a sharp watch ahead, they climbed a path which soon brought them to the edge of a mountain torrent. They followed up along the rim of its rocky gorge to where the spray of a waterfall rose in rainbow colors. Just beyond them the trail disappeared among high rocks.

Alan must have glimpsed something there, for he pushed David down behind a boulder. After a short pause he moved cautiously ahead. David followed him. Together they climbed the mossy side of a great, leaning slab till they could see over the top of it. The pass was filled from wall to wall with a line of advancing horsemen.

"Come on," Alan whispered, sliding down from the rock. He raced to the edge of the shallow gorge, and with scarcely a pause leaped into it.

Briefly the fear touched David that his friend had deliberately chosen drowning in the face of certain capture. Then he looked far down and saw Alan standing on a foam-wet rock near the base of the falls. The Stewart was waving, urging him to come. David took a long breath, gauged the distance as well as he could, and leaped.

His feet struck the rock with numbing force. He slid off into the water, but Alan's hand pulled him back.

"One more jump, and we're safe," the Highlander shouted above the thunder of the falls.

The jump to the side of the gorge was a long one, but David made it. Alan's grip steadied him as they raced along a slippery ledge to the back of the waterfall. There his guide led him through a white veil of spray to another ledge under the airy arch of the cataract.

"We'll bide here till the last dragoon has left the pass," Alan shouted.

The Bridge

FOR TWO nights and two days Alan and David had pushed through the wildest part of the Highlands. They had stopped only to eat cold bannocks and snatch a few hours of sleep. From time to time they had spotted a file of redcoated soldiers, or caught the dull flash of steel from a squadron of dragoons. Now another enemy—exhaustion—dogged their steps. As they halted in the pale light of moonrise, David was too weary to care if they were caught or not.

Alan seemed tireless, though his face looked leaner under its new stubble of beard. After scanning the timbered slope ahead he turned to the thickets nearer by. David followed listlessly.

A twig snapped in the coppice to the right. Alan whipped out his sword. A dry branch cracked behind him. He faced that way—and from the first thicket a man sprang cat-like onto his back.

David started forward to help, but another form struck him and sent him sprawling. The darkness was suddenly full of men.

Two of them pulled Alan to his feet, while a third man held a dirk six inches from his throat. Moonlight glinted on the blade. But Alan, far from showing fear, was shouting furiously in Gaelic.

The dirk was sheathed. Alan shook himself free, and at his call the fellow holding David released him.

"All's well," Alan said in English. "These are Cluny MacPherson's lads—his out-sentries. We'll wait here till they get word to their chief."

With a sigh of relief David sat down against a rock. He dozed, while Alan chatted in Gaelic with the Highlanders—big men with black beards. An hour later the whole company moved up the mountain to a timbered bench where a house of logs blended inconspicuously with the living trees. One tree growing out from the ledge above formed its roof beam.

"'Cluny's Cage,' they call it," Alan explained. "Cheer up, Davie, we're among friends now."

David looked at him, bleary eyed.

"I dinna ken who Cluny is," he mumbled, "and I dinna care for his men; but with his kind permission I would like to get some sleep. I've had next to none for a week."

Fully twelve hours later David sat up. He had been sleeping on a thick bed of heather in a corner of the log house. Alan Breck and a big, bearded man with the air of a mountain king were playing cards at the rough table.

"Cluny," said Alan, rising to his feet, "let me present to ye my friend, the Laird of Shaws—Mr. David Balfour."

David rose, and MacPherson nodded.

"I make ye welcome, Mr. Balfour," he said, "with apology for my queer, rude house. My estate is forfeit and there's a price on my head, but I'm honored to share with ye what I have."

Though the dinner consisted of deer meat and bannocks it was served with rough magnificence,

on silver plate. A toast was drunk "to the restoration of our true king." David, indebted for the chief's hospitality, joined in it, forgetting his political scruples. Afterwards, he slept again.

It was morning when Cluny MacPherson waked him.

"Have ye quite rested enough, Mr. Balfour?" he asked. "The news is that your way is clear to the south, and your friend Alan Breck is anxious to be off. I'm sorry ye must leave so soon."

David thanked the chief heartily for his kindness. Then he joined Alan outside, in the cold mist which blanketed the mountainside.

Forced to avoid beaten tracks, David could only trust to Alan's knowledge of the country. He lost all sense of distance and direction—except when the sun shone. Even the number of days they had spent in the hills became uncertain. When at last the stone buttresses of a great bridge loomed up in the evening light, he was unpre-

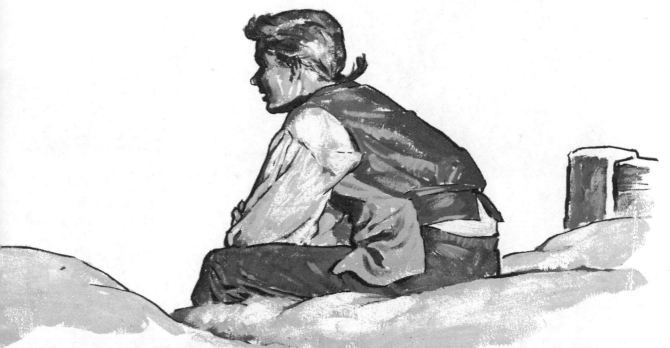

pared for Alan's announcement: "There ye are—the Old Bridge of Stirling! On the other side we can throw our bonnets into the air, Davie—for we'll be safe away from the Highlands."

David stared without speaking at the ancient structure, at the river, and at the dim castle on the hill beyond it. Then he broke into a run.

Alan trotted at his side. On the bridge itself they slowed to a walk—and it was well that they did; for out of the sentry box in the middle stepped a red-coated sentry.

They drew back into the shadows unseen.

"Could we swim across?" David suggested.

"I swim like a stone," his companion answered, "and a boat would not do, for its theft would alarm the conutryside . . . But look—look! There's our answer!"

He pointed to an old woman with a bundle, who was just crossing the bridge.

"Ye see, Davie," Alan explained with a chuckle,

"it's a trick that has won many a battle—to go where you're least expected. So this is where we cross. Observe, yon old crone is smoking a pipe. We'll buy it off her—along with her tinder box and a twist of tobacco if she has it. I'll wander onto the bridge, lean against the parapet and light my pipe, as if I had all the time in the world and a redcoat meant nothing to me. I'll seem the very opposite of a hunted man. Then you saunter past me, Davie, and after a while I follow ye."

"I hope," murmured David, "that it works out the way you've told it—since there are now *two* sentries on the bridge. Look there! The other just came out of the sentry box."

"Hoots-toots! Twice the redcoats, half the risk! They'll be gabbling to each other like two geese, with no thought of us . . . Now, here's the old woman with her pipe; so stop your worrying."

The Signal Gun

THE REDCOATS, David saw, were both idling near the parapet. He watched his friend stroll across almost to the middle of the bridge, stop not far from the uninterested sentries, and knock out the newly purchased pipe on his palm. David realized it was time for him to start.

Everything went as planned until he was about to pass the soldiers. At that moment their talk took a turn that froze his blood.

"We chased the two blokes wot done it over half of Scotland," one of them grumbled. "I saw them both, near enough to know them again, but wot good is that—unless they happen to cross this bridge while I'm on duty?"

The other sentry turned, his firelock clinking against the stonework.

"*If* they was to cross and you nabbed them, cully, it would be worth a hundred and fifty quid. A hundred for the big 'un and fifty for the little 'un."

"*Blimey!*"

At the sharp ejaculation behind him David tensed, barely controlling an impulse to run. For long seconds there was no sound but his own de-

liberate footsteps, and the pulse pounding in his ears. He listened, breathlessly, for the command to halt.

Again there came the clink of metal against stone—and a long sigh.

"Blimey," the soldier's voice repeated, now wistfully, "wot I could do with a hundred and fifty quid! I'd buy myself a nice little pub and sit outside in the sun, and drink my own beer from morning to night, so I would."

* * * * * * *

It was still early in the morning when David reached the door that had been described to him, in a busy street of the town of Queensferry. When his knocking brought no answer he stepped back —and nearly bumped into a brisk old gentleman in a powdered wig. They begged each other's pardon. Then the old gentleman produced a key and unlocked the door.

"You—you are Mr. Rankeillor, the lawyer?" David asked. He added quickly, "I am David Balfour, sir—son of the late Alexander Balfour. I've come—for advice."

The lawyer's unhurried gaze took him in from head to foot.

"I think you have come to the right place," he said at last. "Pray, come in, Mr. David Balfour."

Seated in Mr. Rankeillor's dusty little law office, David told of what he had discovered in the

254

house of Shaws, of his kidnapping and a little of the adventures he had met in trying to return. When he had finished the old gentleman's eyes were twinkling.

"You have been open with me, Mr. David," he said, "and I will be equally frank with you. Your uncle did not steal the estate of Shaws. It came to him as the result of—a love affair.

"Your father and your uncle, Mr. David, loved the same young lady. When she accepted your father, his brother Ebenezer made a great show of his disappointment—he even took to his bed—until everyone pitied him. He kept it up until your father, whom he blamed for all his woe, took the young lady who became your mother, and went away, leaving the entire estate to his younger brother.

"Your father's foolish generosity helped nobody, not even Ebenezer. Common gossip hinted that Alexander had been murdered. A time came when your uncle's friends avoided him. Lonely, selfish, he grew to love only money. He became what you have seen—too miserly even to finish the building of Shaws. As for the estate, your father could give up his own rights to it, but when he died it became yours, by the law of *entail*.

"You, Mr. David, are beyond doubt the present Laird of Shaws—but getting possession is another matter."

"I'll fight for what's mine," David burst out.

"Quite so," Rankeillor agreed. "Of course, law suits can be expensive. The quicker way would be to force your uncle to admit having you kidnapped, before witnesses. But there's a trick that only a violent man could turn—one without too much concern for what is mannerly and proper. I doubt if you could manage it, Mr. David."

David jumped to his feet.

"*I* might not manage it," he said with a smile, "but I know just the man who could."

* * * * * * *

An elegant young gentleman with silver-laced hat and gold-headed cane stood at the window of the Queensferry Inn, looking out at the harbor. For all his look of wealth he did not seem happy. His well-tailored shoulders drooped.

"That's a braw new suit, Mr. Balfour of Shaws," a gay voice remarked, from the doorway.

David turned, his face lighting up.

"Alan Breck!" he exclaimed. "I've been waiting for you since noon, man! The tide's on the turn, and your ship will be signaling you to go aboard, any minute now. I hoped we would have a little more time . . ."

"Time for what, David? Time for gabbing like old wives? Or telling again how I baited your miserly uncle, until he was so rattled that he swore he'd paid no more than twenty pounds for your kidnapping—?"

"—with Mr. Rankeillor and me behind the gate listening to it all!" David finished. "Oh, I'll never forget the look on Uncle Ebenezer's face when the lawyer popped up like a jack-in-the-box and said, 'Thank you, Mr. Stewart, I think we have just what we need!'"

They both laughed, and then David grew serious.

"Alan," he said, "whatever I have I owe to your friendship—yes, even my life. And now you are off to France. How can I tell if I'll ever see you again? There's a world of things we have never talked of . . ."

The muffled "Boom!" of a ship's gun cut David short.

"The signal! I must leave now," said Alan, "and it's just as well. I hate lengthy partings."

They went out and walked to the slope which led down to the harbor. Now that the last moment had come, David searched for words and found none that would help.

"Alan," he blurted, "when will ye be back?"

The other's laugh rang out gaily.

"The Highlands will be no safe place for Alan Breck for a while," he said. "But when the noise has died down—perhaps one day ye'll come on me behind a heather bush, or watching ye from the wood of birches . . . And now, good-bye, Davie."

"Good-bye, Alan Breck."

David watched him down to the ship's boat which waited at the shore. He saw Alan wave. Then he turned to the road which led back from the town to the distant hills.